Dark Swans
Stephen Jackson

First edition published in 2023

Book cover design by Diego Alcalá

ISBN 9781739332013

www.stephenjackson.info

For Jenni and Matt

Prologue – 3 July 1976

When the fortune-telling machine proclaimed, 'An untimely ending will usher a divine beginning,' little could Albert Taylor have grasped the significance of its prophecy. But within twenty-four hours, his life would change forever.

Albert's granddaughter, Chloe, giggled as the animatronic soothsayer froze and whirred back to life. Its glowing eyes and luminous crystal ball sought to lure further gullible holidaymakers to part with their cash.

'What does she mean, Grampy?' Chloe asked.

'I've no idea,' said Albert as he mopped sweat from his brow with a handkerchief. 'It's all nonsense anyway.'

Chloe's dad, Paul, interjected, 'Why don't we find somewhere more fun to spend your pocket money, Darling?'

Chloe scanned the fairground and focused on a stall near the entrance. 'Can Grampy win me a Womble, please?' She signalled towards a shooting gallery with a jumble of cuddly toys dangling from the roof.

'Why don't we give your daddy a chance to earn you a prize this time?' Albert replied.

Paul pointed the air rifle at a row of 5-inch tall, metal soldier silhouettes. He fired. Nothing. The soldier figures remained stubbornly still. Albert groaned and grabbed the gun. 'Ahh, let me do it,' he rebuked. 'We still have three shots left to claim a prize.'

Albert aimed the rifle with a sure grip and a steady hand. His taut posture, neatly trimmed moustache and sideburns contrasted with his son's ungroomed shoulder-length hair and languid slouch. Each shot Albert fired provoked a tinny clang as it felled a soldier. Chloe whooped in delight. 'Hooray, we won. Can I get Madame Cholet, please? Then I'd like to go on the Helter Skelter.'

Chloe climbed the lofty spiral slide that functioned as a beacon for Hunstanton's fairground. She sped down the twisty chute like a fireball in her vivid orange sundress, shrieking excitedly. Albert and Paul rested on a bench in the tower's shadow, shielding themselves from the blazing sun. Unusually, Albert had forgone his jacket. Still, he wore smart brown trousers with razor-sharp creases, held up by braces over a cream button-up shirt. Albert emitted a long breath. 'I don't know where Chloe gets all her energy from,' he said.

Sitting with his legs crossed, Paul, wearing flared jeans and a brown polo shirt, replied, 'From her mum, obviously. She has the same dynamism and infectious spirit. It's uncanny how much Chloe resembles Juliana, isn't it? They even have identical golden hair and hazel eyes.'

Albert scoffed as he stuffed tobacco into his pipe. 'Chloe is wonderful, without a doubt. But it's not because she's just some carbon copy of her mother. You're infatuated with your wife, so you can only recognise Juliana's traits in Chloe. But Chloe reminds me of you at her age: smart, fearless and full of life. Sadly, the antithesis of what you've become. What exactly is your role in life nowadays? A glorified secretary? A housewife?'

Paul sighed. 'Look, Dad, how many times have we been through this? I'm supporting ground-breaking research.'

'And what does "supporting" mean? A man of your talent should be the one leading the research. You achieved the highest scores at your grammar school, a top degree from Cambridge, but then flunked your doctorate. Now you're approaching thirty, relying on your wife as the family's breadwinner. I'd reached factory supervisor level at your age.'

'Dad, you know it's not like that,' Paul replied. 'Juliana is leading the world in her field. She's uniquely gifted, with a drive that leads others to deliver truly astonishing results. I can't do that. But we're a great partnership because the way we share our work and family responsibilities brings out the best in both of us.'

'So where is she this weekend, then? It looks to me like the responsibilities are clear. Juliana does the real work while you perform the childcare.'

Paul grimaced, 'Juliana was desperate to be here this weekend. She knows how much Chloe loves the seaside, especially when it's so sunny. But the facility has an important event on Monday. Juliana's presenting the results of our research to the press. She needs to prepare. It's confidential and sensitive – so I can't tell you about it now, Dad. But, trust me, it's extraordinary – it will change the world when it's revealed.'

A dog's bark interrupted their bickering. Albert's wife, Peggy, had returned with Rocky, Paul's family golden retriever. Peggy wore a flowery dress and permed greying hair bulged from under her floppy sun hat. 'He hasn't been teasing you again about being a housewife, has he?' she said. 'I think your dad's forgotten sex discrimination is illegal nowadays.'

Paul rolled his eyes, then asked, 'Is Rocky all right, Mum? Did you find him some water?'

'Yes, he's fine for now. But he's struggling in this heat, like the rest of us. They say it could get to a hundred today.'

Chloe skipped towards Paul and her grandparents and hugged Rocky. She pointed to the Womble peeping from Paul's rucksack. 'Look what we won, Grandma,' she exclaimed.

'Has Grampy been showing off his shooting skills again?' said Peggy.

Chloe nodded.

'They'll ban him if he keeps hustling their cuddly toys.'

Chloe turned to Paul. 'Can we go to the beach now, Daddy? Please?'

'Of course we can,' he gratefully replied.

Sunlight glistened off Albert's polished black shoes as the family entered the promenade. They witnessed a scene reminiscent of Nice rather than Norfolk. The walkway buzzed with life – chiming arcades and roaring speedboats transcended the hubbub of animated holidaymakers. The varied aromas of seafood, candyfloss, and sun-tan lotion drifted across the seafront, blown by the gentle sea breeze. Albert grinned at Chloe's wide-eyed wonder, eagerly taking everything in.

Once decamped on the expansive sandy beach, Paul, Chloe, and Rocky sprinted to the seafront, seeking relief from the heat in the icy North Sea. Chloe braved the cold and was swimming within seconds. After drying, Chloe asked Grandma to build a sandcastle with her.

Albert leaned back into the striped deck chair. 'You know, Chloe could do with a brother or sister,' he said. 'But I don't suppose you're planning another one? How old is Juliana now, forty-five?'

'Forty-four,' Paul replied. 'No, we're not planning another one. Chloe's all we want – look how happy she is.'

They both turned to observe Chloe chuckling as Grandma attempted to dig a moat while trying to stop Rocky from joining in and destroying the castle.

'Time for an ice cream?' Albert yelled at Chloe.

'Yes, please, Grampy,' Chloe called back. As they capered hand in hand to the nearest vendor, Peggy said, 'He does adore her, you know?'

Paul replied, 'I know, that's why I bring her to see you as much as possible, but I wish he'd tone down the continual niggling.'

'It will take time. He's still getting used to your situation.'

'It's been five years already. How long does he need? I'd like him to at least accept it's how we wish to live our lives.'

'He respects Juliana, but I will try to get him to drop the criticism.'

Paul paused, his brow furrowed, leaning in to face Peggy. 'Listen, Mum. Monday's going to be an important day for us. It will be a seminal moment for science and significantly elevate Juliana's profile…our family's profile. I need you and Dad to be prepared for that. Juliana will receive international respect but also – possibly – condemnation. Some of it could be cruel. We'll shield Chloe as much as possible, but I need you and Dad to help look after her if things turn nasty.'

'You're scaring me now, Love,' she said. 'But, of course, we'll do anything to help Chloe.'

'Don't worry, Mum, I'm probably being overdramatic. The research will have an incredibly beneficial impact on humanity. I'm sure the reaction will be overwhelmingly positive. I can't wait for you to find out about it.'

They packed away the beach gear and returned to Albert and Peggy's static holiday caravan. On their way back, Peggy walked with Paul and said, 'Do you have to go early tomorrow? We're staying until late evening. Your dad hoped to take Chloe to the boating lake.'

Paul replied, 'I need to get back by lunchtime to help Juliana with a final run-through of her presentation. And you could see a lot of Chloe over the next few months.'

Paul was packed and ready to leave at 10.30 a.m. He and Chloe hugged Peggy and Albert, and they said their farewells.

Paul managed to manoeuvre Rocky into the back of his Ford Cortina Estate. However, before Paul and Chloe entered the car, Albert approached. He momentarily stared into Chloe's hazel eyes before hugging her again. 'Come back and see us soon,' he pleaded as he surreptitiously passed her a tube of Smarties.

'I love you, Grampy,' Chloe replied.

Albert turned to Paul and opened his mouth as if he had something to say. Paul waited for him to speak. Albert wasn't usually tongue-tied. Finally, after thirty silent seconds, he simply said, 'Good luck tomorrow, Son.'

Getting back to Juliana's home, their home, near St Ives in Cambridgeshire, usually took a couple of hours. But, after they passed Downham Market, it was evident the journey would take longer. Traffic dawdled southwards, held up by frequent roadworks and the volume of vehicles. They were stuck behind a Mini. Slender straps fastened a stack of holiday paraphernalia onto its roof, including two hefty wooden deckchairs. Paul shook his head in disbelief. How could they fit so much on such a small car?

They finally picked up speed. Paul glanced in the rear-view mirror. Chloe snoozed, cuddling her Womble. Her unwavering trust in him tugged at Paul's heart. He flinched, startled out of his contemplation. The deckchairs on the car in front slipped loose from their bindings. They broke free and hurtled towards the windscreen. Paul thrust the steering wheel to the right but went too far. The blaring horn of the onrushing lorry signalled a futile warning. A head-on collision was inevitable.

Part 1: April 2001

Chapter 1. Jamie – 25 April 2001

Although the knowledge to outwit death could have elicited extraordinary possibilities, in my experience, its main effect was to shorten people's lives. But, unfortunately, it took me a long time to understand this.

Three heavy knocks on my front door marked the commencement of my life's startling deviation from comfortable inertia. Caroline and I were on the sofa, the ten o'clock news had just finished, and we were about to go to bed. We shuddered at the rapid thuds from outside. Unexpected visitors this late were rare in suburban York. 'Be careful, Jamie,' cried Caroline as I stood up to investigate.

'Perhaps one of the neighbours is in trouble,' I said.

I squinted through the peephole viewer. The image before me caused my heart to thump. Initially, I didn't recognise him. Maybe it was the 180-degree lens's distortion. But more likely, it was his sallow complexion, gaunt cheeks and patchy stubble. He looked like he hadn't eaten or slept in days. 'It's Nick,' I stammered as I opened the door.

'Jamie, thank God you're in,' he said. 'I need someone to talk to.' He wore a dark blue work suit with a striped tie that dangled below his open top button.

'Sit down, Mate, you look shattered,' I said. But he continued to stand.

'Oh, hi Caroline, good to see you.'

Caroline said, 'I can go home if you need space to speak to Jamie.'

'No, don't go on my account,' replied Nick.

'Let me get you something to drink. A beer? Tea?' she offered.

'I'd love a black coffee.' Caroline went to the kitchen. But caffeine was the last thing Nick needed, judging by how he manically paced around the parquet floor.

'I'm sorry to call so late,' he said. 'But I've just finished work and need to get things off my chest.'

'No problem,' I said. 'I'm always here for you. It's a shame we don't bump into each other as much since you left Ebor Assurance.'

'Yeah, I know. My job at The Cygnus Foundation is all-consuming. That's what I want to talk to you about.'

'Why? I thought you loved it there.'

'Yes. In many ways, I'm privileged – making a real difference, helping new biotech startups...' Nick paused and stared at the magnolia wall. He shuffled his rectangular gunmetal glasses to the bridge of his nose, then peered up to look me in the eyes. 'You won't believe what I've seen, Jamie. It's incredible. Science is on the cusp of delivering mind-blowing changes to our lives. Frightening, even.' He slumped on a chair and folded his arms.

'I don't understand, Nick. What do you mean?'

'I can't say. That's part of my problem. Everything I work on is bound by strict confidentiality clauses. There's so much I want to tell you. All the moral dilemmas and unintended consequences my work entails. But I have to keep it bottled up.'

'Come on, Nick, how long have you known me? You can count on my discretion.'

'This isn't like the office gossip we used to trade in the café at Ebor Assurance. I'm talking about cutting-edge scientific breakthroughs companies spend millions on protecting.' Nick sounded a hollow chuckle. 'It's ironic; remember all those lunchtimes we used to meet with Patrick to discuss the next hot dot com enterprise to invest in? We never really had a clue, did we? But I could make millions now with what I know.'

'Isn't there someone at work to talk things through with? Your manager, maybe?'

'It's no good. I'm not like them. Everyone there has a zealous devotion to the progression of science, whatever the costs. I'm just the accountant, but I'm meant to have the same conviction. The Foundation pay for a counsellor who is meant to help me. But his main job is to brainwash me to their way of thinking.'

Crimson forks sprouted from Nick's steely irises, and the table lamp glinted in the tear on his cheek.

'I can't carry on anymore. I want it to end,' he whispered.

My stomach turned. What should I say? I wasn't equipped to deal with an emotional crisis. I was desperate for Caroline to return and help me out. All I could think of was to seek clarification.

'You mean you want to end your time at The Cygnus Foundation?' I said.

'Of course. What else did you think?' he snickered. 'Yes, I'm considering handing my notice in tomorrow.'

I calmed a little. 'You should, Nick. Honestly, you're not looking well. You could get a job anywhere with your qualifications. Ebor Assurance would bite your hand off to have you back.'

'But even if I resign tomorrow, it won't solve things immediately.'

'Why not?'

'Because of the nature of the work, I have a twelve-month notice period. But they won't put me on garden leave. I'll have to work the whole time so they can monitor me. And I can't cope with another year there.'

'Why don't you explain your situation? Surely they'll let you go sooner? It doesn't help anyone having an unhappy employee.'

'You don't understand how far they'll go to protect their secrets, Jamie. These are serious people.' Nick unfolded his arms and leaned forward. Behind the chunky lenses, his eyes seemed the size of saucers. 'What am I saying? Talking to you is helping me see things differently. Maybe keeping everything suppressed is clouding my judgement. I will speak to my boss tomorrow. Tell him how things are. I'm sure we can come to an amicable arrangement.'

'Yes. You'll feel better if you stay positive,' I said. 'I'm sorry I haven't been around for you as much recently.'

'No, It's my fault. Work takes up most of my time. And I'm too knackered to do anything else when I'm not working.'

'It's quiz night at the Old White Swan tomorrow,' I said. 'You haven't been for ages. It would be great to chat over a few beers.'

'Yeah, I'd love that. I think Vicky's going. I'll try to make it if I can get away from work. Will Patrick be there?'

'I hope so. We don't have much chance of winning without him.'

Caroline sensed the right time to come back with the drinks. She placed the mugs on the oak coffee table and said, 'I'm off to bed now.'

Nick smiled and nodded.

'What does Vicky think?' I asked.

'I'm not sure,' he said. 'I find it difficult to know what she really wants

9

nowadays.'

'But you have told her you're considering leaving The Cygnus Foundation, right?'

'She knows I'm not happy there.' He frowned. 'Honestly, Vicky and I are currently going through a rough patch. Of course, the long hours don't help, but there's some other stuff. It's all connected, really.'

'Shit, sorry, Mate, that's terrible,' I said. 'Is there anything else you want to talk about?'

'Yeah, there is something. We've not told many people about it. Vicky and I have been trying to have children for years. That's one of our main causes of stress. But we'll get nowhere when I'm in this state.'

'Wow, I didn't know. I thought you were both career types,' I said.

'Sorry, Jamie. I guess it's not the kind of thing blokes talk about, is it? We've been through countless IVF attempts without success. But ironically, recently, I've started to believe it's possible again. I've discovered an exclusive new fertility clinic with amazing success rates. The problem is they're extortionately expensive, which is another thing that makes leaving The Cygnus Foundation tricky. They pay well, and I need the money if we want to go down that route. We remortgaged the house to fund all the treatment we've had already.'

'It sounds like you need to speak to Vicky, Mate. Quitting Cygnus is a decision you should make together.'

'Yeah, I know. Thank you so much for being there for me. I'll go home now to speak with Vicky. It's getting late, even for me.'

'That's fine. Anytime. And remember, 8 p.m. at the Old White Swan tomorrow.' Nick man-hugged me before he walked to his car.

Caroline sat in bed reading. With flowing black hair and wearing my Metallica tee shirt, she emanated a seductive rock chick vibe. Her discreet smile and sepia eyes beckoned me. I put my arm around her, and she rested her head on my chest.

'Thanks for making yourself scarce,' I said.

'It looked like Nick needed to speak with you alone, and it might have been awkward with me there as I'm Vicky's best friend.'

'I've never seen him like that,' I said.

'What did he want?'

10

'I'm not sure, really. I think he just wanted someone to listen to him. He's not having a good time at work, but I couldn't make sense of some of the stuff he said. To be honest, he sounds a bit delusional. Talking about secret, scary shit developed by the biotech companies he works with. He wants to leave, but he thinks they have some hold over him. He's best off out of there if you ask me.

'He's having marriage problems too. Did you know they've been trying to have a baby for ages?'

Caroline kissed me. 'Yes, Vicky told me. But she swore me to secrecy. They didn't want others to know their business.'

'I've been such a rubbish friend, haven't I? There's all this stuff going on in his life that I know nothing about.'

'Don't blame yourself, Jamie. You can't make people share their problems if they don't want to.'

'Well, I will ensure I'm there for him now. Hopefully, he'll make it to the quiz night tomorrow.'

Caroline turned the light off, and I held her close.

'I hope we don't end up like that,' I said.

'One step at a time,' Caroline replied. She kissed me and squeezed my hand. 'We don't even live together yet, so trying for children seems a long way off. But maybe one day.'

Chapter 2. Nick – 26 April 2001

Nick stared at the framed wedding picture on his desk. He and Vicky looked so happy then. Why was it still there? No one else at The Cygnus Foundation cluttered their workspace with personal keepsakes. It was probably a culture hangover from his time at Ebor Assurance. There, smug parents typically displayed cheerful school photos for everyone to see. Perhaps he subconsciously marked out the space for when he could show off his own kids. He hadn't yet given up hope.

His office door opened. It was Claudio, Nick's boss.

'My secretary said you wanted to see me,' Claudio said.

'I was hoping to get away early today,' Nick replied. 'I want to go out tonight.'

'That shouldn't be a problem. Just ensure you have the reports ready to check before you leave. Also, how are you getting on with the programme? Dr Gillespie tells me you have constructive sessions, but he's not sure you're taking the medication. You need complete commitment, Nick. There are no half-measures.'

'That's the main thing I wanted to talk to you about,' Nick said. 'The programme's just not working for me. I've tried. I really have. But if anything, I'm becoming more stressed.'

'Perhaps if you took your medication?' Claudio offered.

'I really don't think so. I've concluded that I will never be a good fit for The Cygnus Foundation, so it's best for all of us if I leave as soon as possible.

'I'm happy to finish work with my existing clients. After that, I'd be grateful if I could forgo the twelve-month notice period. I won't expect any severance payment, and you can be assured that everything I worked on here will remain confidential.'

Claudio tensed his facial muscles and sucked in a slow, noisy breath. 'I'm not sure things can be as clean-cut as that, I'm afraid,' he said. 'You know the security of client information is of the highest importance to The Cygnus Foundation, and then there's the matter of your investments to consider.' Claudio looked out of the office window towards the Jaguars and BMWs in the car park as if pondering his response. 'Listen, Nick. I want to help you. I know you've tried your best, so I'll see what I can do about cutting your notice period. But can you do me one favour first, please?'

'What do you want me to do?'

'Dr Gillespie's visiting later. Please can you have one more session with him? I'd like his input into the best course of action.'

'Yeah, okay, but I doubt it will change anything from my point of view.'

'Great, what time do you need to leave tonight?'

'Before seven if possible.'

'All right, I'll ask Dr Gillespie to see you at six.'

Nick looked at his watch. Seven o'clock already. He'd lost track of time finishing the reports. Where was Dr Gillespie? Nick marched to Claudio's office to ask if he knew why the doctor was late. But Claudio was absent. Strangely the whole office was empty. This wouldn't have been unusual at his previous employer, but most Cygnus employees worked late into the night.

Nick returned to his office. Should he wait? He really wanted to attend the quiz, but he needed to play along with Claudio's game to maximise his chances of a quick release from his contract. So he texted Vicky and Jamie to tell them he'd be late.

Half an hour later, Nick's desk phone rang. It was the office security guard. 'The doctor's here to see you, Nick.'

'Okay, send him up.'

A tall man with slicked-back hair, wearing a dark suit, entered Nick's office.

'Hello, who are you?' Nick stuttered. 'I was expecting Dr Gillespie.'

The man replied, 'Dr Gillespie can't make it. But I'm here instead to ensure you take your medicine.'

Chapter 3. Jamie – 26 April 2001

A CALM MISDOER. 'No idea,' I said, my puzzle-solving skills blunted after four pints of Black Sheep ale.

'I didn't expect you to get it,' teased Patrick. 'But I hoped for inspiration from Caroline or Vicky. We normally achieve a perfect score in the anagram round – we've no chance of beating The Gladiators if we can't solve this one.'

'Imelda Marcos,' I blurted out, my subconscious finally deigning to kick in, most likely to spite Patrick.

'Yay, well done, Jamie, brilliant', enthused Caroline.

'Welcome to the party,' said Patrick. 'Right, I need to focus. History round next.'

It was Thursday pub quiz night at the Old White Swan, a quintessential York tavern, all ancient exposed beams, open fireplaces and tales of hauntings. The four of us worked in financial services at the Ebor Assurance Company. A career choice that requires a Faustian bargain to sacrifice any semblance of professional excitement for a steady income, pension scheme and private healthcare. Caroline, Patrick and I joined the company five years ago on the graduate trainee programme. Nick, and his wife, Vicky, started at the same time, moving to York from jobs in London. They were a few years older – childhood sweethearts who'd qualified as accountants together. But since securing his role at The Cygnus Foundation, Nick hardly ever came to the pub. And, so far, tonight was no exception. He texted earlier to say he would be late.

Patrick was smashing the history round. Fortunately, he still joined us for the quizzes. After his recent promotion to departmental head, we half expected him to be schmoosing with the senior management crowd. But we needed his encyclopaedic knowledge to beat our pub quiz nemesis, The

Gladiators – a bunch of old blokes who were probably hustlers on the York pub quiz scene.

'Which symbol of triumph did Julius Caesar establish in Rome to obscure his baldness?' Patrick spontaneously brushed his hand through his hair. A pale crown peeked through the thinning thatch as he tilted his neck to write the answer. I subconsciously mirrored the gesture. Satisfyingly, my fingers skimmed the rigid, prickly clumps cemented with gel – a look which Caroline compared to a hedgehog. The spikey sensation continued as I ran my hand over the stubble on my cheeks and chin. I liked to picture myself as stylishly unkempt. Still, tonight my appearance had degenerated into just scruffy – wearing a wrinkled white tee shirt and tatty blue jeans.

The final round was general knowledge. 'In which year was Black Wednesday, when the UK Government was forced to withdraw the pound sterling from the European Exchange Rate Mechanism?' This was one I should know. It happened when I was studying Economics A-level at school. '1993,' I suggested.

'It's 1992,' insisted Patrick.

'I think we should go with Jamie's suggestion. He has an A-level in economics,' said Caroline. Frustratingly, I had to double down on my answer because of Caroline's support – even though my confidence waned.

'I have a Business Management degree from Warwick,' retorted Patrick. 'Anyway, we need to get our answer sheets in, so we'll go with 1993. But it's Jamie's fault if we lose.'

It was strange how we all gravitated to York from different parts of the country yet made little effort to broaden our social circles beyond our office acquaintances. When we first moved to York, the company paid for us to stay in a bed and breakfast for a month, automatically creating our social group. We unconsciously replicated our friendship networks formed at school and university, deepening our dependence on Ebor Assurance. I had been jealous of Nick for escaping its clutches. Even though he was still an accountant, his work appeared much more rewarding. He was helping new ventures achieve their dreams rather than reconciling cash flow on thirty-year endowment policies. Yet, after our chat, I realised I should be grateful for what I had.

I kept scanning the door, hoping Nick would arrive. He used to have a knack for stealthily mocking Patrick. It would be great to experience his mischievous humour again. But Patrick had free reign tonight.

'Have you seen the new girl in Admin?' Patrick asked me.

'No.'

'If she took off her glasses, she'd be a split for Angelina Jolie. I wouldn't mind some of that.' Patrick often dated the new graduates. Presumably, they were seduced by his management grade and BMW Z3 Roadster.

Vicky was usually central to the banter, double-teaming Nick to fire barbs at Patrick. But she was understandably subdued this evening. Vicky was in solemn conversation with Caroline. Caroline's calming countenance hinted she was acting the role of counsellor. As ever, Caroline exuded composure and elegance, predominantly dressed in black, complementing her shoulder-length raven hair. I thought Caroline was mismatched for a career in marketing with an insurance company in York – simultaneously too urbane and too empathetic, better suited to a caring profession where she could directly make a real difference to individuals.

The clang of spoon striking glass quieted the pub. 'I have the results. It's a close one this week,' bellowed the quizmaster. 'As is tradition, I'll read the answers before revealing the winners.'

We were doing well. Patrick nailed the history round, correctly identifying that Julius Caesar wore a laurel wreath to hide the onset of baldness. Although chuffed to have contributed to the perfect score in the anagram round, I dreaded the remaining answers.

'And Black Wednesday occurred in September 1992.' Nooo. Patrick said nothing but glared at me and Caroline like a father might do to his children when he is not angry but is disappointed.

'So, the results are: in third place *May Contain Nuts* with 41. In second place with 45 is *The Ebor Handicap*. Jamie Glover, team captain, please come up and collect your prize.'

The team moniker was Patrick's doing. A play on our employer's name and the famous horse race at York Racecourse – Eboracum being the Roman name for York. Given the captaincy choice, I remained convinced he invented it with me in mind.

'And the winner is...*The Gladiators* with 46.' Pleasingly the announcement was greeted with a chorus of jeers from across the pub, not just our table.

I brought back the beer vouchers. 'Well done, everyone,' said Caroline.

'Nice one Jamie,' said Patrick. 'We should have learnt by now. If in doubt, go with my answer. Come on, Vicky, let's spend the vouchers at the bar. Oh dear, there are only three for second place. Jamie will have to miss out.'

'How's Vicky?' I asked Caroline.

'I'm not sure. I told her about Nick's visit last night. She's worried about him, of course. But I think she's in two minds about him leaving his job. It's not a good time for them to lose his income.'

'I hope she's okay tonight,' I said. 'She's drunk a lot. Another pint's probably not a good idea.'

We both peered towards the bar. The straight lines of Vicky's chestnut bob made her conspicuous. Patrick stood beside her in beige chinos and a pink Oxford shirt, looking like he was at a corporate away day. Patrick slipped his hand across Vicky's slender waist as he ushered her to the front of the drinks queue.

'I'll go and check on them,' I said, fearing Patrick might sense an opportunity with Vicky. He'd tried it on with Caroline in the past. 'I need to buy my drink anyway.'

'Do you want to stay at mine tonight?' Caroline asked.

'Yes, sure.'

'I thought we could share a taxi with Vicky to ensure she gets home okay.'

I returned to our table after buying my fifth pint. I would feel it on Friday, but I could doze through the end-of-week team meeting. Patrick and Vicky had already staggered back with the proceeds of our second-place finish. Caroline glanced at her watch and turned to Vicky, 'Jamie and I are getting a taxi back after this one. Do you want to share it?'

Before she had a chance to answer, her mobile phone chimed. Vicky's demeanour implied she was speaking to someone with magical sobering powers. I jumped at the shrill clatter of glass as her Nokia crashed on the table. With a haunting expression, Vicky turned to Caroline and said, 'I think something's happened to Nick.'

Chapter 4. Jamie – 26 April 2001

'Please hurry,' I yelled at the taxi driver as we travelled to Vicky's house, off Fulford Road. Fortunately, traffic was light in York after 11 p.m.

The police car waited outside. Two uniformed officers emerged. 'Hello, I'm PC Rosemary Slater, and this is PC Kieron McQueen. Can we speak to Victoria Shepherd, please?'

'It's Nick, isn't it?' Vicky replied.

PC Slater's silence implied Vicky was correct. Vicky collapsed into Caroline's arms.

We perched around Vicky's oak kitchen table in their Georgian villa. Caroline poured Vicky a glass of water, striving to calm her.

PC Slater shuffled in her chair, clearly uncomfortable about delivering the message. 'Mrs Shepherd, I'm sorry to inform you that we have identified a body found in the offices of The Cygnus Foundation, as Mr Nicholas Shepherd. He was confirmed dead at 9.30 p.m.' PC Slater's face was youthful with bright skin and high cheekbones. She was younger than me. Probably with scant experience in communicating such grave news. 'We are treating the death as suicide, but we are investigating further, and there will be a post-mortem.'

'Why do you believe he committed suicide?' asked Caroline.

'He was found with an empty bottle of medication prescribed for anxiety. We suspect he deliberately took an overdose.'

I couldn't begin to imagine how devastating this news was for Vicky. They had been friends since high school. Nothing can be worse than being told your husband has taken his own life.

PC McQueen informed Vicky that they could provide a counsellor. Vicky declined because she wanted Caroline to stay with her. I checked Caroline was okay with that. She said, 'It's fine. I want to be with you, but Vicky needs me more now. You should go home.'

I decided to walk back to my house in New Earswick. It would take over an hour, through the centre of York. But I needed to clear my head. And it was troublesome finding a taxi after midnight.

I tried to make sense of the previous two days. Was Nick's visit the night before a cry for help? Were his concerns about his employer justified? I had thought he was delusional. But could his death have been suspicious? His short text earlier indicated he was in a positive frame of mind. Whatever happened, I wondered how he might still be alive if I had acted differently. Was my advice a death sentence?

As I trudged past the looming York Minster, tourist throngs long since departed, the fuzziness cleared from my brooding. Perhaps the alcohol was wearing off. I perceived holes in PC Slater's articulation. She'd not mentioned a suicide note – I couldn't believe Nick would abandon Vicky without any explanation. It also seemed odd that he would do it at his office. I understood why Nick didn't want Vicky to find his body at home, but wouldn't he have gone somewhere more out of the way? I promised myself to find out what really happened.

At 2.30 a.m., emotionally and physically shattered, I collapsed onto my bed, eager for sleep to spirit me away from the sorrow. I awoke to the stench of smoke on my clothes – an instant reminder of the pain from the night before. I couldn't face work, so I called them to deliver the tragic message. They didn't know. Nick was popular when he worked at Ebor Assurance, so the news would stun colleagues throughout the company.

Caroline texted me that she was staying at Vicky's in the morning. She would try to help her cope by undertaking essential tasks such as calling close family. Fortunately, Vicky's sister from Manchester was due to arrive that afternoon, freeing Caroline to go home.

I'd neglected Nick in the preceding weeks because I'd become consumed by a project to landscape my garden. My house was in New Earswick, a suburb to the north of York, originally designed to be a garden village for the employees at the Rowntree's confectionery factory in the city. I'd bought a red brick early 1900's two-bedroom workers' cottage a year before. It was in a shabby state but liveable. My ambition was to refurbish it, both inside and out. I hadn't started on the house because my real passion was the garden. So, I embarked on a complete redesign of the

19

gardens to return them to former glories. I needed to purge the shoddily laid patio in the back garden. So I smashed concrete slabs with a sledgehammer to dissipate my despondency.

I yanked off my t-shirt and tossed it on a garden chair. Taking a deep slug of ice-cold lager, I admired the pile of broken patio slabs. God, that felt better. But I couldn't stop mulling over whether Nick had taken his own life. I needed to find out more, so I texted Caroline to let her know I was coming over, hoping Vicky's sister had arrived to relieve her.

Half an hour later, I parked outside Caroline's two-up, two-down, period terraced house, just off Bishopthorpe Road. I knocked on her door, as we hadn't reached the stage of exchanging keys. She answered. I shuddered backwards. Caroline looked like a zombie vampire, with puffed eyes and smudged mascara. She still wore the black jeans and blouse from the night before. I realised this was her first opportunity for emotional release without the need to appear strong in front of Vicky. She pulled me in for a long embrace. 'How are you coping?' She whispered.

'It's difficult. I keep thinking I should have done more to help him.'

'Don't feel guilty, Jamie. None of us could have really known what Nick was thinking.' Her soothing voice instantly calmed me.

'Are you okay?' I said.

'Not so good. Vicky told me more about what was going on with Nick, but I'm still confused. The police have asked her to speak with them. So, we might find out more after that. It's hard for Vicky to process what's happened and communicate it to others. Her sister, Julie, will let the rest of his family and friends know.'

'What did Vicky say about Nick?' I asked.

Caroline tenderly clasped my hand before speaking, 'She admitted they've had a strained relationship for a while, but it became much worse after Nick started at The Cygnus Foundation. She told me more about their fertility problems. They have been trying to have children ever since they moved to York. That was the plan: move out of London, buy a nice house in a good school catchment area, back up north, in a great place to bring up kids. But Vicky didn't conceive, so they started fertility treatment.'

'Did they find out what the problem was?'

'Vicky didn't explicitly say, but I think Nick was diagnosed with a low sperm count. So, they decided to go down the IVF route. They used up their NHS-funded attempts without success. This further strained their relationship, but they wanted to keep trying and fund the treatment themselves. Private IVF is really expensive – well over £5,000 a go. That's one of the reasons Nick changed jobs. He was after a big pay rise to fund treatment.'

'That's consistent with what he told me on Wednesday. He also said they remortgaged the house to pay for treatment.'

'I know. But did Nick tell you about his investment losses?'

'No, he just said he could make millions using what he knew about The Cygnus Foundation's clients.'

'Well, he might have tried, but he failed. Vicky told me he lost a fortune when the dot com bubble burst. And things escalated badly. Nick was under disciplinary action at work. They were investigating him for buying shares in the companies funded by the Foundation. Basically, insider dealing. He was trying to make up his losses.'

'I can't believe Nick would commit a criminal act. He had too much integrity for that. He was an accountant.'

'Yeah, I struggle to believe it too. But then you saw what Nick was like this week. He looked desperate.'

'How far have the investigations gone?'

'The Cygnus Foundation haven't called in the police yet, I'm not sure what evidence they have, but he could have faced a jail sentence if convicted. Vicky thinks Nick saw suicide as the only way out.'

Caroline's phone buzzed. 'Vicky's texted. Her sister needs to go back to Manchester tonight. Some problems with childcare. She wants me to go over later.'

'Caroline, you need to rest. I'm worried about you. Vicky needs professional help.'

'She needs to be with someone she knows. She hardly sees her neighbours. I'll be okay. I'll shower, rest and go later, and take some overnight things in case she needs me to stay.' Caroline noticed my face drop. 'We can get together again over the weekend.'

'Okay, I need to get back and sort out the mess in the garden anyway. I'm going for a run tomorrow morning. Do you want to come over to New Earswick and see how the landscaping's going tomorrow afternoon?'

21

Part 2: August 2020 – June 2021

Chapter 5. Wes – 26 August 2020

Wes Myers followed the arrows along the one-way aisle. He rigorously obeyed the convenience store's regulations. A fellow shopper doubled back towards the refrigerated section, brushing Wes in the process. 'Sorry, I forgot the milk,' she said.

Rita was at the till. Wes had spoken more with Rita during the past five months than anyone else. Happily, she ignored the prevailing sentiment, which frowned on contact between human beings, always eager to chat. Rita was remarkable. She worked there most days – indoors, unventilated, subjected to the public – at maximum risk of exposure to a deadly new virus. In contrast, Wes had been paid to stay home and do nothing. Yet Rita retained a joyful demeanour, forever interested in the welfare of her customers.

Wes had never observed Rita's entire face. Her mouth and nose remained masked. She was probably in her forties – with greying, curly hair and wrinkles around her eyes. But those eyes, alert and cheery, hinted at an inner satisfaction with her occupation.

'Wesley. How are you? I've not seen you all week,' Rita called out through the mask.

'I've been venturing further afield; now some restrictions are relaxed.'

'I hope you've not been two-timing me at the Monks Cross superstores.'

'No. I don't have a car. So I stay local. But sorry, I did visit the Co-op on Hull Road.'

'But you must come here to see me. I need you to tell me when COVID is over. Is it all over now, Wesley?'

'I wish I could tell you it was, Rita. But I'm not so sure. They've lifted some restrictions, but that growth rate is still troubling. The summer weather and school holidays should be keeping it down, but they're not.'

'Will you publish anything on your Twitter feed soon?'

'Yes. I've written a fascinating piece with strong local interest, ready to publish. A super spreader event that no one knew about because they hadn't linked the data. I'm just waiting for an expert to review it.'

'Ooh, I look forward to that. I love your Twitter COVID analysis.' A socially distanced queue formed behind Wes.

'Better go. Keep crushing that R-Rate. See you soon, Rita.'

Wes's phone beeped. A Direct Message from The Exonerator. He'd review it at home.

Wes hauled the groceries in two recyclable carrier bags along Melrosegate and around the corner to his bedsit. It was in a converted house – originally built for the council to accommodate local families. But now, it was privately owned by landlords adept at extorting the lucrative student market. Only Wes wasn't a student. He used to be, five years ago. But Wes liked it here, so he stayed – even after he graduated and qualified as a teacher.

Wes resided in the Tang Hall suburb, an area with a dubious reputation in York. The kind of place that touring comedians insert into template bad-neighbourhood jokes to make them relevant to the local audience.

But it wasn't too bad. Nowhere in York is. Just a little scruffy and lacking character. A mixture of red brick and rendered flat-front houses, terraced in blocks of three. A few boasted well-tendered gardens, but most were overgrown, with weeds sprouting through the concrete driveways. Wes swerved past the rust-spotted cars that obstructed the pavement; the road was too narrow to allow kerbside parking.

He lived upstairs. A self-contained bedsit of two rooms. A kitchen/lounge/bedroom. And a tiny shower room. Cheap and convenient. But a depressing place to isolate for five months. The students in the other bedsits had long since fled to the comfort of lockdown with their parents.

Before arriving home, he stopped at Mrs Cartwright's, next door. The Cartwrights bought their house from the council forty years ago to own the family home. But their children had grown up and departed for more upmarket locations. Her husband died of COVID-19 in April – leaving Mrs Cartwright alone, holding off the student housing entrepreneurs.

'Here's your shopping Mrs Cartwright. I've bought that chocolate you asked for.'

'Thanks, Wesley. Make sure you always remember the chocolate.' Mrs Cartwright didn't say much. All she wanted was chocolate and cakes. Had Mrs Cartwright once mentioned she had diabetes? Perhaps chocolate and cakes weren't a good idea. But Wes couldn't deprive her of all enjoyment.

Once home, Wes put the kettle on. He settled on the sofa and opened Twitter on his iPhone. The message from The Exonerator (Twitter handle @exonrrater) wasn't what he wanted to see: *'The data doesn't justify your conclusions. DON'T publish. I will explain in a message tomorrow.'* Wes was disappointed. He was sure the data warranted his findings with a high degree of confidence. But he wasn't an expert at interpreting medical or mortality data.

It was essential to remain credible in the Twitter COVID data community. The Exonerator's insight helped build Wes's profile – they (he didn't know their pronouns) had followed @mathsywes since the start. They'd reviewed his forecasting models and even pointed him to super spreader events the media overlooked. Wes's forensic COVID analysis was widely shared on social media, boosting his followers to more than five thousand. But much of his success was thanks to The Exonerator.

Who was The Exonerator? It was an anonymous account. But they'd conclusively proven their expertise. Were they an epidemiologist or an actuary? Maybe they worked for the government. But why had they gone cool on his latest piece? It's not as if he hadn't posted most of the data already – he just hadn't revealed the super spreader event that caused it.

The pandemic hit Wes hard. His life's purpose was to educate young minds – to help them appreciate the beauty of numbers, as he had as a child. To Wes, maths was a refuge from his callous parents and spiteful school bullies. The bullies used to call him Velma, after the Scooby-doo character, because of his jam-jar glasses and pudding bowl hair-cut, shorn by his mum. It irritated him that the insult wasn't even accurate. Daphne was the ginger, not Velma. After the seizures started, they just called him 'Spaz'. But Wes could escape their venom by immersing himself in the logic and purity of mathematics. Wes wanted to steer others to this enlightened existence (without the bullying), so he embarked on a teaching career – in contrast to many of his fellow maths graduates from York University. They snapped up high-paying jobs in technology or finance in London.

As well as teaching maths at a York state secondary school, Wes ran a voluntary club for local schoolchildren who expressed enthusiasm for mathematics. The objective was not just to academically stretch talented young mathematicians but to expand their outlook – introducing them to exciting concepts absent from the formal examination syllabuses. He hoped the club would function as a platform to inspire youngsters from disadvantaged backgrounds like his own. But it was overrun by brainy kids from private schools and affluent families.

However, the pandemic shattered everything that Wes loved. The teaching. The maths club. They all ended after lockdown in March. It was terribly unfair on the students, who had been preparing for life-defining examinations. To end up effectively abandoned, at the mercy of the bungling policy-makers dictating their futures.

On a practical level, the prospect of lockdown was unappealing too. He had no close friends and little contact with his parents in Essex. Medication kept his seizures under control. And although he didn't have to shield, his doctor recommended extreme caution. So, how would he spend his time?

But Wes quickly comprehended the true nature of a pandemic. Sure, the medical professionals were at the vanguard of fighting the disease. The scientists developing vaccines would ultimately take credit for suppressing the virus. But mathematicians wielded the true power. A mathematical model could explain and therefore forecast the pandemic. People needed mathematicians to answer their fundamental question – *What's going to happen?*

But the problem was the incomplete data. COVID-19 was a novel virus with new information emerging all the time. Yet politicians were still making momentous policy decisions based on imperfect modelling. This captivated Wes. He realised he'd found the ultimate practical application of mathematics to engage young minds.

He immersed himself in his new obsession, devouring new data sources and academic papers. Examples like the Diamond Princess cruise ship, quarantined in Japan after it was discovered that a passenger who disembarked in Hong Kong had tested positive for COVID-19. It functioned as an inadvertent experiment into the prevalence and fatality rate of the virus.

Wes found a community of experts already existed on Twitter, analysing and debating every snippet of information that furthered their understanding. This fulfilled not only his need for knowledge but also social interaction.

He started by building his own forecasting model. Wes found a vast appetite for COVID forecasts from people who'd realised that following the right accounts on Twitter satisfied a need for timely and balanced analysis. This was in contrast to the partisan government press briefings or the hyperbolic media. But he also knew that forecasting the future path of the virus would become more complex. Factors like new variants, seasonality, and (hopefully) vaccines would come into play. So, he dived into the detail of any country, city or locality whose data exhibited unusual characteristics – hoping this could provide greater insight and generate better forecasts. This was when he started corresponding with @exonrrater, firstly via replies to posts, then by direct message. The Exonerator found several instances where cases or the fatality rate spiked unexpectedly. So they worked together to establish the source – often a super spreader event.

But Wes was most proud of his recent analysis. He'd identified a spike in hospitalisations, especially at younger ages, which was strange because the severity of COVID-19 is strongly correlated with age. However, the spike was so subtle that it could easily be a random fluctuation. Wes was convinced he'd found the source. But The Exonerator reckoned Wes's analysis was flawed. Should he post the link to his findings regardless? Wes decided not to. It could wait another day, and he was going out for pizza later.

Chapter 6. Wes – 26 August 2020

'What's the volume of a pizza of thickness A and radius Z?' David Perkins asked the waitress bringing his Hawaiian thin crust.

'Err…PI*ZZ*A…pizza! Mr Perkins,' giggled the waitress. Obviously one of David's former students, familiar with his brand of mathematical dad jokes. David was head of maths at Wes's school. His boss. They were also out with Judy Thomson, a fellow maths teacher. They didn't often dine together outside school hours. Still, David wanted to celebrate the conclusion of this year's singular exam process and rally the troops before the return of face-to-face teaching in September. And, it was the last day of the *Eat Out To Help Out* scheme – a government bribe of £10 per meal to encourage people to leave their homes and spend money after lockdown. However, Wes believed it would do more to stimulate the R-Rate than the economy.

'Cheers.' They clinked their glasses of Frascati. 'Well done, team. I think the outcome of this year's A-level results was pretty good, all told, given the circumstances. Seventy per cent of our students are going to Russell Group universities. Two are going to Oxbridge,' said David.

'In some ways, I think teacher-assessed grades are fairer than exams, anyway,' replied Judy. 'Especially after that ridiculous algorithm, which so flagrantly favoured private schools, was ditched. We know the kids' capabilities best. So, reward for consistent attainment is better than a one-off assessment.'

'What about Nathan Fosdyke?' Wes responded.

'He was lucky to get a D,' David replied.

'Nathan's one of our most gifted students. As good as Tasha McDonald, and she's going to Oxford. He could have achieved an A or A-star in the exam, but now his future's in tatters,' said Wes.

'Remind me, what did he get in his mock?' said Judy.

'You know he failed. But that was because he turned up 45 minutes late

28

due to family issues. He didn't know then that the mock result would heavily influence his actual grade.'

'No one did,' said David. 'But that's not the only component. It was also based on assignment scores throughout the year. And Nathan only completed half of them. We had to follow the guidelines. There's no way we could have pushed him any higher. We only upped his grade to a D because you argued so hard for it.'

'But did you review the assignments he did complete? He's a natural. He picks up challenging concepts like complex numbers far more quickly than his peers.'

'He can always retake in October if he thinks he can do better,' said Judy.

'He needs the motivation to do it. He'll think everything's stacked against him. Especially when he sees average students from other schools scoring As.'

'Doesn't he go to your maths club?' Judy asked. 'You could use that as a springboard for a retake.'

'He came a few times. He didn't fit in. His brother, Troy, is a bad influence too. I'm worried he'll slump into his brother's lifestyle of petty crime and drugs.'

'You know Troy Fosdyke came to the school to plead on Nathan's behalf to increase his grade?' David said.

'That was the first time he'd been back at school since being expelled for breaking a boy's nose,' Judy scoffed. 'He also said he was going to "destroy" you if Nathan didn't get accepted to Loughborough University,' she said, turning to Wes.

Wes said nothing.

After the meal, Wes rubbed antibacterial sanitiser gel, from one of the numerous dispensers, into his hands. York was lively in the setting late-summer sun. The world was waking up. One of the few positives from the pandemic was the emergence of an outdoor dining culture. He unlocked his bicycle from a stand on the buzzing Parliament Street. He cursed. He'd forgotten his lights but could manage to cycle home in the twilight.

He had been looking forward to going out and meeting people at a social dinner. Why was he now so dispirited? Was it Nathan? David and

Judy meant well, but they were comfortable accepting one or two students falling through the cracks of an imperfect system. Wes wasn't. He would try to help Nathan realise his potential.

Wes cycled along an off-road cycle path, tracing a dismantled railway line, towards Tang Hall. The path was narrow, with thick unkempt greenery on either side. It was a shared space for pedestrians as well as cyclists. Wes usually had to clang his bell to maintain momentum, but it was mostly quiet tonight. Up ahead, two tall young men in dark jackets idled towards him, side by side. They didn't divert from their line of travel. Wes braked. 'Excuse me, please.'

'Get some fucking lights, man.' They were now only two yards ahead of him. 'Hey, it's fucking speccy Myers,' said the taller one. 'It's that cunt that fucked you up, Nath.'

Wes was facing Troy and Nathan Fosdyke. 'Hi, Nathan…Troy. Have you sorted a university place yet, Nathan?'

'No. I'm not going now. Thanks to you. I'm not getting a loan to go to some shithole uni that will accept someone with a D in maths. You gave fucking Flynn Harries an A, for fuck's sake.'

'I understand your frustrations. It's the guidelines we had to work with. But you can do resits. It will probably be better to skip a year anyway. You won't get a proper university experience this year with all the COVID restrictions. Let me help you. You can come back to school. I can give you personal tuition.'

'Don't listen to him. He's a nonce.' Troy was now inches from Wes's face. Wes's glasses were steaming up. 'It's always the same with people like us, Nath. They fucked me. Now they've fucked you.'

'How about some social distancing?' Wes implored.

'All right then, you asked for it.' Troy shoved Wes. He fell sideways, losing balance, off his bike – engulfed by the dense shrubbery. Twigs and thorns clawed his face and arms. Blood trickled down his cheeks.

'Is that fucking two metres?'

'Leave him alone, Troy,' cried Nathan.

Wes started shaking. Uncontrollable, wild. Shrieks of laughter from Troy as Nathan tried to pull him away. A mist descended. Wes was in a school playground, surrounded by a sea of contorted faces – some terrified, some cheering. 'Look, everyone. Velma's spazzing.' Then

30

everything disappeared.

Where was he? What had happened? Why did his face smart so much? He grimaced. His skin fractured as if encrusted in dried mud. He made out a series of sharp monochrome lines illuminated by a streetlight piercing the curtains. It was a wall poster – *Escher's Ascending and Descending*. A wave of relief momentarily dulled the aching. He was home.

The floorboards creaked. He wasn't alone. Who was there? Nathan? 'Is that you, Nathan?'

'Hello, Wes. You had a nasty fall.'

'You're not Nathan. Who are you? What are you doing in my home?'

'You've been too clever for your own good, Wes.' Wes pawed his face. 'Does it hurt? Don't worry. It will all be over soon.'

Chapter 7. Millie – 22 June 2021

'Mind if I sit here?'

'Yes, if you're going to eat that. And we're still meant to be social distancing,' Millie Kumar replied. Kyle Hill ignored her and flopped onto the seat opposite Millie. He opened the buff paper bag and withdrew a Big Mac, large fries, a strawberry milkshake and nine chicken McNuggets.

'Who else is joining us?'

'No one, it's just for me. Want a chicken nugget?'

'No, I'm vegetarian. And it smells disgusting. Did you get me a coffee?'

'Thought you hated McDonald's.'

'I do. But the coffee's okay. Better than the shit they serve here,' Millie said, pointing to the drinks machine, in the corner of a canteen area at York Police headquarters. The room contained three tables, two vending machines, a microwave, kettle, big fridge and a sink.

'I was hoping to bump into you, Mill. Got a puzzle for you to solve.'

'Isn't that literally your job, Detective Sergeant Hill, you know, to solve things?'

'Yeah. But this one's right up your street. There's a data slant. Officially it's case closed – pressure from upstairs. But the governor won't let go. To be honest, I think it's a waste of time – most likely suicide or an accident, but not suspicious – though there are a couple of loose ends. We thought you might spot something. Come at it from a different angle.'

'What's with the "we"? Don't you and DCI Slater think data science in the police is like snake oil?'

'No. It has its place. Facial recognition technology is awesome. But law enforcement won't turn into Tom Cruise in *Minority Report* like the Home Office think. If we used your predictive algorithms to solve crimes now, I'd be collared for every other misdemeanour in York. They're basically another form of systemic racism.'

Millie spat out a mouthful of her insipid coffee. 'Whoa, do you want my help or not? And, anyway, it's not like that now. Our AI algorithms are super advanced, with full inherent bias monitoring. It's not early 2000s Quantico. We're all about complementing traditional law enforcement, not replacing it.'

Millie was a data scientist for York Police. She started six months ago. Previously she worked at Ebor Assurance. It was a weird time for a career change. After endless months working from home, she yearned for the buzz of workplace interaction. But January brought another lockdown with updated home-working orders. She met her new colleagues over dispassionate Zoom calls. Millie's only face-to-face contact was her support bubble, Shiv, her mum. So, the call to return to the office was a blessed relief. But human interaction brought new problems. She worked in a newly created position for York Police but detected hostility towards her function. Some people just had a natural aversion to new methods. And perhaps the traditional coppers thought she was a harbinger of new technology to replace their roles and cut costs. That was disappointing.

Millie was cognisant of the power of data because of her previous work as a data scientist at Ebor Assurance. But she recognised its enormous potential in other areas – one of them being law enforcement. So when the job at York Police popped up on LinkedIn, she decided to go for it. The pandemic had piqued her interest in opportunities away from finance. And she needed to escape the sex pest at Ebor Assurance.

'So, tell me about the case then,' said Millie.

'It's a body of a maths teacher, Wesley Myers, found at his home in Tang Hall in August last year.'

'I remember. The York Press reported it. It made a change from articles about COVID and people finding big chips.'

'Yes, an anonymous 999 call reported Westley Myers was "having an epileptic fit" on the Tang Hall cycle path. The caller named the victim. The ambulance arrived but couldn't locate him. Uniform went to his home the next day and discovered the dead body on his bed. He was in a grisly state. Crusted with blood and covered in scars. But the forensic report concluded the cause of death was an overdose of the medication Myers took to control epilepsy.'

'Presumably, finding out who made the call was the first priority?'

'Yes, we traced it to an eighteen-year-old, Nathan Fosdyke. He was one of Myers's students. He initially denied making the call but then changed his story. He said Myers had a "fit" and fell off his bike. He was scared, so he ran away.'

'Does that account for the scars?' Millie asked.

Kyle slurped the rest of his strawberry milkshake through a straw. 'Crashing into the bushes could have caused them. But, according to medical reports, he'd not had a seizure for more than five years. His medication kept it under control. So we suspected something else, possibly traumatic, happened. Especially as elevated stress levels can trigger seizures.'

'Did you find anything?'

'Well, Nathan Fosdyke has an older brother, Troy, who has a string of convictions, including assault. Troy recently threatened to "destroy" Wesley Myers.'

'What? Why?'

'Because of Nathan's maths A-level result, of all things. It caused his preferred university to reject him. They held Myers responsible. Teachers set the grades because of COVID. Myers was Nathan's maths teacher.'

'Wow. I bet you don't come across that motive often?'

'Troy had a grudge against the school too. They expelled him for beating up another pupil. We suspected Troy's involvement. Eventually, Nathan admitted Troy was there too.'

'So, what happened?'

'His revised statement made more sense. Myers was cycling towards Tang Hall. Nathan and Troy Fosdyke blocked his path. It was dark and quiet. They challenged him about the A-level grade. Troy moved too close. Myers told Troy to socially distance, so Troy pushed him away, hard. Myers fell off his bike and plunged head-first into the dense undergrowth. That caused the scars and presumably brought on the seizure. Troy told Nathan to run, so they did. Nathan later called 999, supposedly overcome by remorse.'

'But then, if he did have the seizure on the cycle path, how did he get home, and why did he overdose?'

'Cleanest theory is he recovered and made his way home. He overdosed as a reaction to a return of the seizures. I think that's the most likely scenario. It could have been accidental or deliberate.'

'Well, I assume he fits the profile. Let me guess. Male, twenty to thirty, living by himself, isolated by weeks of lockdown?'

Kyle nodded. 'There you go with your profiling again. But he had no record of depression, and the school said he was an excellent teacher who loved his job. Highly popular with the students.'

'What were the other loose ends?'

'His bike, phone and laptop were missing. We've still not found them.'

'Couldn't Troy have just stolen them? He does have a criminal record, after all.'

'Maybe. Troy denied it. And we don't think Myers had his laptop with him at the time.'

'Troy could have carried out an opportunistic burglary, knowing Myers was incapacitated?' Millie suggested.

'Again, that's possible. But there was no evidence of a break-in at Myers's bedsit. Only Myers's fingerprints. There's no security camera footage. We only brought an assault against Troy for pushing Myers.'

'Anyone else have the motive to harm Myers? I presume you've checked friends, family, finances?'

'Couldn't find anything. Myers lived a lonely existence. No close friends, girlfriend or boyfriend; estranged from his family; spending within his means; no gambling debts; no drugs. The only contact from outside teaching we could find was his next-door neighbour, Ada Cartwright, an old-timer. Myers did her shopping.'

'What about social media?'

'That's where we could use your help. Myers didn't use Facebook but built a large Twitter following. Posting about COVID. He was a bit like you, a data nerd.'

'Thanks,' Millie grinned.

'He was part of a Twitter community of mutual back-slappers. But a Rita Shuttleworth called the station after reading about Myers in the paper. She works at his local convenience store. She seemed devastated. They used to have long conversations about the progress of the pandemic.'

'I bet the other customers loved that.'

'She'd spoken to him on the day he died. Said Myers told her he was about to publish "fascinating" new COVID research. We've no idea what it was about. And, of course, we don't have his laptop to examine. It's probably not relevant, but DCI Slater wants someone with a data analysis background to take a look. It's a long shot, but there could be clues that we missed.'

Millie was grateful for the opportunity to get her hands dirty. The work in her first six months had been peripheral. Tasks like familiarising herself with HOLMES 2, the system UK police forces use to investigate major incidents, reviewing data query methods, and reading various academic papers about data science in law enforcement. Big data could be a potent tool for crime-solving. But it was scary just how much data was available about individuals in the modern world: social media, smartphones and watches, fitness trackers, satellite navigation, ride-hailing apps, DNA ancestry tests, census, electoral register and much, much more. An abundance of data was publicly available. Power rested with the custodians of that data and those that could exploit it – whether for benevolent, commercial, or even nefarious purposes, such as voter manipulation. Millie was wary about the big brother overtones of her new role. Especially when the police had access to even more information – security camera footage, facial recognition technology, DNA and fingerprint databases. But data could be used as a tool for good too. And Kyle had given her a chance to show what she could do.

'I'm off duty later, so I'll give you all the details tomorrow,' Kyle said.

'Are you? Fancy a drink when you get off to discuss it further?' Millie asked.

'Could do a quick one. But I'm watching the England match with my mates later.'

What was wrong with men of her age? Did their emotional intelligence evaporate around women? Initiating a relationship during a pandemic was hard enough already. It was obvious Kyle liked her, yet Millie had to make the first move. It was understandable for males in financial services – an industry that attracts its fair share of shrinking violets. But surely the police force would be different? Kyle was on the promotion fast track. He'd cultivated a tough-guy image and was in decent shape (despite his appalling

36

diet and long hours). But put him next to a woman he fancies, and his detective skills dissolve – incapable of discerning the clearest signals. Maybe those skills were redundant in the age of Tinder. Contrast that to a particular senior manager at Ebor Assurance – unfortunately, he wasn't a shrinking violet. One drunken snog at the 2019 Christmas Party, and he wouldn't give up – flowers, emails, inappropriate messages, dick pics. She'd long since surpassed the communication by subtext stage. But he still wouldn't accept an unambiguous, 'Fuck-off. I'm not interested.' What made him think she'd be into a tubby, balding man twenty years her senior? Well, maybe the money and power. But they were qualities that bored Millie.

'Never mind,' Millie responded.

'Are you free next Monday evening? I'm off duty then.'

'As long as it's not McDonald's.'

Chapter 8. Millie – 28 June 2021

Millie glanced at her Apple Watch. Ten past seven. Ten minutes late. Had he misheard her and gone to The Old White Swan? Or perhaps even just The Swan, on Bishopgate? Why were there so many swan pubs in York? Millie was in The Black Swan Inn, white-washed walls carried by a crisscross of black timber beams and window frames bearing lead lattice panes. The fifteenth-century building was like an antique chessboard stranded in an Ikea furniture display. It appeared incongruous in this corner of the city – juxtaposed with modern offices and the densely fabricated apartments of the Hungate development, where Millie lived.

She scanned her phone for messages – nothing, that was partly good news. Her digital stalker seemed to have finally taken the hint. She stared at the iPhone, aimlessly checking social media apps, avoiding direct eye contact with the other punters. Of course, a single female at a table in a pub can attract unwanted attention. But, in truth, it felt safe enough. The other drinkers were minding their business. The oak-panelled walls and patterned carpet generated the homely ambience of a quaint tea room rather than an edgy boozer.

Kyle entered the bar and scanned the room. His gaze lingered when he located Millie's table. She was wearing a shimmering rubescent top and black trousers. A waterfall necklace and silver bangles glowed on her tawny skin. Dark hair cascaded down her back, complementing her body's curves. 'Wow, you look stunning,' Kyle said as he kissed her on the cheek.

'Thanks. You're lucky I'm still here,' Millie replied with a mischievous glint in her eyes.

'Sorry I'm late,' said Kyle. Let me buy you a drink.'

'Thanks. I've already had two. Needed to fill the time.'

Kyle returned from the bar with a pint of Guzzler and a glass of Pinot Grigio.

'Turned anything up on the curious case of the dead maths teacher?'

'Yes, I'm starting to build an understanding of Wesley Myers. He was a smart cookie. I think I'd have liked him.'

'See. I knew you'd have a fondness for another data geek.'

'He made a real name for himself in the COVID data community.'

'A bit like being a famous train spotter?' he snarked.

'You'd be surprised. Remember, in the first half of 2020, people craved anything to help them make sense of what was happening. The government press briefings were rubbish. No forecasts – probably because the public doesn't understand uncertainty. And the media crucified the first official projections published. So, the public devoured the musings of anyone that could fashion a decent forecast. And Wesley was good. He wasn't spot on. No one can be with forecasts. But he was adept at recognising trends – where we would be in a few weeks – far more quickly than the government or media. Just before he died in August, he tweeted his concern about rising case rates. Prescient, if you consider what transpired over autumn and winter.'

'Okay, so you've a hard-on for Wesley Myers. But are you any closer to finding out why he died?'

'I'm getting there. As the pandemic progressed, Wesley realised forecasting was getting harder. More factors came into play. Variants, vaccines, immunity and so on. To increase his understanding, he accessed data sources from across the world. But he gained an edge by creating his own data. Trawling the internet for connections to COVID cases.'

'How do you mean?'

'Well, he'd studied research proving a single event could seed a country. For example, nearly half the cases in Malaysia were traced to a single religious event. Wesley built algorithms to search for COVID-19 references, using sources such as Facebook, Twitter, and local media. He tried to link social media mentions to explain spikes in COVID cases or hospitalisations. We all know about the first UK super spreader events – the Cheltenham Festival and the Liverpool Champions League match.'

'Against Atletico Madrid.'

'Yeah. Wesley started there. He searched individual posts that mentioned a COVID case and the particular event. But he progressed to smaller, unknown super spreader events. He matched people that belonged to certain groups, like sports clubs, churches, offices, or factories – to pinpoint likely sources of mass spreading.'

'Very clever. Is all that information public?'

'Yes, he was simply smart enough to process free big data. As a result, he advanced public understanding of how the virus spread.'

Kyle sipped his beer. 'Do you think he could have angered anyone, or any organisation, enough to want to silence him?' he asked.

'There's no indication. Feedback was overwhelmingly positive. But Wesley's posts shortly before he died were different.'

'How so?'

'He thought he had found a spike in hospitalisations at younger ages, in local hospitals. One striking thing about COVID is that hospitalisation rates follow an almost perfect exponential relationship with age. They double every 16 years. So, it was curious to see higher rates for younger adults and children. However, many followers thought he was reading too much into small data samples. It was just random fluctuations. But interestingly, Rita Shuttleworth said he was about to publish some new "fascinating" analysis. I wonder if he was poised to reveal what he thought caused the spike.'

'Have you worked out what he was thinking?'

'Err. Not yet. I can't establish any connection to his data. And even if I did, I'm not sure it would get us closer to discovering why he died.'

'You disappoint me. I thought you were the shining star of modern law enforcement.'

'I've thought of a couple of avenues we could explore, which might help me solve it.'

'You need my help?'

'Yes. I reviewed all the Twitter accounts that regularly networked with @mathsywes. Most are named and identifiable. But the account that interacted most with Wesley was @exonrrater or The Exonerator.'

'Sounds like a Batman villain.'

'Wesley and The Exonerator collaborated on many of Wesley's findings. But interestingly, The Exonerator didn't respond to Wesley's most recent posts. And The Exonerator's only tweets are responses to @mathsywes. He or she doesn't tweet about anything else. It's like they set the account up solely to communicate with Wesley. I've tried to search them, but the handle's non-existent elsewhere on social media. Can you find out who it is?'

'No, that will be a dead-end. It's hard enough to identify anonymous trolls on Twitter. We'll never uncover the owner of a responsible account who's not broken any rules. So, what's your other avenue?'

'Have you investigated whether there have been cases with similar characteristics?'

'What, you think there might be a serial killer bumping off maths teachers in York?'

Millie sniggered. 'No, but presumably, you think there's a possibility it could be suspicious. So did you investigate other local deaths where phones or laptops were stolen?'

'There's nothing else recent I'm aware of that fits the profile of Myers's death.'

'That's a pity,' said Millie. 'It often helps to put additional factors into the algorithm. For example, there might have been something I could use to find a link to Wesley's COVID data analysis. Sometimes you discover data links in the most surprising places.'

'Well, all crime incidents are digitised now, so why not search for links yourself?'

'Okay, I'll have a look tomorrow.'

'Sorry, I won't be able to help you. I'm off duty.'

Millie flicked her hair away from her eyes and tilted towards Kyle. 'I'm sure I can manage. But it might look like I'm doing your job for you. Are you ever at work?'

'First full day off in two weeks. Criminals are running amok after lockdown.'

'You don't want to talk shop anymore then, do you? It's been a crap date so far.'

'Who said it's a date?' Kyle replied. 'Another Pinot Grigio?'

'Tell me about Millie,' said Kyle. 'Have you any brothers and sisters?'

'No. It was just my mum and me when I was growing up. Mum kicked my dad out when I was four – exasperated by his serial cheating. He lives in London now.'

'That must have been tough. Do you ever see your Dad much?'

'I sometimes met him for dinner on work trips to the capital. But not since the pandemic. We get on okay, but we're not that close.'

'So, you're close to your mum, then?'

'Yeah – she's done a brilliant job combining the mother and father roles. Mum was obsessive about my education. She wanted to ensure I could always provide for myself if necessary.'

'Did she mean to turn you into a nerd, though?'

Millie kicked Kyle's ankle and then grinned. 'Fuck off. I'm baring my soul here.'

'Go on then,'

'It wasn't easy for Mum. She was diagnosed with breast cancer when I was in the sixth form.'

'God, Mill, I had no idea.' Kyle touched Millie's hand. She entwined her fingers in his.

'How is she?'

'Cancer free now, thankfully. But even when she was going through the mastectomy and treatment, her primary focus was me. Making sure I achieved good A-levels and went to university.

'But although I gained good grades, I decided not to go to university. I wanted to repay Mum for everything she'd done for me. Be there for her and bring in an income. So I followed in her footsteps and took a job at Ebor Assurance.'

'So, how did you end up crunching data for the police force?'

'I stumbled into the data science career path at Ebor Assurance. And I was lucky. They funded my training. So I got a degree anyway. I even started earning enough to afford a mortgage. And Mum, ever the pragmatist, encouraged me to get a foot on the property ladder. But I fancied a change – I didn't want to work in insurance forever, and there was some shit going on that made me want to leave. I thought this job looked exciting, and here I am.'

'What was shit at your old work?'

'Oh, just boring stuff I needed to get away from. But I don't want to talk about it now.'

'Okay, what about your property? Where do you live?'

'You can see it if you walk out of the pub door. It's a third-floor apartment. The buildings are crammed, but it's right in the city centre.

There's even a reading café where I can chill with a book and a latte. And, if I crane my neck, I am just about able to glimpse York Minster from my bedroom window.

'Anyway, I'm starting to feel like I'm in one of your interrogation rooms. Talk to me about DS Kyle Hill. How did a big city boy like you end up in sleepy York? It's hardly a hotbed of urban crime.'

'Not much to it, really. The chance for promotion to DS came up in York. So I transferred from Leeds in 2019. But I still live there. I prefer it to York, both on and off duty. More energy. More grit. But you have to take the opportunities when they come along. I also like the governor. She moved to York Police in 2019 too. From Newcastle – a promotion to DCI. Even though she started her career at York Police, DCI Slater is still considered an outsider, like me.'

They finished their drinks. 'I'd better go. I've drunk too much. I'll need to get an Uber,' Kyle said.

'Do you want to come and see my Minster view?' Millie replied.

Part 3: April 2001 – May 2001

Chapter 9. Jamie – 28 April 2001

I drove to Castle Howard, a magnificent stately home (paradoxically, not a castle) fifteen miles northeast of York. The eccentric follies, bridges, and graceful landscaping created a fairy-tale vista – a perfect location to train for the Great North Run half marathon. And emollient escape from my recent trauma.

I planned to cover a 10-mile circular route around the estate's myriad of public footpaths. Starting south of the house, then along a trail to Coneysthorpe, a picture-postcard village of cottages horseshoed around a green.

An ephemeral mist carpeted the adjacent fields as I ran along a gravel track. A pyramid peaked through the fog, like a faraway mountain emerging from the clouds. A sparrowhawk hovered above. Occasionally, it swooped and soared like a rollercoaster, its intermittent warble disturbing the early morning silence. I trotted over the New River Bridge. To my right, The Mausoleum stood tall, like an elaborate half-domed wedding cake, elevated by a circle of columns. Below, a single majestic swan, its nest like an island kingdom in the reeds, guarded seven eggs.

As I approached the village, a cyclist knelt by her bike, inspecting a tyre. She was the first person I'd glimpsed since starting the run. 'Are you okay?' I yelled as I jogged past.

'I think I have a puncture,' she said. I was mindful that the attention of a dishevelled man (I hadn't shaved all week) might appear menacing to a woman stranded on a lonely road. But from painful experience, I understood the frustration of a puncture, miles from home. I wanted to repay the previous kindness offered by passers-by.

'I'll have a look if you like. I've had loads of punctures before, so I might be able to help.'

'Thanks. Typically, it's my first long cycle on this bike, and I get a puncture.'

'It's really easy to get a flat around here. There are still lots of thorns on the roads from hedge cutting.' I stooped to examine the front tyre. It was unquestionably flat. I inflated the tyre utilising the pump attached to the frame. But we watched the air swiftly empty. I felt around the tyre and eventually located a substantial thorn protruding from the rubber. 'This is the offending article,' I said. She knelt beside me. Even though she wore a cycle helmet, I couldn't help but notice her facial beauty. Her eyes were extraordinary. They were an indefinable colour, with hints of green, brown, gold, and grey – engendering an aura of enigmatic curiosity. 'Do you have anything to fix a puncture?'

'No, I'm so stupid to come this far without preparing. And I don't have a phone.' She was well-spoken with a faint foreign accent, which I couldn't place. Possibly Italian but with a slightly harder edge.

'Don't worry; I never cycle with a spare inner tube. So I've often pushed my bike back home for miles, although once I was lucky, passing cyclists fixed it for me. How near are you to home?'

'I'm not sure, but I think it's more than ten miles.'

'I have a phone in my car so you can call someone to pick you up. It's in the car park a couple of miles away.'

'I don't know anyone who can come.'

'Okay, we can push your bike to the car park, and I can drive you home or take you to a bike shop to get a new inner tube. I should manage to get your bike in the car if we take the front wheel off.'

'As long as you don't kidnap me.' She didn't appear too menaced. 'But I don't want to spoil your run.'

'No problem,' I said, shocked at her sense of humour. 'I'm training for the Great North Run. But it's not for another six months, so I have plenty of time to get in shape.'

Her eyes lit up. 'Are you? I'd love to do that; the atmosphere must be amazing. I've watched it on television.'

'You should. I think they are still accepting entries.'

'I don't think so.' She said without explanation.

We took turns pushing her bike along the country roads toward the car park. Her name was Renata. She removed her helmet to reveal shimmering flaxen hair tied in a ponytail.

She carried the athletic figure of a frequent cyclist. I was 6 ft. Renata stood only an inch or so shorter. She asked what I did. It's peculiar how our employment defines us. I replied, almost apologetically, that I worked in pensions. At parties, it's a calamitous mistake to admit to a vocation in financial services. It usually results in your interlocutor concocting a polite excuse to exit. I wished I'd fashioned a thrilling alter ego. But Renata appeared enthralled.

She quizzed me about what it was like in an office and then, unfathomably, eagerly interrogated me about pensions and the economic dilemmas of ageing populations. 'Why do countries continue to rely on the young to fund pensions for the old?' she challenged. 'People are living longer, but birth rates are declining in rich countries. Society strives to increase lifespans, but it can't afford the consequences. As a result, state pensions will collapse in fifty years. There won't be enough people working to pay for older-age pensions.'

'My job's about helping people build up their own pot to allow some independence from the state.' I tried to explain.

'But why would you and I forgo money now to prepare for a world that will be unrecognisable in fifty years?'

'Because the government gives big tax breaks to encourage saving,' I said meekly.

'But that's exactly my point. It's such a waste of resources. The money squandered on tax breaks would be better allocated to help people stay economically active. Future medical advances mean that common debilitating conditions in older age will become ancient history. Why prepare for retirement when there's no need to retire?'

'So people will have to work 'til they die then?' I objected.

'No, governments and companies like yours should focus on helping people achieve a balance throughout their lives, mixing work and leisure. Policymakers still assume forty years of work, sandwiched in between twenty years of education at the start, ending with twenty years of torpid retirement. The prelude to a grateful passing. That thinking belongs in the last century.'

A muntjac deer sprang across our path. Renata instinctively grabbed my arm. My heart started pounding, and I wasn't sure why.

We'd reached the car park. 'Where's home?' I asked, taking off the front wheel of her bike. It just about fitted into my Golf GTI.

'Can we find somewhere to fix it, please? I haven't any spare inner tubes at home.' I drove to Malton, the nearest town, to find a cycle shop. It was half an hour before the shop opened, so I suggested breakfast at a nearby café.

Over a full English in a traditional market square tea shop, I tried to probe Renata's background. What did she do? What was driving her trenchant views on the unproductiveness of long-term saving? She wasn't exceptionally forthcoming but did disclose she was born in Italy and came to the UK as a young girl. Her mother brought up Renata and her two sisters (she didn't reveal what happened to her father). I remarked on the similarities with my upbringing. My mother struggled to raise my sister and me after my dad died of a brain aneurysm when I was twelve. Renata used this to switch the conversation back to my life adeptly.

'That must have been traumatic, especially at that age.'

'I've tried to bury those memories. The day my Headmaster at school called me out of a maths class. My dad, Keith, was on a job in Slough. He owned a building company in Reading, down south. He just collapsed on site unexpectedly. The ambulance arrived too late for the medics to help him. We were fortunate he didn't die at home in some ways because that would have been even more distressing. The next couple of years were tough for the three of us – me, my mum, Susan, and my younger sister, Erica. Dad hadn't left much money, but his endowment policy paid off the mortgage on our house, in Tilehurst, near the football ground. Mum toiled to pay the bills, working on the tills at Sainsbury's. However, she still needed to sell the house to make ends meet, and we ended up in local authority housing in the south of Reading. Mum and Erica shared a bedroom so I could have my own room.'

'Your mum sounds like an incredible person.'

'She is. My dad was too. We were a happy family. The three of us relied on each other to get through that period. Mum then secured a job as an administrator at Prudential in Reading. That's where she met Mike, an actuary, and her future husband. They married, and we moved into his four-bedroom 1930s detached house in Caversham, near the Thames.'

'How did you and Erica cope with a new stepdad?'

'We were lucky. He couldn't replace Dad, but Mike's a terrific bloke, and I think he truly cares for Erica and me. He's ten years older than Mum, but he's a bit geeky and awkward in social situations and never married or had children. I think he was seeking a ready-made family, so it worked for all of us. He helped me focus back on schoolwork. If it weren't for Mike, I wouldn't have achieved the grades I needed to attend university. I think it's also because of him that I ended up in financial services. I'd experienced first-hand what life can do to you if you don't have protection – insurance, I guess. Living with Mike revealed the cocoon a career with a large corporate can provide – nice house, nice car, benefits package – who wouldn't want that?'

I paused, waiting for a challenge from Renata. But none came. I think she could sense it was an area I found difficult to discuss. I couldn't believe I was expounding quite so much about my dad's death to a stranger. It was a topic I usually tried to skirt around, even with Caroline – she'd learnt it was a subject to avoid.

I glanced at the clock on the café wall. It was past 10.00 a.m. We'd long finished breakfast and a refilled pot of tea. 'Shall we check if the shop can replace your inner tube?' I suggested.

They stocked the right inner tube, and Renata's bike was fixed and ready to use after a few minutes. 'Are you okay cycling home?'

'Yes, fine.'

'Well, best try and stay away from thorny hedges,' I counselled. 'It was good to meet you, Renata.'

'What's your number, Jamie? I'd like to take you out to thank you for rescuing me.' Without thinking, I gave it to her.

When I returned to the car, I took my phone from the glove compartment to check for messages. Three missed calls from Caroline and a text that said, *'Please come to Vicky's as soon as you can.'*

Chapter 10. Jamie – 28 April 2001

The letter had arrived that morning. Caroline passed it to me and said, 'What do you make of this?'

Dear Mrs Shepherd

PRIVATE AND CONFIDENTIAL

It was with extreme sadness that we learnt of the death of your husband, Nick, at The Cygnus Foundation offices. We wish to offer you our sincere condolences. Nick was a highly valued member of the Cygnus family, and his colleagues will greatly miss him.

I know this is a challenging time, but I also wanted to inform you of the position regarding Nick's workplace benefits. The Cygnus Foundation provides a life insurance benefit of four times salary. However, a condition of the insurance is that death by means of suicide is excluded for employees within their first twenty-four months. Nick had served seventeen months at The Foundation, so, unfortunately, you are not eligible to receive the life insurance payment if the cause of death is confirmed as suicide.

However, we do wish to recognise Nick's contribution to the Foundation. In respect of this, as a gesture of goodwill, we would like to offer you a single payment equivalent to twenty-four months' salary. This would be paid directly by The Foundation. If you wish to accept this offer, we request that you sign a document confirming your consent to abide by the terms and conditions of the payment. These include an agreement that you will not discuss the circumstances surrounding your husband's death with the press.

You may be aware that your husband was supporting internal investigations regarding private investment in some of The Foundation's partner organisations. Agreement to accept the payment offer will bring this matter to a close regarding your husband. The payment terms also prohibit the discussion of any matters relating to the investigation.

Once again, we offer our condolences for your tragic loss. We hope you accept the goodwill payment in recognition of Nick's service to The Foundation, but we require a decision within the next seven days. Please contact me at any time on the above number.

Yours sincerely
Claudio Macina
Chief of Staff, The Cygnus Foundation

'It's a strange letter,' I said. 'It's almost as if they're trying to buy you off.'

'They sent me some flowers too,' Vicky pointed to a vase of white lilies beside the fireplace. 'I think it's a genuine gesture. I know Caroline's filled you in with some of the background. They knew that Nick and I were undergoing fertility treatment because of the number of odd days he was taking off and that it was exerting a heavy financial toll. They want to do something to alleviate my financial situation because they realise they should have done more to recognise Nick's issues and help him.'

'But I don't understand the part about the internal investigation,' I said. 'I hope you don't mind me being too blunt about it, Vicky. But it's as if they're saying take the money and keep quiet about anything linking The Foundation to Nick's death. If you don't, there's an implied threat about the consequences of some kind of nefarious activity Nick was up to, which I don't believe. But it's almost as if they're worried about further scrutiny on Cygnus. Surely if they thought something illegal was going on, they would have involved the police already?'

'The Cygnus Foundation are extremely sensitive about disclosing where they're investing and managing their external image. They're involved in several innovative, confidential, and sometimes controversial initiatives. So, their threshold for an investigation wouldn't necessarily be the same as for the police.'

I was surprised at Vicky's lack of animosity towards The Cygnus Foundation, given its involvement in Nick's death – especially when I'd experienced how scared he was of his employer. I was concerned she may make a rash decision when at her most vulnerable. But I could also understand why she would want to bring matters to a close. 'Well, if you're going to take the payment, please ensure you get someone with legal training to review what you're agreeing to.'

'I think I need to take the money. I can't afford the mortgage on my salary alone, and our savings are pretty much exhausted.'

Before I thought, I said, 'Don't you have a life insurance policy to pay off the mortgage?' I immediately regretted it, not wanting to labour the circumstances of Nick's death.

'We did. But the conditions are the same as his life insurance at work. We remortgaged this year to realise some equity to pay for IVF. We took out a new life policy at the same time, so it won't pay out for suicides in the first 12 months.'

'Have you reviewed Nick's investment dealings? Do they shed any more light on what Cygnus were investigating?'

'Yes, I have. But I haven't managed to glean anything other than he squandered all our savings and left us mortgaged to the hilt. However, always the accountant, he maintained scrupulous monthly records of his positions. But I wanted you to have a look. You might spot something – I know you and Patrick used to play the markets with Nick. Perhaps that seeded his hunger for speculation.'

It comforted me to see Vicky more composed than after the quiz. But I now sensed a bitterness towards Nick for his profligacy. And even some hostility directed at me – maybe for encouraging his recklessness, or, more likely, because I did nothing to stop it. She handed me a folder of trading statements.

I leafed through the folder. It contained monthly statements listing the amount and value of Nick's stock holdings. They started in early 1999 when he'd amassed around £50,000 worth of shares, primarily in large-cap stocks like BP, IBM and ICI. However, his investment profile transformed throughout the year, with an increasingly heavy weighting of internet stocks, presumably seduced by their seemingly perpetual ascent. Initially, these performed well, almost doubling the value of his portfolio by the start of the millennium. But, heavily exposed to the dot com collapse, it dropped to less than £10,000 by the end of 2000.

But his troubles worsened. In early 2001, £120,000 was deposited into the account. Presumably from the remortgage. Did Vicky know what was going on? Over the next few months, this was invested in a motley bunch of entities, some listed in alternative markets overseas, others initial public offerings. Two things were instantly evident. Firstly, I'd never heard of any of them; secondly, they'd all bombed.

I asked Vicky if I could use her laptop to look up some of these companies. The financial information was sparse – explaining why they weren't listed on the leading indices. But the ones I could locate were all involved in innovative research in areas such as genetically modified crops, animal testing and gerontology (the study of ageing). These were precisely the kinds of companies I'd envisaged The Cygnus Foundation financing. However, there was no mention of The Foundation in my searches, which might be explained by their desire to keep a low profile.

I was surprised at quite how poorly his portfolio had performed. Modern biotech stocks can be volatile – if they demonstrate a breakthrough to the market, they often skyrocket, but if not, they frequently plummet. I guess Nick was undermined by poor market timing. From the last statement, the current total value was just over £20,000. But some of the investments were illiquid, so whether Vicky could recoup the full book value was questionable.

Although there was no explicit evidence of insider dealing, Nick's new employment had influenced his investment strategy. And if Nick was insider dealing, he'd used the insider information egregiously. So Vicky's acrimony was understandable, as was accepting the monetary offer from The Cygnus Foundation.

'I'm so sorry, Vicky. I had no idea what he was up to. Did you know your remortgage proceeds would end up in his investment account?'

'Of course not. It was meant to stay in our savings account to fund IVF.

53

I don't think I can ever forgive him for squandering our savings. Or leaving me,' she sobbed.

As Caroline wrapped her arm around Vicky, my phone rang. Unidentified number. 'I need to take this,' I said, skulking into Vicky's hallway – hopefully out of earshot.

'Jamie, it's Renata.'

'Err…Hi'

'Are you okay to speak?'

'Yes, fine,' I fibbed.

'I want to thank you for rescuing me this morning. How about I treat you to fish and chips at Whitby next Saturday? We can meet at the train station at midday?'

'Sounds good.'

'Okay, see you then. Bye.'

'Who was that?' Caroline asked as I returned to the lounge.

'Oh, just Patrick checking I'm okay for five-a-side on Wednesday,' I lied. 'Listen, I need to get home and shower.'

'Shall I come over later?' Caroline asked.

'No, probably best not. I'm tired and don't feel like company tonight.'

Chapter 11. Jamie – 30 April 2001

I passed the statue-endowed turrets of Bootham Bar on my way to Ebor Assurance's office. I'd become inured to the allure of this ancient place. Corporate life in York was a contradiction. A city conquered by tourists – it lacked the morning rush of besuited bodies typical in commercial centres like London, Leeds or even Reading. Yet here I was, venturing toward another day in that most corporate of corporates – a financial services company. The historical backdrop made no difference. But today was different. Nick was dead.

It was Monday. My first day back at work. I'd spent Sunday in the garden, smashing concrete slabs and clearing rubble. I hadn't spoken to Caroline again. The way I'd brushed her off on Saturday was inconsiderate. But Renata represented a thrilling refuge from the gloom engulfing me in York. Whereas Caroline was, blamelessly, embedded in that despondency. I'd speak to her at the office.

I laboured to my desk. Patrick was already in. 'Hey Jamie, shit times, man. How's Vicky holding up?'

'Not good, but it's starting to sink in.'

'Okay. I put a message on the works intranet on Friday and have organised a collection and card for Vicky.'

'Thanks, Patrick.'

The death of a colleague, or a colleague's partner, is challenging to handle in the workplace. It's a rare occurrence in an office with an average age in the mid-thirties. I was thankful Patrick took the initiative, releasing Caroline or me from the task. But a card and collection seemed to trivialise such a solemn occasion, putting it in the same bracket as birthdays, retirements, and new babies. But I knew people wanted some way of letting Vicky realise they were thinking of her.

I checked my emails. One missed day and more than a hundred had accumulated in my inbox. A message told staff to dispose of the magnetic paper clip holder the company had gifted us to celebrate their stellar results. It turned out it might corrupt a computer's hard drive – typical waste of money. And, they were nowhere near as useful as the previous year's present – an Ebor Assurance branded USB pen.

The morning passed uneventfully. Some colleagues came over to find out more about what had happened to Nick. Shiv Kumar, who once worked in Nick's team, hugged me and said, 'I can't quite believe it.' But most people kept their distance. I hadn't seen Caroline, but she worked on the floor above. Then I noticed the diary invite. Lunch?

We decided to eschew the charms of the office canteen and head for Café Concerto, near the Minster. We sat at a corner table in the narrow coffee shop with music scores plastered on the walls. We ordered the lunch deal – sandwiches with crisps and a drink.

'What did you do on Sunday?' Caroline asked.

'Oh, just working in the garden. How about you?'

'I stayed with Vicky on Saturday night and most of Sunday.'

'Any more news from the police?'

'No, but PC Slater is going to Vicky's at 5 p.m. to update her. They've completed the autopsy.'

'Will you be there?'

'Yes. I think it would be helpful if you came too. We need to make sure we ask the right questions.'

'Okay, I'll come over if Vicky's all right with that?'

'Of course she will be. How are you coping, Jamie? You seemed distant on Saturday.'

'Sorry, I was tired after my run. And my emotions are scrambled. I realised how little I knew Nick – I was such a shit friend. But also the shock of the swiftness with which our lives can disintegrate. It's bringing to mind what it was like when Dad died. And it's prompted me to re-evaluate my life – I think I was stuck in a rut, even before Nick.'

'Am I part of that?' She asked nonchalantly.

I agonised over what to say next. Caroline looked so classy – dressed and made up for work, in a black tailored blazer and a white blouse, sipping a cappuccino. 'It's mainly work. It's not going anywhere, and I think I'm bored. But maybe we're part of that. Everything's become routine.'

56

Caroline ripped open her crisp packet, scattering potato chips over the table. Her eyes were welling. I'd disregarded how tough the previous few days had been for her.

'This sounds like a break-up to me,' she said. 'I thought you liked how things are, keeping your own space but having a girlfriend on tap.'

I placed my hand on hers. She flinched. 'I don't know,' I admitted. 'I suppose I just want to take control of my life, rather than just let stuff happen. I still need you as a friend. Especially now Nick's gone.'

'Ah, so you're demoting me from fuck-buddy to bar-buddy, now there's a vacancy?'

'You just pipped Patrick for that position,' I feebly joked.

'Look, I have a meeting at two. I need to go. I'll see you at Vicky's later.' She slammed £5 on the table and marched out. I had a meeting too. But I waited a couple of minutes before paying and leaving.

I wasn't expecting that. I hadn't gone to lunch intending to split up with Caroline and was already regretful. I reflected on my new found isolation. I had thought of Nick as my best mate. We enjoyed chatting about football and cars and making jokes at Patrick's expense. But Caroline was my best friend, my muse. We talked about everything (other than football) – politics, movies, travel, garden design. Had I lost her now too?

I left work at 4.30 p.m. and took the bus to Vicky's. Caroline answered the door. 'Hi Jamie,' she said coolly. No kiss or embrace. Vicky offered me a cup of tea, and we waited, mainly in silence, for PC Slater's arrival. She was on time and showed herself to the same kitchen chair she'd taken on Thursday.

'We've concluded our investigations,' she said. 'The results of the post-mortem show that Mr Shepherd died of an overdose of a barbiturate he'd been prescribed due to stress and trouble sleeping.'

I glanced at Vicky. 'Yes, I knew he was taking medication to treat anxiety. But he stopped going to our normal GP in Fulford. Instead, a doctor was treating him through work.'

PC Slater continued, 'We have no evidence that the death was suspicious, so it will be recorded as a suicide by means of deliberate overdose. Unless additional evidence comes to light, we will not be investigating further. You are free to arrange the funeral and collect the body.'

'But don't you think it was strange that he died in his place of work?' I said.

'Not really. It's not uncommon for suicides to happen in the workplace. A cleaner found Mr Shepherd's body at 8.30 p.m. in his private office. We've investigated the circumstances, and we were aware he was being treated for anxiety and was having financial difficulties.'

'So that's it? Case closed. Nick died by suicide, and Vicky loses her life insurance payments,' I replied.

'Yes, sorry. Unless you know any evidence to the contrary, we've not considered?'

'Look at the text he sent me that evening,' I said, holding up my phone. 'He intended to come to the pub later. Does that sound like someone who's about to take their own life? It's just so out of context. Nick wasn't capable of doing anything like that. Isn't that right, Vicky?'

'Sadly, that's not true. Nick did talk to me about ending it all. Our inability to have children, investment losses, pressure at work, and the fact that our relationship was struggling, were getting to him. That's why he was on the medication.'

I wish I'd kept my mouth shut. I was just making it worse for Vicky. And he'd said the same thing to me, but shamefully I'd ignored his cry for help. PC Slater left. Vicky and Caroline said they needed to sort out the funeral and speak to The Cygnus Foundation about the goodwill payment. I offered to help, but Vicky said, 'We're okay, thanks, Jamie.'

Chapter 12. Jamie – 4 May 2001

Psychologists say having something good to look forward to reduces stress and boosts mood. For me, the anticipation of Saturday's rendezvous with Renata just about kept me going. I drifted through work (which I did most weeks). I drank too much beer by myself. I turned up to five-a-side football on Wednesday but expended my latent aggression by unreasonably taking out an opponent with a late tackle, which caused a scuffle. Patrick told me to calm down. Talk about hypocritical.

I hadn't spoken to Caroline. We'd bumped into each other a couple of times in the office but just said hello. She sent out a group email to people who knew Nick and Vicky, informing them that Nick's funeral would take place the following Thursday at York Crematorium. I was disappointed not to get a personal invitation. Still, Vicky later texted me to ask if I could read a eulogy, which I was pleased to do and would help me focus on something else.

By Friday, I was getting nervous about my date (was it a date?) with Renata. I hardly knew anything about her. No number. No address. Our phone conversation lasted less than 30 seconds. I started to wonder whether our meeting was a figment of my imagination – manufactured as a release from the distress of Nick's death.

I looked in the mirror. The week had taken its toll. My designer stubble transformed into an unkempt beard, my mousy hair a bedraggled mess, and my eyes bloodshot through too much alcohol and lack of sleep. I awoke early on Saturday, shaved, and then journeyed into York for a haircut and eye drops. We were only having fish and chips, so I wore a casual look – jeans with a button-up shirt over a tee shirt.

It took over an hour to drive to Whitby. I arrived at 11.45 a.m. and parked near the station in the Marina car park. The aroma of fish on the chilly sea breeze and the squawks of circling gulls signalled my arrival at a working coastal town. The abbey perched on the hill to my right, majestic, like a shadowy lion king surveying his savanna.

I wasn't sure where Renata was coming from. I scanned the passengers disembarking the 11.55 a.m. from Middlesbrough – none were Renata. I waited in the station until 12.15 p.m., but there was no sign of her. Was she a fantasy?

I exited the station to examine the surroundings.

'Jamie, sorry I'm late.'

I took a second look. Renata sported a blue dress, patterned in black and white swans, under a pink fleece jacket. A white designer rucksack on her back. Her cheeks were flushed as if she'd hurried here in her white sneakers. Her enigmatic eyes and golden hair scintillated as the sun peeked past a cloud. I noticed a flower stall outside the station and wished I'd bought her a bouquet. She was worth the wait.

Renata reached over to kiss me on the cheek.

'No problem,' I said. 'I wasn't sure where you were coming from.'

'Okay to eat now?'

'Yes, I'm hungry. I was up early.'

We secured a table at Trenchers fish and chip shop near the station. It was busy. The clientele was a mixture of holidaymakers and locals.

'How's the tyre holding up,' I asked.

'Well, it got me home. How about you? Still having fun at work? Have you solved how people can afford long and happy lives?'

'Err. Not yet.'

'Get on with it then,' she said with a smile. 'Why are you working there? There's no point coasting along with no objective. We're all here for a reason. You just need to find out what yours is.'

'Why are you here?'

'To thank you for rescuing me.'

'And what's your bigger purpose?'

'To help people lead better lives.'

'So, what are you, a social worker? A medic?'

'Kind of. When I'm not working, I help look after my sisters. They've become poorly, so they need more support now. When I have time, I help at a clinic.'

I was pleased Renata had revealed more about herself, but I was

60

reluctant to pry about her sisters.

'Did you go to university?'

'No, I didn't get the chance. I've had an unusual education. When we came to England from Italy, my mother wanted me to be home-schooled. She was concerned I'd fall behind as English wasn't my first language, so she organised a tutor. That arrangement persisted throughout my education. It worked for me. I'm knowledgeable. But I didn't go to university. I had too many commitments at home.'

'Maybe in the future,' I suggested. 'Didn't you miss the company of other kids at school?'

'No. I don't think so. My sisters were, are, enough. Oh, and our dog Sandy, of course.'

'I'd like to meet them sometime.'

'I hope so. Anyway, enough about me, tell me what you're going to do. Let me help you discover your life's purpose.'

There it was again. Renata was deflecting the conversation back to me. I told her about Nick, how the experience had resurrected interred memories about my dad's death, and how I felt in a rut and wanted to take control of my life. Essentially what I'd told Caroline. However, I didn't mention Caroline's part in my turmoil.

I found myself freely chatting about the events that had conveyed me to where I was. Getting to university. Taking geography at Lancaster. The shock of the transition to life in northern England. Drifting into a job in financial services via the university milk round (I didn't want to become a geography teacher). Moving to York. Buying my house. How my social life revolved around Ebor Assurance. My glacial career progression.

'Living in York is strange,' I said. 'It doesn't feel like living in a northern city. More like a theme park once you're inside the city walls.'

'Are you going to eat those?' she enquired as I massaged the mushy peas with my fork.

'Mushy peas are something else about the north I've never understood. What's wrong with petit pois?' We'd been in the restaurant for over an hour and a half.

'Shall we wander up to the abbey?' she suggested.

We crossed the swing bridge, a causeway that unites each half of the town

61

and establishes a natural harbour in the River Esk. Next, we ascended a quaint cobbled thoroughfare of shops selling Whitby jet jewellery and Dracula-themed souvenirs. Then climbed the 199 steps to the church and abbey ruins at the hill's crown. Renata wanted to rest, which surprised me because I'd assumed she was in better shape than I was. So, we sat on a bench by the church, overlooking the town. Renata tilted into me, hopefully not just as protection from the biting wind. I sidled my arm around her as we scanned the spectacular vista.

We progressed toward the grey, ruined abbey looming ominously ahead. It's easy to comprehend why it inspired Bram Stoker's *Dracula*.

'You're not a vampire, are you?' I quipped.

'I wouldn't be out in the afternoon sun, would I?'

'No, but you did need to rest when we reached the church.'

'Maybe I am, then. That Bram Stoker was a prescient chap. We'll all be like vampires one day.'

'Err. How do you mean?'

'In the 1890s, he wrote of Count Dracula feasting on the blood of his victims to retain strength, vitality and even immortality. Organ transplants are enhancing people's lives today. Essentially the same as Dracula. They use someone else's body parts to boost strength and increase lifespan. Technology will inevitably improve throughout this century to make replacement organs readily available, artificially grown or mechanically manufactured. Some people even believe that transfusion of a young person's blood can slow ageing.'

'But people aren't going to become immortal, are they?'

'There's no theoretical limit to human lifespan. But immortality shouldn't be a goal. The world couldn't cope with that. But people will live longer, more productive lives. That's why your industry needs to adapt.'

'I don't think that I could face working forever. An eternity in front of spreadsheets at Ebor Assurance would be a hellish nightmare.'

'That's why you need to find your calling. Seek a noble quest to become your life's ambition. Or pursue new learnings and achievements. But don't stay still.'

'It didn't work out for my friend Nick. The allure of life expired for him at thirty. Do you know your plan?'

'Yes, I'm clear on what I'm here to do.'

Waves crashed into the rocks to our left. As we chatted, we continued walking, losing track of time. We were now on the coastal path, which undulated and zigzagged across the cliffs and craggy outcrops southwards. We eventually reached Robin Hood's Bay, an old fishing village of sandstone and white-rendered houses with red-tiled rooftops clinging to narrow, twisting streets.

Walking and talking was thirsty work. So, I suggested a drink at a pub on the main street down to the tiny cobbled slipway. We sat at a window table facing the front and shared a bottle of Sauvignon Blanc and a jug of water.

'I think we'd better get a bus back to Whitby,' I said. 'We'll be lucky to arrive before dark if we walk.'

She looked across the street. 'Let's stay.' I choked on my wine. 'You're not doing anything tomorrow, are you? Look, there's a vacancy across the road at the bed and breakfast.'

This day with Renata had transported me to a magical place, far from my despondent existence at Ebor Assurance. Away from reality. I was thrilled it wouldn't end. But the first thing I said was, 'I think I only have a ticket on the car for today.' What was I thinking?

Her face dropped. 'You can get a taxi back to Whitby if you like. I'll pay.'

I peered into her unfathomable eyes and kissed her. 'Renata, there's nothing I want more than to stay here with you. Even if it turns out you are a vampire. I've no idea why I was thinking about a parking ticket. I've lived up north too long. I'm transforming into a skinflint Yorkshireman.'

I crossed the street and booked the last room at the bed and breakfast. Renata ordered us food at the pub. We both chose lasagne and salad. Perhaps the garlic bread was a mistake. We speedily devoured our second hearty meal of the day, our appetites expanded by exercise and sea air.

We explored the village before checking in to the B&B. We were allocated a small front-facing room with a partial sea view. It was tastefully furnished. Brown painted walls, with auric towels and cushions atop white linen on the double bed.

I awoke in an unfamiliar place. Was I dreaming? The sun peeped through the side of the blinds. Renata was still snoozing. A strand of hair clung to her cheek. I was spellbound. But she was a conundrum – assured, intelligent and sophisticated – yet she savoured every experience as if new to her but fleeting. Was she waiting for a jailor to return her to a vicarious dungeon?

I slipped out from the duvet, gently nudging her naked arm, trying not to wake her. I studied the mark on her wrist. She sported a small tattoo of a black swan – it further enhanced her air of mystery and elegance.

I entered the ensuite bathroom. It turned out Renata's rucksack was actually an overnight bag. Had she planned to stay over? Her washbag was open next to the sink. I didn't want to be nosy, but I noticed boxes of pills and tablets. Unusual for someone in her early twenties, especially as she appeared so healthy. I glanced in the mirror. At least there were no fang marks. And I could still see my reflection.

She stretched her arms and blinked as a shaft of sunlight brushed her face. 'Come back to bed,' she said.

At 10.30 a.m., we emerged to share our second full English breakfast. Yorkshire sausages, bacon, black pudding (which, like mushy peas, I still didn't understand), eggs (fried and scrambled), mushrooms and tomatoes. With hash browns and toast. 'I need to curb these breakfasts,' I said, thinking about how much I'd drunk over the preceding week. 'I'll be in no shape for the half marathon.'

'You'll be fine. You've had sufficient exercise this weekend. And you can wear it off on the hike back to Whitby.'

Renata paid for the room with a clutch of twenty-pound notes from her rucksack. The receipt was addressed to Mr and Mrs Glover.

'Let me at least go halves,' I implored.

'No, my treat,' she insisted.

We trekked back up the coastal path. Hand in hand. Deep in conversation. I was conscious I wore the same sweaty clothes, but she didn't seem to mind. Or, at least, she ignored the smell.

Whitby Abbey appeared into view. Now a portentous beacon, signalling the untimely termination of our exquisite sojourn. As we entered the town, I asked Renata if she could stay longer. She said she needed to get back.

'Can I give you a lift anywhere?' I asked.

'That's okay. I can make my own way.'

'I don't even know where you live or have any way of contacting you.'

'I'm sorry. I can't tell you now. It's complicated. But I will. I promise.'

'When can I see you again?'

'I'm coming to York next Friday with my sister, Fleur. Can you take time out of work to meet us? Maybe go for a walk along the Ouse. Shall we meet at the new Millennium Bridge at one o'clock?'

'Of course,' I said. Knowing I'd manufacture an excuse to decline any meetings I might have at that time.

After Renata left, I wandered the streets of Whitby for a while. I passed the row of Whitby jet jewellery shops. Something caught my attention that was perfect for Renata. So, I bought it, praying I'd see her again to give it to her.

I drove back to York, developing a severe case of Sunday blues. The start of the working week would bring my euphoria crashing down. Even though I was still buzzing after the weekend with Renata, I harboured a nagging reservation that something unsaid thwarted any prospect of a blossoming relationship.

Chapter 13. Jamie – 10 May 2001

I'd reached the age of twenty-six and only ever attended one funeral. Not my dad's. Mum thought it would be too disturbing for Erica and me. At seventeen, I went to my stepdad's mum's funeral (was she a step-grandmother?). I'd only met her once, at Christmas, so I was pretty detached. She seemed ancient. In her eighties. The wake was mostly an excuse for a few old dears to have a natter over a sandwich and a complimentary glass of sherry.

This would be grimly different – a talented man terminated in the prime of life. The cause of death, unspoken but ever-present, loaded a further gloom to the proceedings. This was the context under which I had to deliver a eulogy. I arrived at Vicky's with trepidation.

A blue BMW Z3 was parked outside. What was Patrick doing here? Caroline answered the door, natural and graceful in her black dress. An embrace was appropriate under these circumstances. Vicky had asked me to take her and Caroline to the funeral, but I hadn't expected to bring Patrick. Hang on, was I second choice for chauffeur duties? My black Golf deemed slightly more suitable for the occasion than Patrick's two-seater knob-head Beamer.

'Thanks for coming, Mate,' said Patrick, emerging from the kitchen. 'Mate' emphasised in the most alpha-male way possible. Why wouldn't I come? It was my best friend's funeral.

'I thought you'd make your own way,' I responded.

'I want to ensure Vicky has as much support as possible.'

They followed me to my car. The hearse arrived on Vicky's road. Caroline sat in the front, next to me, which I found surprising given our situation. I expected her to be in the back, consoling Vicky.

I glanced in the mirror. FUCK. FUCK. How had I not figured this? My knuckles whitened as my hands strangled the steering wheel. Patrick had placed his hand on Vicky's thigh. Her hand was on top of his. Scarcely a gesture of comfort. More like the body language of lovers. Events immediately fell into place; the principal reason for Nick's despair – usurped by rutting buck Patrick for failure to impregnate his childhood sweetheart. And why Vicky was comfortable going along with the suicide verdict. I was sure Caroline knew. Why hadn't she told me?

We followed the dawdling hearse. Fortunately, the short journey to the crematorium in Bishopthorpe only took ten minutes. A large crowd gathered outside the chapel, including several of Nick's former colleagues from Ebor Assurance. Had anyone come from The Cygnus Foundation? Vicky asked me to sit in the front row with her parents, sister, and Caroline. I was relieved Patrick kept a low profile, seated with some of his work team behind us.

The celebrant enunciated what I assumed was a standard calming funeral homily. He spoke a few words about Nick. Vicky had sent him a copy of my speech, so we didn't overlap. Now it was my turn.

I trudged up to the wooden lectern. The celebrant gave me an encouraging nod as I climbed up to look out over the mass of friends and family gathered before me. Shiv Kumar caught my eye. She was sitting with Nick's old team. Her eyes were wet, but she gave me a reassuring smile. I started by saying, 'Nick was loved by so many people.' Then I looked down at my notes and choked, recognising the hypocrisy of the following line. 'But no one loved Nick more than his wife, Vicky, his sweetheart since high school in Manchester.' Vicky stared forward, stony-faced, as Caroline held her hand.

I then talked about Nick's intelligence, ambition, quick-wittedness, loyalty, and friendship. I also mentioned his love of football, particularly his passionate support for Manchester City. But City's relegation from the Premier League was confirmed the previous Monday after a defeat to Ipswich Town. So I joked that one consolation is that Nick wasn't around to witness that – which seemed to hit the right note.

At the wake, in a Bishopthorpe pub, I eventually managed to corner Caroline. 'How long's it been going on?'

'I don't know.'

'But before Nick…?'

'Yes'

'When did you know?'

'Not 'til after Nick died, but I have suspected for a few weeks.'

'Why didn't you say anything to me on the night Nick came to my house? He needed to speak to someone about it, but it was too tough for him to acknowledge Vicky's infidelity. I could have made it better.'

'What would you have done, Jamie? When was the last time you spoke to Nick before then? Vicky was going to leave him, which, to be frank, is what he deserved after squandering Vicky's savings and drowning her in debt. You don't have a time machine.'

'But with Patrick? Vicky and Nick used to poke fun at him constantly. We did too.'

'Patrick's charismatic and ambition is an attractive feature in a man.' I assumed that was directed at me.

'Really?' I spotted Patrick splitting off from his work colleagues, manoeuvring in our direction.

'Everything all right, Caro?' he asked.

'Perfect,' I said. 'I'm going to get a drink.' But then remembered I was driving. I couldn't wait to get home.

As Vicky's chauffeur, I was amongst the last to leave. Fortunately, Patrick opted to catch a lift to his car in Fulford, so at least I wouldn't have to endure another journey with him. I didn't challenge Vicky about Patrick. That was for another day.

I dropped Vicky and Caroline off at the house. I was aching to be liberated. But, as I was about to drive home, Caroline rushed back out of the house and screamed, 'Wait, Jamie. Vicky's been burgled.'

Caroline and Vicky were standing by the front door. Vicky sobbed uncontrollably as Caroline held her. I cautiously entered the house to witness the emptied contents of drawers and cabinets scattered around the floor. The door to the French windows, at the back of the house, into the lounge had been forced open. The intruders must have also broken through the back gate, the only way to access the rear garden. I assumed the burglars were long gone, but I needed to check all the rooms. I grabbed a rolling pin as an improvised weapon.

I jumped at each tramp on the rickety staircase. My footsteps echoed throughout the house, making them sound like movement elsewhere.

Upstairs, all the bedroom doors were closed. I gingerly twisted the first doorhandle. My heart thumped, and I flinched as a nearby clatter shattered the silence. But no one was there. It was just a precariously scattered box falling from the bed. Household detritus was strewn over the carpet, just like downstairs. My sympathy for Vicky had cooled. But this was the last thing she needed.

I called 999 and suggested it would be sensible not to touch anything and wait for the police. They arrived within half an hour. It was PC Slater and PC McQueen. The two officers who had delivered the news of Nick's death. They managed the situation professionally, concluding (as I had) that the intruders entered from the back garden. They asked Vicky if she could see anything of value missing. 'I can't see the laptop,' she said. 'But it looks like most of my jewellery is still there.'

They asked us to wait for the crime scene investigators to arrive. PC McQueen spoke to neighbours. While Vicky tried to assess the damage, I told PC Slater that this was an unlikely coincidence, occurring so soon after Nick's death. She didn't share my worry. She looked at me as if I'd just insisted the moon landings were faked or that MI5 ordered a hit on Princess Diana. A crazy conspiracy theorist.

'Why do you think it's connected to Mr Shepherd's death? There have been a series of burglaries in this area recently, conforming to a similar MO. Forced entry. Opportunistic. The funeral cortege clearly suggested the house would be empty.'

To reinforce my foolishness, PC McQueen returned to report that several neighbours noticed 'suspicious-looking teenagers' loitering in the vicinity. I wasn't convinced, especially as Nick and Vicky's personal laptop was missing. Was there something on it that The Cygnus Foundation wanted to erase?

Vicky's parents and sister arrived for assistance, so I decided to leave, comfortable that Vicky and Caroline could manage without me. Vicky could stay at Caroline's if she needed to. And she could always call on Patrick for comfort, of course.

Chapter 14. Jamie – 11 May 2001

When did bring your child to work day become a thing? I could understand why Ebor Assurance wanted to propagandise the financial services industry to potential future recruits. But surely exposing the ennui of Mummy's or Daddy's daily office existence would scar them for life? Shiv Kumar approached my desk. 'I thought your speech at the funeral yesterday was beautiful. Nick would have appreciated it.'

'Thanks, I hope so,' I said, genuinely touched.

A timorous-looking girl, dressed in a school uniform, emerged from Shiv's shadow. 'This is Millie. She's five. Can you tell her about pensions?' Just what every 5-year-old girl wants to know about.

'What's your favourite subject at school, Millie?'

'Maths.'

'Well, perhaps you might become an actuary here someday.' I noticed Shiv had wandered off to talk with a colleague. What was I meant to do with Millie? I saved and closed my spreadsheet and asked, 'Have you played Minesweeper before?'

'No.'

Minesweeper is a classic game on Microsoft Windows. Crucially, accessible on work computers, so perfect for idling through a fallow hour or two.

'It's brilliant fun. Here's what you do.' I showed her the grid of grey squares. I clicked a block, which opened out to reveal some coloured numbers in a few adjacent squares. I explained what the numbers meant and how she could use logic to deduce which squares were clear and where the mines were. Shiv was still chatting, so I let Millie sit in my chair and play the game. Unable to work, I sneaked to the café to get a coffee – probably breaching numerous security protocols by leaving my computer unlocked, under the control of a 5-year-old. But then that was Ebor Assurance's fault for allowing a herd of children to roam the office. 'How are you getting on?' I asked.

'Look, I've done it,' she said. Millie had located all the mines and completed the hard level in less than two minutes. Way faster than my PB.

'Amazing,' I said. Truly amazed. Shiv was still chatting. So I went over to tell her I was finished with Millie, conscious that I needed to take an extended lunch break later.

'She's a smart kid,' I said.

'I know. Did you learn about pensions, Millie?'

'No. But I can play Minesweeper.' Shiv glared at me as if I'd condemned Millie to a lifetime's torment, addicted to computer games.

'Thanks, Jamie.'

Millennium Bridge had opened a month before. A pathway for cyclists and pedestrians spanning the River Ouse, suspended by what looked like a futuristic lyre, charming the track to transcend the water. It connected Fulford with Bishopthorpe Road, meaning Caroline could walk to Vicky's in twenty minutes, halving the journey time. I scouted my surroundings as I approached the bridge on the west bank of the Ouse. I instantly recognised Renata's poised stature, traversing the river from the Fulford side. She was alongside a woman with a slight hunch and lugubrious gait – making her seem lethargic compared to Renata, even though they moved in tandem. Fleur, I presumed. And Sandy too. A golden retriever bounded down the ramp, barking in anticipation of meeting a new friend.

'Hi, Renata. And you must be Fleur? You look so alike.' And they did. Facially they could almost be twins – eyes and hair of the same colour. But where Renata effervesced, Fleur was sullen. Her eyes were flat, skin sallow, hair listless and cropped short. Renata had implied she was the elder of the three sisters, but Fleur appeared senior in years. The comparison extended to attire. Renata was clad in jeans and the pink jacket and white sneakers she wore at Whitby. Fleur's coat was a dull blue, her footwear – grey plimsolls. It was as if Renata had drained the vitality from her alter ego, like Count Dracula sucking the lifeblood from his victims.

'Hello, Jamie. You must be Renata's little project.' That was ominous. In my professional experience, a project was synonymous with unfulfilled objectives.

'Well, I hope I deliver.'

'Sorry Jamie, we can't be long – we need to get to the station. But I know you have to return to work,' Renata said.

'I can take as much time as you have. What brings you to York today?'

'Fleur had an appointment. And Sandy loves it by the river.'

We strolled along the bank toward the city centre. The conversation was humdrum compared to when I was alone with Renata: the weather and the previous year's York floods.

I asked of their other sister. 'Hazel can't go out much. She needs to be careful as she has an immune system disorder,' Fleur explained. 'Will you be coming to see us all in the happy house?'

'That's up to Renata. But I hope so.'

'Well, come prepared. It's a bit like *Hotel California*. You can check out any time you like, but you can never leave.'

'Stop teasing him, Fleur,' interjected Renata.

When we arrived at the train station, I found myself relieved that I was returning to work. There seemed to be a covert agenda between them. Renata asked, 'Can I see you tomorrow? Just me this time.' Why did she always assume I had nothing else on?

'Yes,' I said.

Chapter 15. Jamie – 12 May 2001

We met at The Judge's Lodgings, a historic hotel on Lendal. She was already at a table in the bar. Resplendent in a vermilion dress and white sandals. She would have effortlessly outshone the racegoers dressed to the nines who usually flocked to the May meetings at York racecourse. But foot and mouth disease had curtailed the year's racing so far.

'I bought this for you,' I said, presenting her with a small box. She opened it to reveal a Whitby jet swan on a silver chain. She beamed. A pearl of moisture escaped from the side of her eye and snaked down her cheek.

'I love it. Thank you, Jamie. No one's ever bought me a surprise present before.' I unlocked the chain and placed it around her neck.

We instantly slipped into a more intimate dialogue than the previous day's. 'Did you like Fleur?' asked Renata.

'Of course I did. Fleur's so much like you. But she somehow seemed burdened. She doesn't radiate vivacity in the way you do.' Renata blushed at the compliment.

'Take it easy on her. She's been poorly since she was a young child. She's had to contend with heart and liver conditions – and trying to keep up with her big sister.'

'I'm sorry. It must be hard for you. Is it the same with Hazel?'

'Yes, but you don't need to be sorry. That's just how it is.'

A posse of gaudily attired women settled at a table in our basement alcove. A hen do. Drowned out by noise and smoke, I suggested moving on. We strolled the city's ancient streets and snickelways. But it became claustrophobic, bound by the narrow lanes, and hemmed in by hordes of day-trippers. I asked Renata if she wanted to see my house. 'That's why I'm here,' she said.

We ventured north, up Haxby Road. The streets were quieter. The buildings blander. 'The house is a bit of a mess,' I cautioned.

73

'Don't worry. All I care about is potential. That's why I'm interested in you.'

'Your little project?' I questioned. She grinned.

'We've always been quite self-dependent as a family. So it's unusual for one of us to get close to an outsider. Fleur's only jealous.'

'Ah, you don't live in that village at the start of *An American Werewolf in London*, do you? The one with the Slaughtered Lamb pub with pentangles on the wall.' In my worst Yorkshire accent, I quoted, 'Keep clear of the moors. Beware the moon, lads!'

She looked baffled. 'It's not anything sinister. We've just lived a sheltered existence.'

'What happened to your father?'

'He died before I was born.'

'I'm sorry.'

'It's nothing in comparison to what you suffered. I never knew him. You lost yours at a terrible age.'

'Has there been any other male influence on your life?'

'Not really. Our mother's never had a partner. At least, not a lover. There is Franco, of course. He's always been there.'

'Who's Franco? Sounds like a mafia hitman.'

'He can seem like that sometimes,' she said ominously. 'He's like mother's right-hand man. He makes sure her work and our lives run smoothly.' I was becoming concerned about what I was getting myself into.

We entered New Earswick. 'This is it,' I said. 'A genuine attempt to engineer society. A mixed community with housing for both workers and managers. It should be a blueprint for the future. Open spaces, low rent, constructed from local materials. The only drawback is they built it with no pubs.' She spotted my car.

'This is your house?'

'Yep. Come here next year. It will look very different when I've refurbished it. Sadly, everyone is converting their front gardens to driveways. But the houses originally had two fruit trees in the garden. So I'm thinking of planting a crab apple or cherry tree. The blossom will look great in spring.'

'It's lovely,' she said. She'd brought her white rucksack. A signal she

74

was staying, I hoped.

'I haven't prepared much,' I said. I can make a spaghetti bolognaise, or we could get a takeaway.

'Bolognaise would be perfect,' she said. However, I was slightly intimidated, given her Italian heritage. We shared dinner over a bottle of Rioja.

'You seemed disheartened by what I do for a living when we talked before. What's driving that?' I inquired.

Her smile faded. 'Oh, Jamie, don't set me off again. We're living at a dangerous time,' she said earnestly. 'We feel safe. Food and energy are plentiful – at least for those in rich countries. But it can't last. Government, society, and industry distribute resources based on what they've known in the past, with no regard for the future. Your industry is one of the worst. Billions...trillions of dollars of capital tied up to pay for the wealthy in their old age, leaving everyone else exposed to the Ponzi scheme of state pensions.'

'That's a bit extreme, isn't it? What's wrong with setting money aside for the future? It's why companies like mine were formed in the first place.'

'Because it's invested in the wrong places. The custodians of most stocks, shares, or government bonds are motivated to allocate capital detrimentally for short-term gratification. Either profits or votes. Hardly anything goes to organisations genuinely trying to solve future world problems. And no one's properly planning how things will fit together in the future – economic stability is a big part of that.'

'But we don't know what will happen in the future. So shouldn't we react when we know a bit more?'

'Scientists have a fairly good idea of where we're heading, but few in power are listening. There will be unexpected events, but even those can be prepared for with some foresight. Worryingly, society has become complacent. Look at what's happening in this country with Foot and Mouth disease. Thousands of animals are being needlessly slaughtered because the government doesn't know how to react. Imagine if it affected humans. What would we do then? There is no plan.'

'So, we're heading for plague and famine?'

'It's likely. After World War II, developed countries experienced

75

massive industrial and commercial expansion and population growth. It created the cosseted and prosperous existence we live now. But it was executed without thought or planning and resulted in massive resource depletion, which will dominate our future. Some people saw what was happening. But no one wants to acknowledge environmental destruction when life's good.'

'But where do you fit into all of this, Renata? Where's all this coming from?' I was pleased to see her smile return.

'I play a small part. I help to advance medical technology so people can live healthier lives. But that is only one of several key areas that must transform so the world can function effectively. Renewable, clean energy production. Food security. And reduced inequality between nations. But it can't happen without planning, which needs an economic framework to ensure money goes to the right places.'

'So basically, you're dissing capitalism then?'

'Pejorative labels for political ideologies are probably part of the problem.' She finished her wine. 'Look at me. You must think I'm some kind of pretentious zealot. What do normal couples talk about?'

'How long have you had Sandy?' I asked.

We retreated to my striped Habitat sofa with a bottle of Merlot. I deliberately steered the conversation to my life and experiences – where she was more comfortable and relaxed (but less impassioned). I reflected on the night that Nick died. The pub quiz. Our quest to defeat The Gladiators. I even opened up about my relationship with Caroline, although I clarified it was over.

'I'd like to go to the pub quiz with you and meet your friends. I've always wanted to conquer a Gladiator.' I wasn't sure that was a good idea.

'You are staying tonight, aren't you?' I asked.

'If you'll have me.' I kissed her.

'Apologies, no full English breakfast this time,' I said. 'Just toast or cornflakes on the menu.' Munching toast together at the kitchen table offered a tantalising glimpse of what life could be like with Renata as a regular couple.

'Will you come to my house next week?' she asked. That would be the moment of truth.

Chapter 16. Jamie – 31 May 2001

Dispiritingly, Renata called on the following Wednesday to inform me she was ill, so she needed to postpone my visit. She reassured me that she would rearrange as soon as possible. Yet two weeks passed without contact. I still had no way of reaching her. Had her enthusiasm for her little project waned?

In the meantime, my life lapsed back into its routine. Only, I was now shorn of Caroline's companionship. The patio was still unlaid. We hadn't attended the pub quiz since that night. But in one of my rare conversations with Patrick, he suggested attending the following week's quiz. 'I could do with another pop at The Gladiators,' he said. 'Caro's up for it. Vicky won't come, of course. Bad memories. So we need as much help as we can get.' He slapped me on the shoulder. 'You might fluke a couple, like last time.' I agreed to go. Mainly because I was missing spending time with Caroline.

Patrick and Vicky hadn't disclosed their relationship. Presumably, considering it judicious to let more time pass. But in an office, salacious gossip propagates like a virus, so it was soon the stimulus for whispers by the water cooler and hushed discourse in the coffee bar. I really should have confronted Patrick. But would that make anything better?

Just as I'd come to terms with my brief liaison mutating into a wistful memory, an unidentified number appeared on my phone – reigniting hope. My heart leapt when I heard Renata's voice.

'I'm so sorry, Jamie. I've only just overcome a horrible bout of flu. Do you still want to come to my house?'

'Yes, of course. I'm glad you're better.'

'How about I come over to York tomorrow evening? I'll stay with you, then I can take you to where I live on Friday.'

'I should be able to take Friday off, and I'll duck out of the pub quiz tomorrow.' Why did she always assume I'd drop everything for her? But I needed to find out if this was going to work. The following two days would surely be the critical point for our relationship. I hoped she would reveal her secrets.

'Can I come to the pub quiz too?' she asked.

'Er, okay,' I said unenthusiastically.

The Old White Swan was still the same. Five weeks after that fateful night. Black timber beams twisted at impossible angles to support the crooked red-brick walls. It seemed wasteful for such a striking structure to be something as prosaic as a city-centre boozer. But such buildings are commonplace in York. I'd arrived early, with Renata, to secure a good table. She looked stunning in a low-cut green dress, showing off the black swan dangling from her neck. Irrationally, the illness amplified her beauty. Caroline and Patrick arrived together. I introduced them to Renata. Patrick's eyes narrowed, incredulous. 'Love the necklace. How much is Jamie paying you?' he snarked.

'I'm cheaper than you'd think,' Renata replied coquettishly.

'Makes sense,' he said. Eying up Renata's glass of Coke. 'Don't you drink?'

'Usually. It just doesn't mix with the medication I'm on at the moment.'

'Ignore Patrick. He has no filter. He can't function when the most beautiful woman in the room's not with him,' said Caroline.

'But you arrived together,' Renata countered. This was going to be a long night.

'Where did you meet Jamie?' Caroline enquired.

'He was my knight in shining armour. He rescued me when a cycle puncture left me stranded near Castle Howard.'

'Did he? That must have been when I was looking after Vicky.'

'It's bad form to leave a fellow cyclist stranded,' I said, unsuccessfully clarifying that it wasn't just because of her ravishing appearance.

'Well, I hope you're good at quizzes,' said Patrick. 'Jamie needs someone to hold his hand and deliver encouragement.' He looked at Caroline. He then pointed to a table by the fireplace. 'The Gladiators are in the arena, but we're going to win today.'

We started well. Renata was proving her worth in politics and history.

'The next round is on Latin phrases,' said the quizmaster. Jeers from the pub. I hate Latin. I've long suspected that it's deployed as a device to expose your educational background. Academic and legal texts are particularly condemnable, interspersed with Latin expressions to catch out state-school plebs. I painfully recalled fellow students' hysterical laughter at my pronunciation of 'in situ' as in-seat-ooh in a university discussion about soil formation.

'Fantastic. I have a GCSE in Latin,' bragged Patrick.

'*Audere est Facere?*' I know that. It's Spurs's motto. 'To dare is to do,' I yelled.

'That doesn't seem like something you'd know anything about,' said Patrick.

'*Cygnis Insignis?*' 'It's the motto of Western Australia. The black swan state. I think it's something like – bearing the sign of the swan,' answered Renata.

'*De omnibus dubitandum?*' 'Everything must be doubted. Or be suspicious about everything,' Renata immediately responded.

'I think we can all take meaning from this round,' Caroline quipped, turning to me.

Renata carried us through the rest of the round, her Italian heritage outgunning Patrick's GCSE. By the end of the quiz, we fancied our chances. 'She's not just a pretty face, then. Just goes to show that foregoing alcohol does enhance performance,' said Patrick.

We awaited the results. Patrick was at the bar, and Renata had gone to the toilet. 'So, you've traded up then?' said Caroline.

'I wouldn't say that. It's just something that happened. Out of the blue.'

'But she's why you broke up with me, right?'

'I suppose so.'

'Be careful, Jamie. She's lovely, but something about her is not right. Like she has a hidden agenda, or she's using you for something.'

'It's not because of my good looks and sense of humour, then? You're just the same as Patrick. You can't understand why a hot girl would be interested in me.'

'I can understand why any girl would be interested in you. Just be wary. I'm worried she could be your femme fetale.' Or my black swan.

Patrick and Renata returned as the quizmaster was about to announce the results. 'And in second place are *The Gladiators* with 44 points. The invincibles have been defeated.'

Patrick shouted 'Yes' and thrust his right arm in the air like Alan Shearer celebrating a goal. It would have been amusing if we hadn't won after that.

'And the winners, with a record-breaking 48 points, are *The Ebor Handicap.*'

Patrick hugged Caroline, then Renata and even me. 'You can come every week,' he said, addressing Renata.

'You go and collect the prize Patrick,' I said. 'You deserve it.'

Chapter 17. Jamie – 31 May 2001

'You were amazing,' I told Renata, walking back to New Earswick. 'Patrick hardly ever expresses respect for anyone.'

'He's a bully, though. You shouldn't take that shit from him.'

'I think I'm inured to it now,' I lied. 'Nick was a master at winding up Patrick. He was really sharp-witted. You would have liked him.' But Patrick had the last laugh, exacting wretched revenge, I lamented to myself.

'I like Caroline. She clearly still cares for you.'

'We've been friends ever since I moved to York. I hope we won't lose that because we're no longer a couple. She told me to be wary of you. Said you might be a femme fetale.' Renata squeezed my arm.

'Maybe she has good instincts.'

A new black Mercedes E-class was parked on the street near my house. It was incongruous alongside the native 5-year-old Golfs, Mondeos and Cavaliers, and the driver was still in the car. Renata frowned momentarily. Had she seen it before?

We entered the house, circumventing the skip procured for my garden debris. 'Coffee, tea, something stronger?' I asked.

'Just some water, please. I'm not drinking, remember?'

'Ah, I almost forgot. The skip's being collected early tomorrow. There are a few slabs and rocks I need to add. I won't be long.'

'Okay, I can get my drink.'

It took me about ten minutes to collect the remaining rubble in the back garden and put it in a wheelbarrow to transfer to the skip.

When I returned, there was an empty glass on the kitchen table. I assumed Renata was in the bathroom. I made myself a cup of tea and waited in the lounge. After five minutes, I shouted, 'Everything all right, Renata?' No answer. I checked the bathroom and my bedroom. She wasn't there. She wasn't in the house, unless she'd decided on an untimely game of hide and seek. I went out to the street. I shouted, 'Renata, Renata,' as if calling a pet cat in for the night. Still no response. The black Mercedes had gone.

What was going on? Innumerable scenarios ricocheted through my mind. Had an evening in the company of Patrick and Caroline put her off? Had she been kidnapped? Was her disappearance connected to the Mercedes? Was it the family's minder, Franco? Was there another reason for her secrecy – another man? A husband? A fiancé?

What should I do? She was an adult. She could do what she wanted. But to simply vanish from the kitchen at 11.30 p.m. was strange. Although, to be honest, in the few weeks I'd known her, much of Renata's behaviour was perplexing. The rest of the night unfolded as a combination of fitful sleep and lonely contemplation, clinging to the vain hope that Renata would slip into bed with me as if nothing had happened. But in the back of my mind, I sensed I was never destined to become too close to Renata. Caroline's words of caution were all too prophetic.

In the morning, I decided to report her disappearance to the police, given the circumstances were so alarming. But I think they were close to arresting me for wasting police time. Or worse.

'So, sir, you're reporting a missing person – but you don't know her full name, address, occupation, age or even the colour of her eyes? You say she disappeared from your house at 11.30 p.m.? Don't you think that, maybe, she just didn't want to stay the night with you?' At best, they thought I was some kind of crackpot. At worst, I'd come to confess to a hideous crime.

I even asked to speak to PC Slater, as she'd seemed professional when dealing with Nick's death. I went through the same details, including trying to describe Renata's eye colour. 'Hazel eyes, you mean?'

'Yes, I suppose so.'

'I'm sorry, Mr Glover, I don't think we can help you. We've no evidence that anything untoward has happened to her. Or even that she's actually missing – given that you don't know her address. But, look, I'll register your report and description. Then, if anyone else reports her missing – her work or family – we'll speak to you again.'

Over the next two months, I endeavoured to find her myself. I marked a circle of 15 miles radius around Castle Howard on my OS map. I thought she would most likely live in this area, within a reasonable cycling distance of where we first met. I spent evenings and weekends driving through North Yorkshire villages or walking or jogging popular footpaths, hoping to see her cycling or walking her dog. I searched her name on the internet. There can't be many Renatas in North Yorkshire. But, then, was that even her real name? It was all to no avail.

She'd blanked me before, of course. But this was more traumatic – the sudden disappearance, the suspicious Mercedes, the lack of explanation, the fleeting prospect of commitment erased. It was worsened by my lack of a confidante – Caroline, my go-to sounding board, was now off-limits. I was no longer close enough to my mum or sister, Erica, to discuss personal matters. But now, more than ever, I needed some kind of reassurance. Or at least someone to tell me if I was being irrational.

Then, sandwiched in a pile of junk mail, I received a handwritten letter with an Italian postmark. I almost missed it. Who still writes letters? I ripped it open.

Dearest Jamie

I unreservedly apologise for my abrupt departure. I hope it didn't cause you too much anguish. You must think me strange. I will attempt to explain as much as I can.

I know you noticed the black car outside your house. It was Franco, our guardian (for want of a better term). He brought news of circumstances that necessitated an urgent upheaval of our arrangements in England. I judged it less cruel to leave without farewells rather than prolong our departure. We have returned to Italy.

I cannot explain why, but you can't be part of my life. The weekend in Whitby and enjoying a simple breakfast at your kitchen table made me believe we could be a normal couple. But that was foolish. We can't. That's not my role in this life. With all my heart, I wish there could have been another way and that you were with me now. But there is no other way. Please don't search for me.

I will always remember our short time together as my best time. It gave me a glimpse of what could have been.

Live your best life.

Addio R

P.S. Stop taking shit from Patrick. Caroline was right about me. And she loves you. But you know that.

Part 4: June 2021

Chapter 18. Millie – 29 June 2021

Millie brought a coffee into her bedroom and placed it on the bedside table. 'There you go,' she said.

Kyle lazily turned to face her. 'What kind of time do you call this? It's my day off, remember?'

'I know. But I need to be at work early to try and solve your case. Remember? And I have my proper job to do on top of that.'

Kyle pulled Millie towards him and tenderly kissed her. 'I enjoyed last night,' he said.

'Me too,' said Millie. 'Here's the key. Put it back through the letter box after you lock the front door. And don't forget to check out the Minster view.'

At 7.15 a.m., Millie turned on her work computer. She was excited by the possibility of finding another case with similarities to Wesley Myers's death. Millie considered the characteristics she might include in the search: deaths, Yorkshire location, medication overdose, males aged 20-40, professional occupation, connection to a burglary, digital devices stolen. Millie didn't set a date range because she wanted to include as many incidents as possible.

Millie ran the query. The output was a list of cases ranked in order of similarity to the factors included. As expected, the Myers case was top of the list with a perfect match. But then her heart jumped. There was another incident that matched all the characteristics. How had Kyle missed this? But she chuckled to herself when she noticed its date. Twenty years ago, in 2001. She hadn't realised they'd digitised data from that far back.

Millie scanned the other cases on the list. Nothing else was close enough to Myers's circumstances to warrant further investigation. So, she decided to peruse the 2001 incident, even though it was unlikely anything from twenty years ago would be helpful.

However, the resemblances were uncanny. A thirty-one-year-old accountant, Nicholas Shepherd, died of an anxiety medication overdose. The same medication that Wesley Myers took to control his seizures. Shepherd's death was recorded as suicide. But, curiously, his house was burgled two weeks later, and the only item reported missing was his laptop. Millie's heart rate soared. Could there really be a link between two assumed suicides twenty years apart?

But there was more to provoke Millie's intrigue. She spotted the name of an officer who communicated the death and attended the burglary. A rookie PC called Rosemary Slater. Presumably, the same Rosemary Slater, now a DCI and Kyle's boss. However, the most troubling disclosure was that Millie thought she knew Nicholas Shepherd's wife, Vicky.

Millie entered the tiny coffee shop on Walmgate. Her mum was already at the table. 'Hi, Love,' said Shiv as she greeted her daughter with a hug. 'Wow, you're glowing. I thought you'd made a mistake leaving Ebor Assurance for a pay cut and limited career prospects. But you look so much happier now.'

'Thanks, Mum. I needed the change. Not everyone can endure working at the same company for life.' Millie grinned. 'And the men there are more interesting too.'

Shiv raised an eyebrow. 'I see. Anyone in particular?'

'Maybe. But it's early days.'

Shiv smiled and touched Millie's hand. 'I can't wait to meet him. But be careful. I know from bitter experience that interesting men aren't usually suitable partners.'

'I can look after myself, Mum.'

After they had ordered lunch, Millie turned to Shiv and said, 'Do you mind if I ask you something personal?'

'What is it? I won't be much help with dating tips.'

'No, nothing like that. Do you remember a man called Nicholas Shepherd? I think he may have worked at Ebor Assurance.'

Shiv's grin faded, and her brow furrowed. 'Yes, he was my manager at one time. A nice guy. Smart. Funny. But tragically, he took his own life shortly after leaving Ebor. It hit me really hard.'

'I thought I remembered you mentioning him. How devastated you were. He was Vicky Shepherd's husband, wasn't he? She was the director of my old department at Ebor Assurance.'

Shiv nodded.

'I knew Vicky had been married. But I never heard anyone talk about her husband. I understand why now,' said Millie. 'It must have been terrible for her.'

'Why are you asking about this?' replied Shiv.

Millie looked down and hushed her voice. 'I shouldn't tell you. But his name came up on a data query for another case. So I wanted to confirm it was the same person. What did you think when you found out he'd committed suicide?'

'Shocked, obviously. Nick was someone I liked and respected.'

'Did you think it strange that he'd taken his own life?'

'Of course. I couldn't understand why anyone would do that. But especially not Nick. He had so much to live for. However, I hadn't seen him since he left Ebor Assurance, and people change, don't they?' said Shiv.

'Do you know anything about The Cygnus Foundation, where he worked? Unfortunately, they no longer exist, so I can't find out much about them.'

'I think it was a specialist venture capital firm. I remember everyone teasing Nick about his new affluent lifestyle at his leaving do. He was getting a big pay increase.'

'Okay, thanks, Mum.'

'You're not suggesting Nick's death might have been suspicious, are you?'

'No, no. That's not my job; I'm not a detective. I'm just looking for patterns in data. So please forget about this conversation. I shouldn't be talking to you about my work, really.'

Once back at the police headquarters, Millie made a phone call. Kyle answered. 'Yes, I did remember to lock the front door,' he said.

'Did you know a thirty-one-year-old accountant overdosed and died in 2001 of the same medication Wesley Myers took?'

'No, should I? How could that be connected to Myers?'

'There are other similarities, too, such as a stolen laptop. And get this – a PC involved in the case was none other than…'

'Let me guess,' said Kyle. 'Rosemary Slater?'

'What aren't you telling me, Kyle?'

'I didn't know about it, honestly. But it helps explain why DCI Slater won't give up on the Myers case. Maybe Myers's death reminds her of the 2001 incident. Perhaps she feels that merited further investigation, so she doesn't want to make the same mistake this time.

'Still, there's no proof of any real connection between the two events. Everything you've told me so far is a coincidence. I bet if you spread the net further afield, you could find more cases with the same characteristics. Have you discovered anything that could link to the reason they died?'

'No, not yet. But I'll have a look this afternoon. Are you enjoying your day off?'

'It's okay. But I just can't switch off from work for some reason.'

'Ha, sorry. Enjoy the pub.'

Chapter 19. Millie – 29 June 2021

It was nearly 8.00 p.m. Millie was still at her desk at York Police headquarters. She'd reviewed the case file for Nicholas Shepherd's suicide but had made no progress finding links to Wesley Myers. Her search algorithms had turned up nothing – one last try. Millie amended the code to hunt for connections between COVID case references in Yorkshire, from March to April 2020, for people below the age of 35 and The Cygnus Foundation (Shepherd's employer at the time of his death). Her expectations were low. What link could there be between a pandemic in 2020 and an organisation that ceased business more than ten years before? She ran the algorithm.

'What the fuck?' she exclaimed too loudly. A cleaner stared at her, bearing a concerned expression. Millie called Kyle. No answer. No answer a second time. She texted. 'Please call me urgently.'

Kyle called ten minutes later. She could hear his voice but couldn't make out the words. The background noise was too raucous. It sounded like football chants. Oh shit, she had forgotten he was in the pub. 'Second call today. Are you checking up on me? I didn't take you for the possessive type,' he shouted.

'I've found a link, Kyle. A link between Wesley Myers and Nicholas Shepherd.'

Millie was waiting to meet the acclaimed DCI Rosemary Slater. Alone in the meeting room. Did detectives make a habit of being late? They eventually entered, and Kyle introduced Millie to DCI Slater.

'So, Millie, DS Hill tells me you have discovered similarities between the deaths of Wesley Myers and Nicholas Shepherd.'

'Err…yes,' Millie said, frustrated at herself for becoming uncharacteristically tongue-tied.

'I'm pleased that you unearthed the Shepherd case. The circumstances surrounding his death have always bothered me,' said DCI Slater. She stood up and paced around the meeting room. 'It was my first time telling someone's wife that their husband had died. One of the worst parts of our job. But the suicide verdict seemed clear cut. He had the motivation and the means to execute it. But the burglary of his laptop was strange. It was the only item stolen, and all the usual local suspects had alibis. However, we didn't pursue it further because there was no evidence linking Shepherd's death to the burglary. Twenty years later, the same thing has happened to Wesley Myers. An apparent suicide alongside the unexplained theft of his phone and laptop. Given the length of time between them, I never considered that the cases could be linked. But I think the events relating to Shepherd's death spurred me to explore every avenue for the Myers case. That's why I wanted you to look at his data analysis. But, honestly, I expected it to be a dead end. Have you actually discovered a genuine link between them?'

'Yes, I found a connection between Shepherd's employer and Wesley Myers's COVID analysis,' said Millie. 'I was getting nowhere. But as a last resort, I added "Cygnus" to my search, and something came up. Initially, I couldn't find many common characteristics for COVID cases in Myers's spike. But "Cygnus" generated a potential link. A clinic called Pickerton Hall.'

'I've never heard of it. So what's the link?' DCI Slater asked.

'It looks like it's mainly a fertility clinic in North Yorkshire. It was established in 2000. I found a local press article from the time, reporting the launch event. It mentioned The Cygnus Foundation funded the clinic.'

'Okay. But nothing is surprising there. That's what the Foundation did – fund new ventures.'

'Yes, but there's also a connection between Pickerton Hall and Myers's COVID spike data. It's fairly weak, but there is something there. My search algorithm traces social media posts from individuals in the right date, location, and age range, which mention COVID. Some of those individuals also posted about attending an event to celebrate the twentieth anniversary of Pickerton Hall on 29 February 2020, leap year day. Possibly a super spreader event. It doesn't prove anything. But Pickerton Hall links your two deaths.'

'Did you find anything out about Pickerton Hall?' Kyle asked.

'Not too much. They market themselves as an upmarket private fertility clinic. They deal in complex cases. It's all on their website. They charge eye-watering prices. But they claim to use cutting-edge techniques and equipment. And they say their success rates are near the best in Europe, even though they deal with the most difficult cases. The anniversary event was a big celebration of all the new lives they'd helped create over the last twenty years.'

'You said it was "mainly" a fertility clinic,' said DCI Slater. 'What else does it do?'

'On the website, it says it's a research facility too. But they've also courted controversy recently with possible links to animal testing. A woman called Ana Steenkamp runs the facility. She's been in charge since it opened. She would be a worthwhile person to contact for detailed questions.'

'Good work Millie,' said DCI Slater. She addressed Kyle. 'I think we should pay Ms Steenkamp a visit.'

Chapter 20. Rosemary – 30 June 2021

The satnav wasn't necessary. A bedraggled bunch of protesters marked the entrance. Tatty homemade banners expressed their grievances. *'No more animal testing', 'Animal rights now', 'Only God can create life.'* As they turned into the driveway, a few demonstrators motioned towards the car, jeering and gesticulating.

'What's that all about?' DCI Rosemary Slater asked.

'They don't want us to make babies,' replied Kyle. Rosemary smiled wistfully.

'That ship has sailed. Besides, I reckon the queen of numbers fronts that queue now. No, I meant, what are they protesting about? Their presence creates the impression that we're entering the HQ of an organisation with something to hide.'

'It looks like anti-animal-testing agitators. Millie mentioned some recent controversies. We need to find out what they think's going on here.'

'It's not a good-natured protest. They look pretty triggered,' Rosemary said.

'Perhaps they just don't like how the other half lives?' Kyle surveyed the scene ahead – a long sweeping driveway bordered by manicured lawns and a collage of flowering shrubs and mature trees. The cinder road weaved towards an extravagant stately home. Irregularly positioned turrets with domes and pinnacles flanked its façade. 'Are you sure you're not taking me on a minibreak, Guv?'

'You should be so lucky. How many country hotels have this level of security? It's like Belmarsh Prison. Although this lot seem more intent on keeping people out than in.' They spotted at least six security guards patrolling the grounds, dressed in dark blue jackets and baseball caps, as if they were expecting a presidential visit.

A barrier across the road halted their progress. The guard at the checkpoint took five minutes to review their credentials and wave them through, even though they had called ahead to arrange the meeting.

A beaming receptionist greeted them at the main entrance, although her smile faded when they introduced themselves. She said, 'Please follow me. I'll take you to Ms Steenkamp's office.' She escorted them through a lounge furnished with comfy sofas and side tables. A few couples perched nervously on the couches. They climbed an oak staircase to the first floor and entered a smaller lounge area, empty this time, with sofas arranged around a large coffee table. 'Please wait here. Ms Steenkamp's PA will call you when she's ready.'

Rosemary surveyed the room. A window overlooked the grounds. Photographs covered the oak-panelled walls.

'It's a bit like the bar at The Black Swan Inn,' Kyle said.

'That doesn't sound like your kind of place. Is that one of Millie's date venues?'

Something on the far wall caught Rosemary's attention – a display celebrating twenty years of Pickerton Hall. It was probably still there from the celebrations. She moved in closer to study the photographs, one for each year. The first one, the photograph for the year 2000, most interested her. She took her phone out and snapped a picture of it.

'Anything interesting, Guv?'

'Yes, I'll tell you later. Also, don't you find it strange that this is a medical facility and no one's wearing a mask?'

Before Kyle could answer, a besuited man in his mid-twenties entered the room. 'Ms Steenkamp will see you now.' They entered the office. It was larger than the waiting lounge. The window offered another panoramic vista of the variegated gardens. A woman sat behind an enormous antique walnut desk, tapping on her computer's keyboard. She stood up and gesticulated toward a separate meeting table and chairs. 'Hello, I'm Ana Steenkamp, Principal of Pickerton Hall. I hope this can be quick. I'm busy. What do you want?'

Rosemary prided herself on her ability to weigh up new people rapidly. Still, she struggled to get a handle on Ana Steenkamp. Firstly, her age was indecipherable. Her bearing and appearance yielded conflicting clues. Her posture, movement and the cut of her grey business suit conveyed the characteristics of a senior executive in her fifties. She had short black hair, most likely dyed. Her voice was smooth and authoritative with a slight South African inflection. Her eyes, unencumbered by reading glasses, signalled smouldering energy. Yet her skin betrayed a woman of more senior years – the folds and ridges on her neck and wrinkles around the eyes suggested sixties or even seventies. On top of this, Rosemary – who had diligently mastered the leadership skills necessary to be a Chief Inspector over twenty years in the police force – sensed she was in the presence of a natural leader. A true alpha female. Rosemary was respectful and wary.

'We'd like to ask you a few questions about what you do here to help us with our enquiries,' Rosemary said.

'What are you investigating that could have any connection to Pickerton Hall?'

'We're not at liberty to say specifically, but two suicide cases may have links to Pickerton Hall. We want to speak to you to hopefully discount these links from our enquiries. So, can you talk me through what you do here?'

'If that's all you want to know, can I direct you to our website? Or, here, you can have a brochure.' She went to her desk and opened a drawer. 'Yes, I still have some hard copies.'

'We'd like to hear the details in your words. I understand you founded the facility in 2000?'

'Yes, that's right. Okay, we specialise in reproductive technology. Our main objective is to help couples who've struggled to conceive and failed with treatment elsewhere. We deal with complex and difficult cases, but our success rate is good. We also run a research facility – we endeavour to push the boundaries of infertility treatment.'

'But you're not universally popular, are you? I noticed the demonstrators outside – some brandished banners protesting against animal testing. What does that have to do with the activities here?'

'As I said, we specialise in reproductive technology. You may have noticed that animals reproduce too. We can apply learnings about the effectiveness of treatments on different mammals to improve the success of human infertility treatment. We're fully compliant with all the regulations. We don't harm or inflict pain on animals. Sadly, there will always be individuals too small-minded to understand the progress work like ours can achieve for humanity.'

'All right, can you tell me about the event you held here on 29 February 2020?' Rosemary asked.

'What about it? We held an event to celebrate twenty years of the facility. We're proud of what we've achieved and all the couples we've helped. The families want to thank us too. Unlike other fertility clinics, we maintain a relationship with the children after birth; events like this help everyone feel part of the Pickerton Hall family.'

'We have seen data indicating that the celebration may have been a super spreader event for COVID. Are you aware of high COVID rates resulting from the event?'

'Why are the police investigating COVID outbreaks in February 2020? There weren't even any restrictions then.'

'We're just trying to fill in some blanks.'

'There was a COVID outbreak at Pickerton Hall in March 2020. We have a sister clinic in Italy. We suspect some of our staff may have contracted COVID in Italy and brought it to the facility in February and March. Attendees at the anniversary event may have caught the virus, but we don't keep data on that.'

'I noticed that none of your staff are wearing masks. Are you following COVID regulations here?' Kyle asked.

'Are you going to arrest me for not following COVID rules? We treat COVID exceptionally seriously. All our staff must undertake daily PCR tests, and we test all our patients.'

'Okay. Let's move on to funding. Who owns the facility? How is it funded?' Rosemary asked.

'We're privately owned. A consortium of organisations and individuals finance and fund our research. We're a non-profit organisation. The fertility treatment subsidiary funds itself through fees, which are necessarily expensive due to the expertise we provide and the complexity of the cases.'

'What relationship did you have with The Cygnus Foundation?'

'None now. They ceased operations more than ten years ago. They supplied the initial funding, but other investors bought them out — that's how venture capitalism works. Now, you've taken up enough of my time.

I have to be elsewhere. If you have any other questions, please take them up with my PA.'

The receptionist escorted them out of the building through the main lounge. The same couples were still there, anxiously waiting. As they walked to the car, Rosemary said to Kyle, 'I pity those people in the waiting room. Why can't they be content with a life without kids?'

'Do you have an objection to humans interfering with the reproductive process? I didn't take you as the religious type, Guv.'

'It's not that. It's what women have to put themselves through to conceive via IVF, physically and emotionally. They must be utterly desperate to go through that.'

'Can't say it's something I know much about Guv,' Kyle replied.

Rosemary looked in the mirror. She noticed a tall man in a black suit staring at them as they drove down the drive.

'What do you think of Ms Steenkamp?' Kyle asked.

'Arrogant, evasive and downright weird.'

'Agreed. She's hiding something. I'm just not sure whether it's related to Myers or Shepherd. What was your interest in the photograph in the waiting room?'

'It was the opening of the Pickerton Hall facility. Ana Steenkamp was at the centre of a group of people, holding a bottle of Champagne, outside the front entrance. Standing next to her was Nicholas Shepherd.'

Part 5: April 2006

Chapter 21. Jamie – 18 April 2006

I was at a team bonding event at the York Racecourse conference centre, to mark the merger of three departments into one corporate area: Product, Sales, and Marketing. On the wrong side of thirty and a veteran of countless equivalent events, they were now something to endure rather than embrace. I was concerned about turning into that obstinate old bloke everyone hates. The grumpy one who sits in the corner criticising everything but never offers any ideas. Tara Ferguson, the rising star of Marketing, had organised the event, which included the most tortuous fun-fact ice-breaker ever devised.

Tara instructed us to introduce ourselves to as many people as possible and find as many interesting facts about them as we could. But surely nothing could be more cynically engineered as a tool to weed out the plodders? Two prizes were on offer. One for the person who met the most people, another for the person who provided the highest number of interesting facts (although goodness knows how they were going to mark it). Sadly, the most significant two moments of my life involved death. The passing of my best friend, Nick, five years before was still too fresh in my mind. I considered going with, 'Hi, my name's Jamie Glover, and my interesting fact is my dad died of a brain aneurysm when I was twelve.' That would eliminate any further conversation. But in the end, I went with something more prosaic. 'Hi, I'm Jamie, and I fully refurbished a workers' cottage in New Earswick Garden Village.'

'Oh, hi Jamie, I'm Tobias, and I performed a sex act on George Michael.' Tobias, you're going to make it to CEO.

The day progressed with lively team-building exercises designed to foster collaboration and competitiveness. Next came the motivational speech about overcoming adversity, followed by the senior management team telling us how well we were doing. But then, the sting in the tail – we weren't performing well enough to avoid job cuts. They were 'undertaking an organisational redesign to realise efficiency savings,' which meant most of us would have to reapply for our jobs. This revelation understandably sucked the energy from the room. I wasn't too concerned. I'd been through countless restructures before. Redundancy exercises were a fact of life at Ebor Assurance because every new management team needed to justify its existence with cost savings. You usually end up doing the same job under a new role title. Any redundancies were mostly voluntary – old-timers signing off with a bonanza bonus before retirement. At least, I hoped that was the outcome – because I needed to maintain a steady income more than ever.

The day moved on to dinner and drinks. They socially engineered the seating plan to encourage mingling between departments. Each table included a leadership team member to sustain morale and ensure conversation remained on-topic. I was lucky enough to be joined by Sales and Marketing Director Patrick Kemp at my table. Fortunately, I didn't have to make conversation with him. He was basking in the adulation of the fawning newbies, pumped at being in the presence of exalted executive deity – especially the hot girl from Marketing in the red dress. But the departmental cliques began to reform after coffee, and the table thinned. Patrick turned to me and said, 'Hi Jamie, I didn't notice you were sitting there. I hope we've reinvigorated your enthusiasm today.'

'There's no one more committed to Ebor Assurance than me,' I said.

'Are you sure? I've noticed you've turned into a nine to fiver. Does Caroline have you under a tight leash now, eh? Making sure you don't bump into any mysterious women who love and leave you. Where is Caroline today, anyway?'

'You remember she doesn't work here anymore, don't you? She became disillusioned with the management duplicity of corporate life and went to work at a nursery.'

'Yeah, yeah, of course. I thought that would be more your thing – all that gardening stuff.'

'No, not that kind of nursery, a children's nursery, as I think you know.'

'So, is she waiting at home for you now, praying you don't get seduced by some young skirt who flutters her eyelids?'

'I'm not you, Patrick. She's out tonight, too, at her Salsa club.' Patrick snorted on his wine.

'Jamie, Jamie. You know what Salsa clubs are, right? They're pick-up joints. Caroline's looking for someone to sweep her off her feet, literally. I don't blame her, mind. It must be depressing living with you.'

Before I could reply, Tara Ferguson tapped Patrick on the shoulder to inform him it was time for the awards ceremony. He was handing out prizes to people who had outperformed their objectives. Safe to say, I wasn't in line for one.

I called a taxi. I anticipated an unpleasant medical probing the following day, so I wanted to constrain any hang-over. It was frustrating how Patrick still riled me after more than ten years. Thankfully, I hadn't seen much of him lately. But, under the restructure, I was in his reporting line. A disheartening prospect. He was my boss's boss. He hadn't changed much. His hair a little thinner, his waist a little thicker. But still lairy. Still charismatic. Still adept at networking with the right people. Still propagating a string of office affairs – I was surprised Ebor Assurance ignored it. His relationship with Vicky hadn't lasted long. She soon realised Patrick was only seeking spiteful revenge for Nick's ability to humiliate him. And she sought it as a distraction from her failing marriage, temporarily attracted by his charm and ambition. I was pleased Vicky's career was now prospering in Finance.

I directed the taxi to my house in Haxby, a village just north of the York outer ring road. Caroline and I agreed that the location made an acceptable compromise when we decided to make a go of it. Neither of us wanted to leave our beloved homes – Caroline's Bishopthorpe Road cottage and my refurb project. The bipartisan sacrifice was a tacit gesture of commitment. However, it wasn't a complete commitment because we both still owned and rented out our properties. Haxby was nice enough. A self-contained village, almost a suburb of York, with a thriving selection of cafés and shops – probably thanks to a substantial senior population residing in the numerous affluent retirement complexes. But I think Caroline missed the Bishy road vibe, which was more akin to a trendy London neighbourhood. However, we both agreed it was an excellent place to bring up a family, which is why we moved there.

'Hi, honey, I'm home.'

'Hi, how was the conference?'

'Yeah, you know, same as usual. There's another redundancy exercise in the pipeline.'

'I hope your job's safe.'

'Yes, it should be. They value experience.' I entered the kitchen. 'Wow, you look spectacular.' And she did. Still in her Salsa garb, clad in a shoulderless, knee-length black dress and sandals. 'I saw Patrick at the event. He says a Salsa club is just a front for a pick-up joint.'

'Everywhere's a pick-up joint to Patrick,' she grinned. 'But he is correct in this case. Not for me, though. I go because I like dancing, and you don't.' I kissed her.

'I don't deserve you,' I said.

'Ugh...you stink of alcohol. I hope you didn't drink too much. I don't want them rejecting us because you can't whip up a sperm sample.'

I tried to hug her. 'Has alcohol ever restricted me in that department?'

'I won't answer that, but you won't get a chance to prove it tonight. You need to save some for tomorrow.'

It took a full six months after Nick's death (and the Renata episode) for Caroline to take me back. We both agreed it needed to be different from before. So, we had *that* conversation about what we wanted. I showed Caroline Renata's letter as a gesture of honesty and to convince her it was definitely finished. Over time, I think she managed to push it to the back of her mind – to be explained as an uncharacteristic aberration due to Nick's death. Certainly, to me, Renata seemed like a hazy dream. I possessed no photos or keepsakes, other than the letter, to spur recollections. She was a dark swan fading into the distance.

I discovered Caroline wanted the complete works – life under the same roof and a couple of kids. That worked for me too. We stopped short of marriage. Neither of us had religious convictions, and we didn't need rings on our fingers to validate our commitment. We also concurred that we mustn't become lifers at Ebor Assurance. The plan was for Caroline to resign after her maternity leave ended – eventually moving to a career better suited to her personality. I agreed to stay at Ebor Assurance to take advantage of the steady income and workplace benefits. Then, when we were ready, I would start my own garden design business.

It was all going swimmingly. We moved into the characterful cottage on the main street through Haxby. We'd found all the local ante-natal classes and pre-school activities we could utilise. Work was still dull, but we loved living together – utterly comfortable with each other's company. I was happy. The only pieces missing from our idyllic jigsaw were the children. Caroline joked that Ebor Assurance spiked the water supply in the guest house they put us in when we first joined. Administering some kind of drug to render us infertile to ensure an unbroken stint of servitude. We were all past thirty, yet none of our group had managed to parent a child. At least, none we knew about – although, surely, by the law of large numbers, there must be some teeny Patricks toddling around? It concerned me that Caroline and I were turning into a rerun of Nick and Vicky – hopefully without the same outcome.

We'd been trying to have a baby for three years. We'd braved all the tests. The fertility consultants were unable to diagnose anything that would prevent conception. It was a mystery. Shamefully, I admit it was a relief to my manhood when the doctor confirmed my sperm count as normal. We tried everything – timing, positions, I even cut down on beer – but to no avail. Having read up about IVF, we were wary about going down that route – but the longer we went without success, the more desperate we became. So eventually, we decided to consider that option. Unfortunately, however, the local NHS waiting list for IVF was enormous.

Caroline then jumped the gun on one of our planned milestones. She resigned from Ebor Assurance, forfeiting any potential maternity benefit – perhaps secretly hoping that would speed everything else up. She took a part-time job at a nearby nursery, which she loved. But I was worried spending so much time with other people's children would make it more painful to acknowledge our ongoing infertility. Then, a conversation with one of the nursery mums provided a glimmer of hope – her twins were conceived with the assistance of a private North Yorkshire clinic called Pickerton Hall. We'd investigated them already – their IVF success rate was excellent. But at more than £10,000 a cycle, we'd discounted them as an option. But the mum told Caroline that Pickerton Hall offered a free IVF cycle to patients willing to trial a new drug. I was sceptical. But Caroline was keen to talk to them. And they did have an excellent reputation. Caroline even asked Vicky if she and Nick had been there –

Vicky said they were thinking about it, but the clinic had just opened when they were trying for a baby. And the ridiculous price tag also put them off. I realised Pickerton Hall must have been the exclusive fertility clinic Nick told me about the night before he died. The one he was pinning his hopes on. It was a poignant irony that I relied on them to fulfil my dreams five years later.

Chapter 22. Jamie – 19 April 2006

'You can't go looking like that,' Caroline said.

'Why not? I thought you liked my Metallica tee shirt.'

'We must create a good impression to be accepted on the trial.'

'Why? We're not trying to join a country club. They'll assess our medical suitability, not whether we look the part in the clubhouse.'

'I wouldn't be so sure. Have you seen the people Pickerton Hall has treated? Celebrities, politicians, royalty. We need to fit in.'

'You know I hate trying to fit in.'

'That's why you work for an insurance company and drive an Audi, then?' Caroline ruffled around my wardrobe. 'What about these?' She'd extracted a crinkled pair of beige chinos and a cyan polo shirt. 'These will look okay with a jacket. But you'll have to iron them first.'

'What the fuck? You're trying to dress me like Patrick. I didn't even know I owned a pair of chinos.'

'Are you taking this seriously, Jamie? Do you really want a child with me? I wouldn't need to tell Patrick how to dress.'

'Of course I do, my love. I'm just nervous, that's all.' But the Patrick comparison smarted.

Caroline's instincts were spot-on. Pickerton Hall was a clinic dressed as a country club. I expected to glimpse buggies and bunkers on what looked like verdant fairways. We drove towards an elaborate country house – several buildings adjoined the main residence. Some were converted stables. Some were modern extensions. I assumed these were laboratories and offices rather than massage rooms and squash courts. Whoever originally owned the house must have been a keen horticulturist – the gardens contained an eclectic mix of shrubs and trees. I was glad to see they were well-maintained.

We were directed to the main waiting room. Three other couples were already there, seated on separate sofas. But there were plenty spare. I'm not sure why, but I was relieved to see we were the youngest couple in the room by some distance. The others were in their late thirties or forties. We still had time on our side.

In my experience, infertility is an affliction couples keep to themselves. Nick and Vicky had been struggling for years before I found out (in the worst way possible). So I'd not broadcast our problems. I don't think Caroline had either – although, for all I knew, it could be the talk of the Salsa club, with a string of lithesome bucks queuing to help out.

The prevailing attitude to infertility makes it a contentious topic to discuss publicly. I once attended a manager development session at work, where each individual was asked to select a subject – something they vehemently disagreed with. Then, the rest of the group was instructed to persuade the individual that they were wrong. It was an exercise designed to assess your ability to stand up for your principles when assailed with vigorous criticism. One woman chose IVF as her severely detested thing. I just couldn't comprehend how, in a world abounding with malignant avocations, she could choose a procedure that brings happiness to millions as her subject of outrage. Since then, I've always been wary about broaching the topic in company. But, suddenly, we were in a room full of couples in a similar predicament. Just think of the wisdom they could impart. I looked around. Swiftly dipping heads, averting my gaze, indicated we weren't about to form an impromptu self-help group. Maybe that was later.

After five minutes, a nurse led us to separate rooms for our medical examinations. An over-enthusiastic male doctor greeted me. He asked me to undress. Three years earlier, I'd have been horrified at the prospect of exposing my tackle for scrutiny. But, after enduring the same procedure with a GP and consultant, it had become routine. The doctor donned a pair of medical rubber gloves and fondled my balls. 'Everything appears normal.' That's a relief.

'Please can you provide a sperm sample?' He handed me a transparent container, about the size of an individual Ski yoghurt pot, and a brown paper bag. He directed me to a room at the end of the corridor. I'd already had my sperm analysed before, of course. But previously, I was afforded the luxury of jerking off at home. Caroline took the sperm sample to the hospital – she looked at me coolly when I handed her the pot. 'Is that all you managed?' I'm sure Patrick would have filled it. But this was the first time I'd experienced a wank room. An area designated for the explicit endeavour of expressing ejaculate. A green vacant sign on the door communicated it was safe to enter, but I knocked anyway. That was one activity I did not want to walk in on inadvertently. After reading about infertility, I was intrigued by the concept of a wank room. I looked forward to browsing through the reams of pornographic material to select an appropriately arousing image to expedite the outcome. But, to my disappointment, the room was bereft of erotic imagery. It was simply furnished – a chaise-lounge and a coffee table, with a box of tissues considerately placed in the corner. The table had drawers, but they contained no porn, just wet wipes. Perhaps this joint was too classy for such vulgarity. The room had the ambience of the lounge in a show home. Maybe that's what men need to relax. I extracted my dollop of yoghurt quickly – the tricky part was navigating the container's tiny opening. Why didn't they supply funnels? All finished, I proudly handed the brown bag back to the doctor and returned to the waiting room.

As with anything to do with reproduction, the woman gets the worst of it. I waited another half hour for Caroline's return. She joined me on the sofa. 'Everything okay?' I asked.

'I think so, you?'

'Same here. But I got to jerk off.'

Caroline smiled, 'I hope you were thinking of me.'

'Of course. However, I was frustrated by the lack of adult material to get me going. Not that I needed it.'

'Urgh…What's next?'

'I think we wait. The coffee's good,' I said, pointing to the machine in the corner.

A few minutes later, a well-dressed young woman approached and said, 'Ms Steenkamp will see you now.'

'She's the boss lady,' I said. We were led up a staircase and into an enormous, oak-panelled office, probably more than twice the size of the wank room. A dark-haired woman of mature years, donning a smart grey business-style skirt and jacket, stood to greet us. She stopped and stared at me longer than necessary, like a boxer trying to psych out their opponent. It was unnerving. It wasn't just her glare. Something else about her unsettled me. Was it her manner or appearance? There was a familiarity about her. But I was sure we'd never met.

'You must be Jamie Glover,' she said.

'And I'm Caroline Ashby.' Caroline, clearly feeling left out, proffered her hand.

'Yes, hello, welcome to Pickerton Hall. Please sit down. I'm Ana Steenkamp. I'm in charge of this place.'

We sat in silence for thirty seconds. Eventually, Ana said, 'How far are you prepared to go to have children?'

What kind of question was that?

Caroline answered. 'Having children is the aim of our relationship. We're prepared to do whatever it takes.' That answer concerned me – I thought we were bound by more than a desire to have children. Hopefully, she was just laying it on for effect.

'Good, you need to be committed. IVF is a demanding undertaking. What do you know about Pickerton Hall?'

'I work at a nursery, and one of the mums told me how you assisted her conception. She had twins. She mentioned you were trialling a new drug and were looking for patients.'

'We've read about how you pioneer techniques and your excellent success rate,' I added.

'You've not experienced IVF before, have you?'

'No,' we both answered.

'Here at Pickerton Hall, we deal with the most complex cases. Many patients have already received unsuccessful treatment elsewhere. They come from all over Europe, and the world, for treatment here. So, you've come to the best place to maximise your chances of having children.'

'So, are we suitable for the trial if we don't fit the typical profile of your patients?' I asked.

'I need to review your test results. But yes, I believe so.' Caroline squeezed my hand. 'The trial is for a new drug, a follicle-stimulating hormone. FSH increases the number of eggs your ovaries produce. Caroline will have to self-inject it, in her abdomen, rather than her thigh, for two weeks. We need couples that fit the more normal IVF profile for the trial to determine a robust success rate and better understand the prevalence of any side effects.'

'Side effects? Is the trial safe?' I asked.

'All medication has possible side effects,' she said. 'The drug we're trialling is based on a standard method of manufacturing FSH, from hamster ovary cells. Side effects might include nausea, bloating, and headaches – but that would be true for any IVF procedure. Does that put you off?'

'No,' answered Caroline. The prospect of Caroline loading her body with hamster ovaries sounded grim. But I held my tongue. Ana Steenkamp explained the complete IVF process and the terms of the trial. We would receive one free cycle, and they would freeze any unused embryos for future use. But we had to pay for future IVF cycles. I empathised with how Nick must have felt. I needed a pay rise.

'When do we find out if we've been accepted on the trial?' Caroline asked.

'We'll call you in the next few days,' Ana said. 'I'll see you out. It was enlightening to meet you.'

Chapter 23. Jamie – 21 April 2006

We heard nothing for two days. 'Shall we call them?' Caroline said.

'No, let's leave it another day,' I suggested. 'Ana Steenkamp said "a few" days. That means up to three under my definition.' I could see it was torture for Caroline. Like waiting to hear if a top university or college had accepted her. She flinched every time her phone buzzed.

The Ebor Assurance redundancy exercise distracted me. I was scribbling draft answers for the preference form when Caroline's phone chimed. It was the call we were waiting for. As much as her rapid nodding, Caroline's grin and flushed cheeks told me it was good news. I hugged her and opened the fridge to extract a bottle of Champagne. 'We'd better open this while you can still drink,' I said. I hoped my reservations weren't too noticeable.

We sat in the lounge, supping the bubbly, discussing what the next year might have in store for us.

'I'm so thrilled they accepted us,' Caroline said. 'We're going to receive treatment at the most advanced clinic in the world. I'm sure it's going to work.'

'I know it's brilliant, but we shouldn't get too excited yet. Do you know the success rate for an IVF cycle is only thirty per cent? I just want to ensure you're prepared for everything – the strain of the whole process and the disappointment if it doesn't work.'

'Try to be optimistic, Jamie. The process isn't that different to a natural pregnancy anyway. The only difference is that the eggs are fertilised outside the body. Otherwise, it's the same.'

'Yes, but to achieve that outcome, the burden placed on the woman is massive.'

'You might not have noticed, but pregnancy tends to be a female thing.'

'Ha, I realise from the point of conception, the man becomes kind of redundant for a natural pregnancy. Although, at least, conception can be a fun shared experience. But, honestly, I can't imagine a more unnatural process than what you'll have to endure for an IVF pregnancy.'

'It's okay. I'm prepared for that.'

I took another sip of Champagne. A reminder that we were meant to be celebrating. I realised I should carefully consider what I would say next, and that alcohol can severely impair judgement. But I needed to say it.

'All right, here goes. This is my understanding of what you'll have to go through. First, you inject drugs to stifle your natural ovulation – these actually put you into menopause.

'Then, you have to trick your ovaries to hyperproduce eggs. How do you do this? By injecting hamster ovaries into your stomach. Is there an alternative to syringing yourself with rodent glands? Well, yes, there is. It's made from pregnant women's purified piss. Nice choice.

'Next, you'll get different hormones to make your eggs nice and ready. They can harvest the eggs at this point by putting you to sleep and shoving a massive needle up your vagina.

'This is where I get some action. My sole contribution is wanking into a pot. If we're lucky, we'll get some fertilised embryos. They'll insert the most promising embryos into your womb, reversing the egg-harvesting process, but this time you're awake.

'That's it. Hopefully, you won't suffer side effects, which could include nausea, bloating, headaches, cramps, and vaginal bleeding. Then we face the harrowing wait to find out if you've beaten the thirty per cent odds to become pregnant.

'I'm just trying to say, is it worth it?'

'I think I'm in a better position to know what I'm letting myself in for than you are. If women decided to stop having children because they have to bear the inconvenience of pregnancy, not men, the planet would be in trouble.'

'Okay, okay…I'm sorry. I want a child with you more than anything. I just wanted to try to articulate how special I think you are, to be willing to go through all that to have my child.' I put my arm around Caroline. 'But I'll still love you regardless of whether we have a baby.'

We had a slew of paperwork to complete over the next week. First, I finalised my job selection form for the redundancy exercise – it would take

111

management 'up to six weeks' to confirm the outcome, so I could forget about that for a while. We also needed to complete the forms for the IVF procedure. All the treatments and drugs were free, but Pickerton Hall required us to take tests for sexually transmitted diseases before starting. They charged £300 for STD tests, so we decided to get free tests from the NHS.

However, we didn't realise that the NHS tests come with counselling. So, we needed to collect our results in person. We sat in the waiting room full of nervous-looking teenagers and twenty-somethings. I was relieved Caroline hadn't dressed me up for this outing. A cheerful portly woman with dark hair called us into a room. She sat clasping an envelope – as if trying to create suspense before announcing the X-Factor winner. 'Before I look at the results, we need to discuss your sexual history. How many sexual partners have you had over the last ten years?'

What? Why do they need to know that? This process was designed for couples who thought they had contracted a STD. Not those who needed the all-clear to access fertility treatment. I suppose the objective of counselling was to get any potential surprises out in the open – but in our case, it was more likely to harm the relationship.

'Two,' I said. Caroline glowered. I absolutely didn't want to go over that ground again.

'How many years did you say?' Caroline asked.

'Ten,' said the counsellor. I could see Caroline considering her answer. We'd started going out eight years ago, with the break after Nick's death.

'Just Jamie,' she said. I didn't think her answer was truthful, but I loved that she was trying to protect my feelings.

As expected, we were all okay. Now the treatment could commence.

The Ebor Assurance benefits package actually provided time off for fertility treatment. However, I declined to take advantage of it. I didn't want work knowing my business, especially when Patrick could access my HR records. I didn't need much time off, just the odd half-day. Caroline took the process in her stride, as she assured me she would – although I helped her with the abdominal hamster ovary injections.

The momentous egg harvesting day arrived. Caroline would have to undergo an unpleasant medical procedure under general anaesthetic. It was also when I played my minor but crucial part.

It must have been ovum collection day for everyone. Nurses were giving another couple in the waiting room the same pep talk. A nurse provided the pot and paper bag and told me to go to a numbered room to do the necessary. Incredibly, there was more than one wank room. Another nurse gave the man from the other couple the same apparatus. The race was on.

One of the most dissatisfying aspects of IVF treatment for men is producing the seed in a furnished cubby-hole, separated from your partner. But it had to be done. And I did it speedily. I was back in the waiting room twenty minutes before the other bloke reappeared. He must have been nervous.

I wandered the grounds, awaiting news that Caroline's egg harvesting was complete and successful. I marvelled at the variety of shrubs and trees. Perhaps I could apply for a gardener's job if I lost my Ebor Assurance role. They could afford to pay well based on the amount they were charging. Finally, Caroline called to say she was ready to go. The good news was they'd collected sixteen eggs. We now had to wait to find out whether my sperm could do the business.

My sperm worked. Seven days later, they'd fertilised nine eggs. Not a bad week's work. We followed the fertility doctor's advice to transfer two embryos, increasing pregnancy chances. However, that obviously also increased the risk of twins. The clinic froze the remaining embryos, so we could use them in the future if required. Two anxious weeks followed before Caroline was due at the clinic for a pregnancy test. They would perform a blood test, which is more sensitive than the standard urine test. To add to the stress, we didn't find out immediately. We had to wait another day for them to phone us with the results. I took the day off to be with Caroline. Our whole life's purpose was focused on this moment.

It didn't take long. I instantly knew the outcome after Caroline answered the phone. 'Okay, thanks for letting me know,' she stuttered. I felt worse for Caroline than I did about the failed IVF attempt. She looked utterly deflated. I held her as we sat in silence for an hour.

I'd almost forgotten about it. But the day I'd find out about my job had arrived. Caroline and I had come to terms with the unsuccessful IVF but hadn't decided on our next steps. My appointment with my boss was at 11.00 a.m. She'd booked a room for individual appointments with all her staff. I entered the meeting room, precisely on time.

'Hi Jamie, Helen couldn't make it, so I'm going to take you through the outcome of the desk-top selection process.'

'Hello Patrick.' What the fuck? How had I not predicted this? – I bet he'd deliberately sent Helen to another meeting. He read out a lengthy brief, pre-prepared by HR to justify their actions and emphasise how everyone had been treated fairly.

'Okay, Jamie, I can let you know the outcome now. You expressed a preference for the senior product manager role. However, we slotted another candidate, who was a better fit, into that position. Unfortunately, there were no other suitable alternative roles, so I'm sad to inform you we are serving you notice of redundancy today. Your leaving date is four weeks from today. Ebor Assurance will pay the remaining eight weeks of your notice and your redundancy payment when you leave.'

That caught me off-guard. In an instant, my emotions lurched from shock to the unexpected relief of liberation, followed by fear. How would Caroline react? How would we fund another IVF cycle?

'Why wasn't I slotted? Surely I have the most experience for that role?'

'Experience isn't an evaluation criterion. You should know that – the pack we sent you outlined all the competencies required. You did okay for technical knowledge but not so well for project delivery, communication, and networking.'

'So that's it, I'm out the door – after giving ten years, my prime years, to Ebor Assurance?'

'That's how business works, Jamie. There's no such thing as a job for life anymore.'

'How much influence did you have in the outcome, Patrick?'

'I reviewed all the recommendations, but there was also a moderation process. Everything was fair and above board. So don't take it personally.'

'It just bears all the hallmarks of your underhand scheming.'

'No, face it, Jamie, you're not very good at your job. You're a plodder. In today's competitive market, Ebor Assurance just can't afford to keep hold of the dead wood, like you.'

'You've always been jealous of me because of Caroline. She's immune to your dubious charms. Always had you rumbled.'

'Been there, done that, Mate. I shagged Caroline in our first month at Ebor Assurance. When we were at the guest house. Didn't she tell you?'

'Fuck off, Patrick.'

'Careful, Jamie. I could fire you for inappropriate and abusive behaviour. Say goodbye to your redundancy payment.'

'As if you're going to do that. I'd like to see Ebor Assurance explain to the union why one of its directors is handing a staff member his redundancy notice while boasting about nailing his girlfriend. To be honest, I've had enough of cunts like you. I'm glad to be getting out.'

Part 6: June 2016

Chapter 24. Jamie – 23 June 2016

Why did she choose Café Concerto? The location of our break-up chat, fifteen years before, after Nick died. I was impressed at its longevity. The lifespan of many York hospitality venues could be measured in months. I parked in Marygate and strolled the short distance to the café. She was already at a table. She noticed me enter and stood to greet me. I marvelled at her transformation from elegant goth to gentrified boho. Caroline had aged well – her figure maybe a little fuller, her face slightly more rounded, but she could still pass for a catalogue model. She wore a long, carmine flowery dress with a chic handbag, which matched her caramel hair.

'Hi Jamie'

'Hi Caroline, it's great to see you. You're looking well.' Unsurprisingly she didn't return the compliment. The London commuter lifestyle had taken its toll on my body. My once flat stomach had transformed into a flabby bulge, and I'd acquired another chin from somewhere. I needed to start running again. And cut down on the beer.

'Have you voted yet?' she asked.

'No, I'm going to later. Fortunately, I'm still registered in York.'

'Patrick's voting Leave – he wants to take back control.'

'Why does that not surprise me? But I would have thought, as a senior manager at a large UK employer, even he would understand the catastrophic economic impact Brexit would have.'

'He doesn't care. Not being dictated to by a "bunch of European bureaucrats" is more important to him.'

'Well, hopefully, enough people think otherwise, so he won't get his way. So, how's your nursery venture going?'

'It's flourishing. We have a two-year waiting list.'

'I knew you had it in you to be a successful entrepreneur.'

'Patrick helped too. He provided the funding to get me started.'

'I hope you don't rely too much on European staff then. He could be cutting off his nose to spite his face.'

'I paid him back. I'm full owner now.'

We ordered our coffees.

'Why did you ask to see me? Is it just to catch up on old times?' I asked.

'I have something to tell you. I'm glad you're in York. I wanted to tell you in person.' She touched my hand. I started to ache in the pit of my stomach.

'I'm pregnant.'

Ten years before, I wanted nothing more than for Caroline to enunciate those words. But it was devastating to hear them today. I'd not cried in thirty years. Not since my dad died. But I couldn't hold back the tears. I must have looked pathetic.

'I understand how hard this must be for you, Jamie, but you know how long I've wanted a child for – I hope you can be happy for me.'

'Yes, I know. Congratulations, Caroline.' Sheet music adorned the café's walls. I noticed the score of Madame Butterfly. I started laughing. I was living in my own operatic tragedy. The waitress delivering our coffee looked at me with concern, perhaps wondering whether to call her manager to deal with the crazy customer.

'And congratulations to Patrick,' I said through gritted teeth. She said nothing. Caroline had been living with Patrick for around three years now. In his mansion in Easingwold, a well-healed market town, seventeen miles northwest of York. The last time I saw Caroline, to sign papers to do with the sale of our old house in Haxby, she told me she was with him. Patrick had provided Caroline with everything she wanted: a baby, the nursery business. He'd taken my girlfriend and my job. No wonder I found it grimly funny. Yet I still wanted Caroline to be happy.

'Is Patrick divorced yet?' I asked.

'It's still going through. Elaina's trying to milk him for as much as she can. I always knew she was a gold digger.' Patrick met Elaina at Salsa club. The one Caroline went to. I'd never met Elaina, but she looked young and spectacularly attractive in her Facebook pictures. They'd been separated for longer than they'd been married. I respected Elaina. I admired anyone who riled Patrick.

'I didn't know that you still wanted children. Or that Patrick did, for that matter. So you're going to break the class-of-1996 infertility curse.

118

Ironically, when we're all over forty. I presume Vicky's still by herself?'

'Yes. Sadly, I don't see much of her now. She's thrown everything into her career. And I've always held out hope for a baby. But I guess miracles happen at unexpected times. I just pray that everything works out okay with the pregnancy.'

'How does Patrick feel about it?'

'Yes, he's excited too. He hopes it's a boy. To carry on the Kemp name.'

'Surely he'll be an Ashby rather than a Kemp? You can't burden him with Patrick's surname. Patrick's already trying to limit the baby's future opportunities.'

'Don't get me started. He says he's voting Leave to save the next generation. Any chance of you becoming a father, Jamie? Weren't you dating someone in Reading when we last met?'

'Yes, I was seeing someone I knew from school, Fiona. Divorced with two young kids. She was nice. I got on with her children too. But I wasn't ready to take on a whole family – like my stepdad, Mike, had done with my mum. So I couldn't give her the commitment she wanted. And she couldn't hold a candle to you.'

'Hold a candle to Renata, you mean. Have you ever tried to find her?'

'No. You saw the letter. Renata asked me not to look.'

'But that was before social media. Haven't you tried to Facebook stalk her?' I was silent. 'You have, haven't you?'

'I didn't even know her surname. But yes, I did look. I found nothing. She's like a ghost. I sometimes think literally.'

'She was real enough. You paraded her to us all at the quiz night, remember? She was very clever but really weird. It's a pity you didn't settle down with your friend in Reading. You'd have made a good dad.'

'Not much chance of that now. I'm moving back to York.' Her face lit up.

'Really. How come?'

'My contract ended at the pension consultants in London. And forty-one's probably too old to live with your mum and stepdad. But rent-free accommodation has helped me pay off the mortgage on my New Earswick house. So I've stopped renting it out, and I'm moving back. That's why I'm here this week. To sort everything out.'

'Are you going to find a job up here? I could ask Patrick if anything is going at Ebor Assurance.'

'You're joking, right? I might try to find contracting work here or maybe in Leeds or Manchester. Or even set up that garden design business I always dreamed of.'

'You should do. We could go to the York entrepreneurs society together. I'll set you up with a girlfriend if you come to Salsa.'

'I hate dancing. But Elaina does seem interesting. And it sounds like she could be coming into some money.'

'Seriously, Jamie, don't go there.'

'I'd do anything if I thought it would irritate Patrick. But I don't want to make things difficult for you, Caroline. I really do hope everything works out for you. I want you to be happy.'

'I know. Perhaps we can catch up more often now you're back in York.'

'Yes, I'd like that, but I can't imagine me joining you for dinner parties at Patrick's manor house.'

We parted with an embrace. I was genuinely happy for Caroline, but I was empty inside. I returned to the car and sobbed uncontrollably for an hour. I'd returned to York with a vague dream that Caroline and I could be reunited. I hoped we could rediscover that bond without the pressure of trying to conceive hanging over us. I even thought Caroline may have been exploring the possibility of reconciliation with her meeting invitation. I knew she was with Patrick. But surely that wouldn't last, given his record? But news of her pregnancy was a bombshell. It changed everything. What should I do? I couldn't face bumping into Caroline and Patrick, joyfully pushing a pram along Parliament Street.

Going back down south was only meant to be temporary. But I'd been there almost four years. After Ebor Assurance made me redundant, Caroline and I agreed to retry IVF as soon as I'd secured another job. We used the frozen embryos, so Caroline wouldn't have to saturate her bloodstream with hamster ovaries again.

I discovered the world of contracting. To my surprise, there was strong demand for people with pensions experience. The pay was good. But it lacked the convenience of a permanent role at a local office. No workplace benefits. No holiday entitlement. No security. And contractors were usually treated as second-class citizens by permies. Moreover, there were only a couple of other big financial services companies in York. So I often took roles in London or Edinburgh, which required Monday to Friday away from home.

But I was bringing home a steady income. We'd saved enough for a second round of IVF treatment. This time I was entirely redundant in the process. It didn't matter that I was away from home for extended periods. The cryopreserved embryos yielded from my aged seed would be brought back to the future. They thawed four of the nine frozen embryos. The fertility doctor transferred the best two into Caroline's womb. But, unhappily and frustratingly, that cycle failed too.

By this time, I saw less and less of Caroline. More of my contracts were in London. I could save money by staying at my stepdad Mike's house and commute on the fast train from Reading to the capital (although the cost of rail travel is extortionate). My mum was all too happy to have me around, and my sister, Erica, was still in town too – working at an IT company. Caroline and I were leading separate lives. I was slipping back into my teenage life – going on pub crawls down Friar Street with my old mates and bumping into old flames. Caroline was doing her own thing too – I didn't realise it then, but she spent more time with Patrick at Salsa club than with me.

We were drifting apart. The principal danger of a relationship formed to produce babies materialised – namely, not having babies. It left us without a focus. Despondent after the second failed IVF attempt, we agreed to a trial separation. I moved out of the house in Haxby and back to Reading. The trial separation became permanent.

I discovered Caroline was moving in with Patrick when she asked me to agree to sell the house in Haxby. That news was distressing. I thought there was nothing left for me in York, even though I still owned another house there. I tried to plan what my life could be like in Reading or elsewhere. I could have settled down with Fiona in a box house in Lower Earley, a massive 1980s housing estate near the M4 motorway. I could have bought my own place in Reading or London. I could have even tried to start anew somewhere else. There were plenty of opportunities for pensions specialists with the Life Assurance companies in Edinburgh. But none of it felt right. I missed York. I missed Caroline. Property prices in the south made the standard of living I enjoyed in Yorkshire unaffordable. I wasn't yet ready to settle for a dormitory existence, with Fiona, in Lower Earley.

I was forever seeking perfection that fleetingly seemed achievable with Renata and Caroline, only to be scuppered by circumstances. Caroline was right. That brief affair with Renata fifteen years before had permanently affected me. But my love for Caroline was different, more robust, something tangible, not a fantasy. That's why I needed to return to York. The place where I had two lots of unfinished business.

I eventually regained some composure and returned to my empty house in New Earswick. I'd not lived there for more than a decade, and the effects of years of rental occupation were evident. The paintwork was tatty, the carpets worn and stained, and worst of all, the garden had been neglected. The flowers I'd planted in the front garden were long since gone – but I was pleased to see the cherry tree thriving, although I'd missed that year's spring blossom.

I sat in the front room, surveying the house I now wholly owned, unencumbered by a bank mortgage. It looked bedraggled and unloved, but it still had the potential to shine. All it needed was care and hard work. Then, a notion sparked my enthusiasm – the house represented me. If I renovated it back to its best state, perhaps I'd be endowed with an equivalent transformation.

I would stop pimping myself out to the Pensions Consultancy or Life Assurance Company that paid me the most to pretend that workplace pensions could engage employees. It was boring. I answered to no one. I could do what I wanted. What had Renata told me to do? 'Lead your best life.' It was about time for me to get on with it.

I decided to create the garden design and landscaping business. I could use my own garden as an example of what I could achieve to show to prospective clients. I spent the rest of the afternoon drafting a business plan. I had enough spare capital to get started, to buy the necessary equipment, maybe a van. The key would be marketing. I'd need to establish a cohort of satisfied customers; word of mouth was important in York. With my passion for life reviving, I donned my trainers for a run along the nearby River Foss path by way of the polling station. I could perform one small act of defiance against Patrick by voting Remain in the Brexit referendum. Afterwards, I became engrossed in the cathartic process of finalising my business proposal long into the night over a few craft beers – I wasn't quite ready to purge alcohol from my life yet. I didn't stay up for the referendum result.

Chapter 25. Jamie – 24 June 2016

The next day I planned to repaint the inside of the house. It was a good time to do it, as it was empty of possessions. Most of my belongings were in my stepdad's garage in Reading. I'd overslept. It was wonderful not having to wake up at 6.00 a.m. to catch the 7.06 from Reading to Paddington Station. My phone rang. I was happy to see it was my sister, Erica.

'It's a disaster. I can't believe it's happened. They're saying they might move our European head office from Reading to France or Ireland.'

'What's happened, Erica?'

'Err…surely you know? Our country's just voted to isolate itself from the rest of Europe. It's a bloody embarrassment. Irmina from work just burst into tears. She thinks most of the country wants to send her back to Poland.'

'What are you saying? Leave won?'

'Have you been under a rock? 52% of the UK voted to leave the EU.'

'Fuck. I didn't know. I'm immersed in my own stuff here. Personal demons I need to exorcise.'

'Well, I hope you succeeded because the country's just unleashed a massive fucking demon on itself.'

'Yes, I think so. I'm staying in York. I've decided to set up my own garden design and landscaping business. On the bright side, there will be less competition from all the Eastern Europeans.'

'Fuck off, Jamie. That's the sort of comment that makes Irmina believe everyone in England hates her.'

'Yeah, sorry, it was a rubbish joke. I know. It's a disaster.'

'Anyway, talking about demons, how did you get on with the she-devil? Did she beg you to take her back again?'

'Erm, not quite. The opposite, actually. Caroline told me she's pregnant.'

'Fucking hell. I assumed she was barren. Is she still with your nemesis? What's his name? Patrick?'

'Yep. I can't understand it. I always thought she had such good judgement.'

'Ow, that must smart. I can understand why you were preoccupied yesterday. How did you take it?'

'Not well. I started crying in the café. Then sat in the car weeping for an hour, feeling sorry for myself.'

'God, she's a manipulative bitch. She engineered the in-person meeting to get the lie of the land. Now she knows you're still her little puppet. You're her escape ramp when she inevitably breaks up with Patrick, which I guarantee she knows will happen. Either he'll leave her for a younger model, or she'll leave him when she catches him out. Men like that are always the same. You'd better be ready when it happens. You'll get another chance to bring up another man's child. I hope you didn't make the wrong choice turning down Fiona. At least you'd have stayed in Reading with her.'

'That's unfair on Caroline,' I protested. 'She's never manipulated me.'

'Who trekked across the country to earn enough to fund your fertility treatment? Who moved out of their own home? Who came running to York when summoned? You did. Who suggested the separation when you couldn't give her what she wanted? Who shacked up with your antagonist as soon as you were out of the door? Caroline did. Every action's calculated to get what she wants.'

'No, it's not. I let Caroline down a long time ago. I was lucky she took me back. And she was willing to go through the trauma of IVF to have my child.'

'You're so naïve, Jamie. You've always been a sucker for a pretty face. From what you've told me, you had a brief relationship with another accomplished manipulator – at a time when your hook-up with Caroline was only casual. Yet, she's been using it to guilt-trip you ever since.'

'I don't think it was ever just a casual hookup. We just hadn't ever admitted it to ourselves.' My phone started flashing. Another incoming call. As if to justify Erica's conviction, it was from Caroline. 'I'd better go. I have an incoming call from Caroline.'

'Don't answer it. Let her wait on you for a change. I bet Patrick's kicked her out. See, my prediction's materialised quicker than even I expected.'

'That's unlikely. But okay, I'll call her later.'

'Good, you need to grow a pair. Are you coming back to Reading soon? I guess you'll need to collect your stuff from Mike's?'

'Yes, I'll be back next week. But come and see me more in York – it's nice up north and a great place for a family holiday.'

'I will. It looks like you'll need more of your little sister's guidance. It was good having you back in Reading. I'll miss you. Anyway, no one's doing much work this morning, everyone's talking about the referendum result, but I'd better get back to looking like I'm doing something.'

'Say hello to David and Lotte for me. See you next week Sis.'

One positive outcome of spending more time in Reading was getting closer to my family again, particularly Erica. We'd been close growing up, especially after Dad died. But we saw each other infrequently after I took the job with Ebor Assurance. The journey from York to Reading was painful, and we were all leading our own lives. Erica lived near my mum and stepdad in Caversham – with her husband, David, a software engineer from her work, and four-year-old daughter, Lotte. David was good company, and Lotte was fun to be around, so I often went to Erica's when I needed space from Mum and Mike. This led to several long, cathartic conversations with Erica about how I'd ended up living back with my mum at forty. Erica was an excellent counsellor, but I think I'd jaundiced her opinion of Caroline. It was also influenced by Caroline's non-attendance at Erica and David's party to celebrate Lotte's birth. She thought Caroline was disrespecting my family, but it was the start of our trial separation, and Caroline didn't want to make things difficult. However, it was helpful to hear someone else's view of my situation from a different perspective. Was I a mug? Caroline's actions over the years had undoubtedly caused me anguish, but I was sure she still cared for me.

What was Caroline calling about? I thought the farewell at the café had an element of finality to it. Perhaps Erica understands people better than I do. Caroline texted too. *'Patrick's gone mental. Can you come and help me move out?'* This was followed by an Easingwold address.

What the fuck? What on earth could possess Patrick to throw out his pregnant partner? Or had Caroline decided to move out? I phoned her.

'Hi Jamie, I'm so relieved you called back. I need to move out of Patrick's. Can you help me? I will stay with Vicky until I can move back into my house in York.'

'What's going on, Caroline? When we spoke yesterday, you had your perfect life planned out. What's changed everything so quickly?'

'Something's snapped in Patrick. I told him I met you to tell you I'm pregnant. He went crazy. I've never seen him like that before. He called me every name under the sun. I was scared. He said if I'm not out by the time he gets back from work, he'll throw me out himself.'

'I don't get it. It doesn't make any sense. Throwing you out just because you met me seems like a massive overreaction.'

'I don't know, Jamie. He's been stressed lately. With work, his divorce, maybe the baby too. Stress manifests itself in different ways.' I knew that only too well. But, even so, it seemed as if something else, unmentioned by Caroline, was going on. Was Erica on to something? Was this part of Caroline's cunning master plan to manipulate my life? Unlikely. And, whatever the real reason, Patrick's torment lifted my spirits even more, so I didn't pry any further.

'Okay, I will come over as soon as possible.'

'Please do. Vicky's told me where the key is, so I can move in anytime.'

I followed the directions on my satnav along a country road outside Easingwold. Though I was confused, my spirits brightened at the turn of events. Was I seriously contemplating fathering Patrick's child? I steered off the road, down a sweeping driveway flanked by lawns and trees, towards a red brick modern house, with an enormous conservatory and garages. I could see why Caroline had taken a liking to the country lifestyle. She was at the front door when I arrived.

She hugged me. 'Thank you so much for coming, Jamie. I've filled my car with as much stuff as I can. Can you help move the heavy boxes and pack the rest in your car?'

'Yes, sure, I've put the seats down, so we should manage to fit quite a lot in. You're not taking furniture, are you?'

'No, I don't want it. All my furniture's in the Bishopthorpe Road house, but that's still being rented out. So I'm just taking clothes and personal items.'

We'd almost filled Caroline's Range Rover Evoque and my Audi A5. It was weird, shiftily grabbing items from someone else's house. Almost as if we were conducting a burglary.

'You know what you're doing, right?' I asked. 'God knows, no one despises Patrick more than me. But look at what you're giving up.'

'I'm sure. Patrick wants nothing to do with the baby.'

'Why? I just can't understand it.'

'It's complicated, Jamie.'

A deep growl punctured the silence. It swiftly amplified as if Caroline had inadvertently summoned a malignant beast. A blue Aston Martin Vanquish pelted along the driveway. Clouds of dust from the gravel plumed in its wake.

'I thought you said Patrick was at work.'

'He was. Fuck, I don't know why he's come home.'

This was getting interesting. My natural reaction is usually to avoid conflict. But this would be my first interaction with Patrick since he gleefully confirmed my redundancy ten years before, and my adrenaline was rushing. I wasn't quite sure what was happening, but whatever it was, it vexed Patrick.

The brawny sports car slammed to a halt. A crimson-faced Patrick emerged. The effects of middle age had caught up on Patrick too. He was sporting a comb-over now, and his expanded abdomen exposed the evidence of too many late-night client drinking sessions.

'Jamie fucking Glover. I should have known you'd have your grimy mitts all over this. I thought you'd pissed off back to mummy, down south. So typical of a spineless weed like you to turn up when you thought I wasn't here. But I collared you on my security camera app. Take one step in my house again, and I'll wreck you, Glover. Get off my property now and drag that bitch, and the bastard in her belly, with you.'

'You don't scare me anymore, Patrick. What are you going to do, engineer my redundancy again? I'm helping Caroline move out of her home. We still have boxes to collect from inside. I'm going to get them.'

'Oooh, look at Jamie, acting the big man in front of his slut. Do you think you're a tough guy? Take one step in my house, and I'll fucking flatten you.'

Caroline grabbed my hand and tried to drag me towards my car. 'Come on, Jamie, let's go. We've packed the important stuff already.'

'No, I've had enough of Patrick's bullying. This was your house too. You have every right to get your things.'

I weighed up what was likely to happen next if I tried to enter the house. I'd not been in a fight since school, but that seemed the most probable outcome. Could I take Patrick? I was taller, in slightly better shape – but knowing alpha-male Patrick, he was sure to have had boxing or martial arts training sometime in his past. So the odds were in his favour.

But Patrick dictated my next move. To my astonishment, he entered the house and returned, clasping a shotgun. He pointed it at me. 'Get the fuck off my property. Now.'

'Okay, okay, calm down, Patrick. Don't do anything stupid. We'll go.' I stuttered. My deliberate, calm, measured tone had transformed into a whimper, revealing my terror. My appetite for a fight evaporated. I was literally out-gunned. Patrick was always prepared to go one step further. I slowly got into my car, and Caroline entered hers. I let Caroline go first. As I motored along the driveway, I half expected my back window to explode. Was Patrick seriously considering using that thing? I didn't want to wait around to find out. Once out of the driveway, I relaxed and followed Caroline to Vicky's home in Fulford.

I hadn't visited Vicky's house since the day of Nick's funeral, fifteen years before – she was more Caroline's friend than mine. Seeing the elegant Georgian façade again rekindled my powerful memories from that time. A pang of guilt hit me. I'd promised myself to find out what really happened to Nick – but the suicide verdict still stood. No new evidence had emerged. But I'd done nothing to find any, always too engrossed in my own problems. I was surprised Vicky hadn't sold the property. It was a lovely house, but surely its association with Nick and the demise of their marriage would be too difficult to bear. But she'd stayed and, as far as I knew, hadn't entered another relationship. Vicky was at work, so Caroline located the key under a flower pot and let us in.

I looked at her in relief. 'Fucking hell Caroline, what was that about? You said he'd flipped, but that was something else. What's he doing with a gun anyway?'

'Now he lives in a country house; he wants the accoutrements of a country gentleman, including a shotgun. He was never going to use it. I'm not sure he knows how. He was just trying to scare you.'

'Well, he succeeded and had me believing he would use it, so he's either a good actor or gone crazy.'

'You can see why I needed to get out.'

'Caroline, I can't understand what you were doing with him in the first place. I know he has money. And, as we've just experienced, a capricious personality. But he's a cunt.'

'I know. I think I've always known it wouldn't last. But it was fun at the start. After those desperate years we endured going through IVF, just focusing on having a baby. I know it's selfish, but I needed something to distract me from the torment. Patrick provided it.'

'He's like a predator – he can sniff out a woman's vulnerability and pounce. He did the same to Vicky.'

'Yes, this house is turning into a refuge for Patrick's cast-offs, isn't it?' she joked.

'Seriously, are you safe here, Caroline? He knows where Vicky lives. Should we call the police? I'm sure threatening people with a shotgun must be some kind of offence. He should at least get his firearms licence revoked.'

'Yes, I'm sure he won't come after me. Or you. He just wants me out of his life.'

'What aren't you telling me, Caroline? There aren't many things that can cause a reaction like that. Although, there is one obvious possibility. I feel horrible asking, but is Patrick the father?'

We sat at Vicky's kitchen table. Caroline's eyes momentarily averted my gaze.

'He probably isn't,' she whispered. I was starting to see Caroline in a new light. Perhaps Erica had good instincts.

'What? Whose is it, then? And shouldn't he be helping you move out?'

'Sorry, Jamie, I'm not ready to talk about it yet. But he doesn't know. All I want to do is focus on the baby now.'

'It does matter, Caroline. I'd certainly want to know. A man has the right to know if he's fathered a child – even if you think he's not interested. Is he in York? Won't he eventually cotton on when he sees you pregnant?'

'I don't think there's a risk of that. So please, Jamie, can you leave it? Maybe we'll talk about it in the future when the time's right. But not now.'

This was shocking – so unlike the Caroline I thought I knew. Once in a relationship, in my experience, Caroline was faithful. And not telling the father was unfair. My mind raced to try to work out who the father could be. A partner from Salsa club? One of the dads at the nursery? A one-night stand to get revenge for Patrick's infidelity? I had no idea.

'Okay, I'll leave it now. It's been a stressful day. Let's get these boxes unloaded.'

After we'd finished unpacking, Caroline put the kettle on for a cup of tea.

'Look, Caroline, if you want anything or need help, just call me. If you want some space from Vicky, let me know, I have a spare room in my house.' She kissed me.

'Thanks, Jamie. I'm so happy you're back in York.'

Part 7: July 2021

Chapter 26. Jamie – 1 July 2021

'This will look amazing next summer,' I reflected, surveying the pergola we'd just completed at the end of the suburban garden. We were at a 1930s semi-detached house in Acomb, York. 'It will create a magnificent scene with flowering climbing honeysuckle and roses. I can almost smell them already. We'll come back in the winter to plant them.'

'At least they'll have the incentive to pay if they need us to return,' said Marcus. 'Mr Davies still hasn't coughed up for that summerhouse we built in Wigginton two months ago. You know, boss, we really should start requesting money upfront. We have more demand than we can handle, but cash flow will cripple us if we keep getting tardy settlers.'

'I know that makes business sense, but trust and reputation are important to me. I want customers to appreciate that we have enough confidence in the quality of our work to ask for payment on completion.'

'Fair enough, boss,' replied Marcus. 'What do I care if you go bankrupt? I'll be out of your hair soon anyway.'

Marcus calling me 'boss' was ironic as he practically ran the business for me. Impressive for a nineteen-year-old. What would I do without him when he went to university in September?

I set up Gardening Glover in 2016 to operate as a sole trader. I couldn't do with the hassle of interviewing and supervising staff. And I had little ambition for rapid expansion, content only to accept jobs I could complete on my own. The business ticked along over the first few years, but I wasn't making big bucks. Still, it was enough to live on, especially as I had no mortgage to service on my New Earswick house. But I wasn't as inspired as I'd hoped when I first formulated my plans.

I was completing modest assignments such as returfing or paving. If I was lucky, I got to lay a new patio or decking. But I was rarely selected for true grand designs, and I experienced little connection with my clients. It all felt like a chore, even if I was my own boss.

Then lockdown hit. I could have continued working. It was outdoors, and I knew many builders who laboured throughout the stay-at-home mandate. However, I was content to take the furlough payments and even considered jacking it all in when the government handouts ceased. If I closed the business, I wouldn't have any employees to let down, which was a relief.

But, due to COVID, people began to cherish their outdoor space. So, in the summer of 2020, demand went through the roof, and clients sought greater creativity and involvement, which rekindled my enthusiasm. Finally, I could make a difference in people's lives – helping them build their sanctuary from this mad world. Even so, I still wasn't looking to take anyone on.

I was unloading Yorkstone paving slabs from a building supplies lorry outside an imposing house on Clifton Green, when Marcus wandered past and asked if I had any extra work. He was looking for something to tide him over until he went to university in September. I'm not one for impulsive decisions. If I had been seeking a new employee, my cautious nature would have decreed a rigorous selection process requiring full references. But Marcus caught me at an opportune moment. The job was more than I could handle easily by myself. In the tsunami of demand that gushed after restrictions were weakened, I really should have been more judicious in selecting projects. This one involved rebuilding a formal patio with a wall and path, returfing, and new planting. I told Marcus he could help with this job. If it worked out, I'd see if there were any other projects where I could use an extra pair of hands over the summer. I didn't need experience; I needed someone enthusiastic and sturdy enough to do the heavy lifting. On first impressions, he was both of those. He was a couple of inches taller than me and held the athletic build of a rower or rugby player (it turns out he was both).

There was a reason he was cheerful. He'd just collected his A-level results. He achieved three 'A stars' and an 'A'. It was a strange year when no one took any exams because of lockdown, so teachers determined their students' grades. Marcus said he was nervous about the outcome because of the uniqueness of the situation. But in reality, he was bright and went to an exclusive fee-paying school, so he would always benefit from a system that shafted many from more humble backgrounds.

He didn't look back from that first job. I'd only employed him as a labourer, but he soon proved he could offer more than just digging holes and hauling bulky items. He immediately immersed himself, without me asking, into running the business.

At the start of September, he told me he was considering deferring his university start for a year. He was something of a COVID forecast savant and reckoned the prognosis was awful. Further lockdowns were likely, so he wouldn't enjoy a proper university experience. Also, travel restrictions meant the traditional gap year activities were off the table. So, he proposed working with me in the garden design business for a year. 'We can make it blossom, Jamie,' he said. He was also a great salesman.

We invested in new garden design software, enabling impactful pitches for new clients. He also reinvented my insipid webpage as a shiny marketing portal, with stunning photographs of our best work and glowing customer testimonials (I had no idea how he secured them). We created sales material that focused on maximising outdoor space in the post-COVID world and partnered with a couple of companies that produced summer houses, outdoor rooms and offices. Marcus supervised acquiring temporary resource for the large jobs when we needed it. He essentially transformed my business from a gardening odd-job man to a boutique horticultural design consultancy with a forecast turnover of nearly half a million pounds. All this while I was paying him minimum wage. He never asked for a raise, but I suspected money wasn't his issue.

'Are you coming to Caroline's for dinner tonight?' I asked.

'Yes, please. I'm always up for sampling Caroline's new concoctions. It's Mexican this week, isn't it?'

'Yep. Although I'm not sure how Sara will cope with the spices.' Wednesday was Caroline's cookery course night. She'd progressed from Indian to Italian and now Mexican. It meant we had a feast of delicious food that she brought back from classes to devour every Thursday. She usually added to it with her own creations. Marcus was almost part of the family, often joining us for Thursday night dinners. Caroline liked him (although I think she found it strange that my new best friend was a teenager) and Sara loved him. The feeling was mutual.

'Do you want a lift? I can put your bike in the van.'

'You know I always cycle or walk when I can,' Marcus replied. 'When will you replace that diesel smog monster with an electric van? It makes sense from an environmental and a tax point of view.'

'I'm driving to Caroline's anyway so you're not saving the environment by cycling. I need the van for longer trips to Reading, so I'm sticking with the efficient diesel.'

'Okay, I'll see you there, as long as I don't suffocate from your emissions on the way.'

Despite York's clogged arteries, I arrived at Caroline's before Marcus. She was back at her beloved Bishy Road house – expanded to provide more space for Sara. It boasted an extra bedroom in the roof and a resplendent kitchen extension, which occupied most of the walled backyard to create a substantial dining space illuminated by expansive skylights. Caroline considered a garden for Sara to play in superfluous because of the proximity of the verdant Rowntree Park at the end of the road.

I knocked on the door. I could hear Sara shouting, 'Is it Jamie and Marcus?' Caroline opened the door. Her hair was lighter and shorter, as if to mimic Sara's. I preferred it longer, but otherwise, she looked wonderful. Motherhood had been kind – aided by regular spin classes at the David Lloyd gym. Sara rushed to me and hugged my legs. 'Marcus is coming, isn't he?' she pleaded.

'He's cycling here. He doesn't like travelling in my polluting van.' Sara dragged me to the kitchen.

'Can we play Reversi?' she asked.

'Yes please, but you're too good for me.' Sara opened her iPad and started a new game. I noticed the table was laid for five people.

'Who else is coming to dinner?' I asked.

'Just Patrick,' Caroline replied.

'What?' I snorted.

'Only joking. Vicky's coming over. She called this morning. She needs to talk to us about something in person, so I invited her for dinner.'

'That's intriguing,' I replied. And it was odd. Why would Vicky want to speak to both of us? Vicky and Caroline became close after Patrick kicked Caroline out. Caroline lived at Vicky's house for a year before she moved back to Bishy Road when the tenants moved out. And Vicky was

Caroline's birthing partner when Sara was born. So surely if Vicky had anything important to talk about, she wouldn't need to include me in the conversation?

Another knock on the door. Vicky and Marcus arrived at the same time. Caroline introduced Marcus to Vicky. 'This is Marcus, the driving force behind Gardening Glover.'

'More like Jamie's lackey,' Marcus replied.

'I doubt it,' Vicky said. 'I've worked with Jamie before. There's no way he has the initiative to build a successful business by himself.'

A little harsh. I was delighted to see Sara greeting Marcus with a hug, in preference to Vicky, and I noticed it irked her. I was concerned Sara might become disturbed by the confusing relationship structure for the important people in her life. She might have considered Vicky another mum after spending the first half year of her life in her home, but that bond weakened after they moved out. How did Sara perceive me? I yearned for her to see me as a dad. I was the closest thing she had to a father figure. Yet I didn't live in her house; she called me Jamie rather than Daddy. I still didn't know who her real father was. Then there was Marcus. He was becoming increasingly important in Sara's life – something like a big brother. I was worried about the impact Marcus leaving York for university might have on Sara.

But still, you couldn't meet a more effervescent, confident, and smart child. Sara's muddled upbringing appeared to have had a positive effect on her. Perhaps a testament to the one stable traditional relationship in her life – with her mum, Caroline. The product of the parent and child connection that Caroline had rehearsed for so long.

Sara placed her black disk adjacent to the corner square. I pressed the top left corner square, automatically generating a white disk in the space and turning several of Sara's newly flanked pieces white. I recalled hearing the secret of Reversi was to command the corner squares. I now held three. Surely this would be my first triumph over Sara? She played the final black piece, and the game automatically displayed our scores. 'Haha, I won again,' cheered Sara.

Marcus laughed. 'What's it like to be outwitted by a four-year-old? You spent too much time focusing on the corners and ignored what was happening in the rest of the game. It's a good metaphor for life. Don't be blindsided by your inherent biases. Instead, focus on what's important.'

'What would you know about life?' I responded. 'You're only nineteen.'

'You'd be surprised at what I've been through over those nineteen years. And, anyway, I know about Reversi. I programmed it at computer club.'

'What are your plans for the future, Marcus?' Vicky asked. 'You sound like you have wider interests than just continuing to work for Jamie.'

'He's not a bad boss. He's let me make most of the changes the business needed. But he's still digging his heels over the most important ones.'

'Like what?' I asked.

'The name, obviously. We should be portraying ourselves as an upmarket landscape design consultancy. But instead, Gardening Glover is going down the route of a suburban hairdresser. Like Mane Attraction or Blade Runner.'

'Or Lunatic Fringe,' said Vicky

'Or Sherlock Combs,' quipped Caroline.

'What about Hairy Potter?' suggested Sara. Everyone giggled.

'My point exactly,' said Marcus. 'And Gardening Glover is even a rubbish pun. It's not as if it's obvious to everyone that Glover is your name. Call it Glover's Landscape Design if you want to make it eponymous.'

'But that's boring,' I replied.

'Sometimes boring is synonymous with professionalism. There's a time and place for quirkiness. You also need to prepare for when I leave for university. You should consider hiring permanent employees now, with the waiting list size. Maybe even recruit a manager to replace me. You'd have to pay them more, of course.'

'Where are you going to university?' enquired Vicky.

'I was going to Exeter to do Maths and Computer Science. But I deferred it a year because of COVID. And Jamie would have gone bankrupt without me. So I'm starting this September, but I'm going to Leeds now rather than Exeter, still doing the same course. I want to stay local. My mum's not well, and I want to be near if anything happens.'

'I didn't know about the change of university, Marcus. Or about your mum. Is there anything we can do to help?' I asked. It was rare for Marcus to reveal anything about his home life. He'd implied he lived with his mother. But their relationship appeared distant, likely a reason he'd latched on to us as a dysfunctional surrogate family.

'I also figured you might need me nearby to give you a steer on the business occasionally. We're lucky; my mum has full-time carers, so we don't need any extra help, thanks.'

'Just remember, we're here for anything if you need us,' said Caroline. It was good to hear her referring to us as a family group.

'Have you thought about plans after university, Marcus? There are some great career opportunities in data science at Ebor Assurance. We're even offering apprenticeships for the best candidates – we'd give you a grant and pay your course fees,' said Vicky.

'Whoa, Vicky, Marcus has come for dinner, not for a heavy-handed recruitment pitch,' I exclaimed.

'I have considered Ebor. But Jamie told me that working in financial services drains your personality and turns you into an emotionless android,' Marcus jested.

'He can speak for himself,' Vicky countered. 'We have a cutting-edge data science discipline, which I run – it's not like the traditional financial services role that Jamie flunked.'

'One of the reasons I'm doing that degree is to have the tools to master data science. But I have greater ambitions than using it to assess insurance risk. I think taming big data can help us unlock the world's problems to understand what's going wrong and how to fix it. I want to be part of that.'

'What do you mean?' I asked. 'Climate change? Poverty? Pandemics?'

'Yes, all of it. The data exists to give us better knowledge of everything – like satellite images mapping the effects of climate change, human behavioural reactions, crop yields, supply chains, and medical interventions. COVID's a notable example. Countries with the best understanding of data generally adopted the most effective policies. After that, it's just a question of putting it together and interpreting the results to create appropriate strategies.'

'We're not just about assessing risk,' said Vicky. She wouldn't give up. 'Environmental, social and governance criteria are a key focus for our investments. You can make a real difference by encouraging companies to act more sustainably.'

'I need to be careful about what I say next because I'm probably doing myself out of future job opportunities,' Marcus said. 'But isn't ESG investing essentially greenwashing? The intentions are good, but it's trying to paste an environmentally-friendly veneer on a system that's already broken. The world's reaching the brink of collapse because of the continual drive for growth and profits over the last hundred years. ESG criteria aren't going to fundamentally change those motives. The governance benchmarks often harm innovative start-ups seeking to disrupt the paradigm because they straitjacket them into behaving like all the failing incumbents.'

'Aren't you being a bit idealistic?' Vicky responded. 'Where can you transform the paradigm?'

'It's a good point – I truly don't know where I want to work. Perhaps that's why I've spent a year digging holes in people's gardens. Politics is a possibility, but that's in such a wretched state now. So maybe I'll do something myself or find another way.'

Caroline appeared from the other end of the kitchen carrying a tray of delicious-looking, colourful food. 'Time to lighten up, guys. On the menu, we have albondigas, which are Mexican meatballs, rice, chicken flautas with guacamole and salsa dips. Sara, there's a separate, less spicy plate for you.'

'Oow, I want to have the same as everyone else,' Sara moaned. I worried Sara would grow up too quickly, exposed to so much adult conversation. Fortunately, she enjoyed the company of other children four days a week at Caroline's nursery.

We all savoured the meal, washed down with Dos Equis beer I'd brought for the adults. Caroline served sopaipillas, little honey pastry puffs, with fruit for dessert. Sara played on her iPad as the rest of us drank coffee. 'Can you get ready for bed now?' Caroline called to Sara.

'Can Marcus read me a bedtime story, please?' Sara asked.

'Yes, if Marcus is all right with that, but not too long,' Caroline replied.

'What would you like me to read?' Marcus asked.

'Clifford the Big Red Dog, please.'

'Nice choice,' replied Marcus.

'I want a dog, but Mummy won't let me.'

'You know there's no one to look after it in the day,' cautioned Caroline.

'I have a dog,' said Marcus. 'He's called Flint. Well, he's more my mum's, but I take him for walks. I can bring Flint to York if you like. We can take him for a walk in the park.'

'Please, please, please,' Sara whooped.

They went upstairs to read a story.

'Marcus is full of surprises,' I said. 'He never told me about his mum or that he had a dog.'

Caroline turned to Vicky, 'What do you want to talk to us about?'

'Something strange. Do you remember PC Slater? She was the officer who came to tell me about Nick's suicide.' We both nodded.

'She called me yesterday, out of the blue. A DCI now, she wants to talk to me again about Nick's death. She's coming to my house tomorrow morning at eleven o'clock. Can either of you come as well? I'd like some support, and you'll have better recollections of what went on then – I've tried to expunge it from my mind, and it was a haze for me anyway.'

'I can make it,' I asserted. 'Marcus is quite capable of finishing off the Acomb job by himself.'

'Sorry, I need to be at the nursery tomorrow,' Caroline said. 'We're preparing for an Ofsted inspection.'

'That's okay,' Vicky said. 'It makes more sense for Jamie to be there. He was Nick's best friend.'

'What on earth do you think it could be about? Why drag it up after all these years?' Caroline asked.

'I've no idea. The detective said there was new evidence she wanted to discuss with me.'

My adrenaline was pumping. There was no way the police would talk to Vicky again unless they had crucial new information. Would my suspicions about the validity of the suicide verdict, which I'd been so timid in pursuing, finally be vindicated?

Marcus came back downstairs to join us. 'I'm off now. It's a long cycle back home. Thanks for a wonderful meal, Caroline.'

After Marcus closed the front door, Vicky said, 'There's something else too.' She looked at Caroline. 'This is confidential. I shouldn't say anything. But given your past, I think discussing it with you is relevant.

'What is it?' said Caroline, taking another swig of beer from the bottle.

'It's about Patrick. He's under investigation at Ebor Assurance for sexual harassment. But it's sensitive. Her word against his. There's no direct evidence. He turned someone in his team down for promotion. She alleges he told her the job was hers if she slept with him. Naturally, he's lawyered up – so this must go no further. But is there anything from your previous relationship with Patrick, when you were working at Ebor, that you think would constitute sexual harassment?'

'My God, that's awful,' said Caroline. 'What can I say? You know Patrick. You know how he behaves. He's brazen about what he wants in a way few men are nowadays. He's always been flirty and overly tactile with women. He propositioned me countless times over the years. As you know, sometimes I went along with it. But it was always my choice. He never coerced me into anything I didn't want.'

'It's the same for me,' said Vicky. 'It still makes me feel sick when I think about my relationship with him. He took his opportunity when I was vulnerable even though it was what I wanted at the time.'

This conversation made me uncomfortable and angry. Did they expect me to give an opinion?

'Let's be honest about this,' I interrupted. 'Patrick's been a predator ever since he's been at Ebor Assurance. I can't believe HR have continually turned a blind eye to it. At least with you two, there was no power dynamic going on. He wasn't your boss. But he's had a string of relationships with his underlings. Surely that raises alarm bells about the abuse of power? Surely there's someone else who can provide evidence of inappropriate behaviour?'

'We need to be so careful about it. It's not like we can put a communication out on the work's intranet asking if anyone's been sexually harassed by Patrick, can we?'

'So, it's Ebor Assurance's reputation you're concerned about, then?'

Caroline interrupted. 'Look, I can't speak about Patrick's recent behaviour. In that respect, I'm relieved. He's had nothing to do with us since Sara was born – I half expected him to constantly hassle me about her. But our breakup was fraught. It felt like he had changed – his cocky confidence seemed to have transformed into unhinged desperation.'

'I think chasing us down the driveway with a fucking shotgun is unequivocal evidence of that,' I said.

'Okay, I'd better go,' said Vicky. 'I need to be in the office early to make

142

time for the meeting with DCI Slater. Please don't say anything about Patrick to anyone.'

We both shook our heads.

'Wow, that was an eventful evening,' I said. Caroline and I were alone now. 'Can I stay over? I think I've drunk too much to drive back.'

'That was always one of Patrick's tricks,' replied Caroline.

'I've obviously learnt from the master. But it's become serious now, hasn't it? I honestly think it was inevitable he'd get into trouble eventually. I'm surprised it's taken this long. I wonder if he'll keep his job. He'll probably wheedle out of it. His bread always falls butter side up.'

'I feel sorry for him. I know you won't have much sympathy, but what he's becoming is sad. He used to have such a charismatic personality, but he was never satisfied with what he had. So now it's all unwinding.'

'How can you say that, Caroline? The way he behaved when he threw you out was unforgivable.'

'I know. But there are things you don't know about. So part of me understands Patrick's reaction.'

'When are you going to level with me, Caroline? We can't be a proper family until we're fully honest with each other. I'll say it – I love Sara, and I want to be her dad. I don't care that I'm not her real father – even if it's Patrick. Our relationship must be so confusing to Sara.'

'I will level with you. Just not yet. Do you know what's scaring me?'

I shook my head.

'When I tell you, you'll hate me so much you'll never want anything to do with me again.'

Chapter 27. Jamie – 2 July 2021

I'm lucky I've never suffered severe anxiety like Nick did. But when I worked in financial services, I often felt a mixture of dread and apprehension before important meetings. Especially when I was expected to impress clients or had to achieve a positive outcome. I've rarely experienced that feeling since leaving the corporate world. But as I parked outside Vicky's house, it returned with a vengeance. The Georgian villa linked many critical emotional moments in my life – finding out about Nick's death; the funeral and burglary; Caroline's breakup with Patrick; and Sara's early months. Would today be as significant? I'd even put Caroline's cryptic comments about her secrets to the back of my mind.

I arrived half an hour early. I knocked on the door, hoping Vicky would be back from work. She answered and ushered me to the kitchen. 'I decided to work from home today,' she said. 'Are you okay with waiting in the kitchen until DCI Slater arrives? Make us some coffee if you like.'

The kitchen was unrecognisable from the day we sat around the table to receive the tragic news about Nick. High gloss white units and a glass-topped, metal-framed Ikea table replaced the oak cupboards and furniture. I made a fresh cafetiere of coffee and waited in uneasy anticipation. DCI Slater arrived on time and introduced DS Kyle Hill. I tried to imagine what DCI Slater's life must have been like since she was last in this house. I wasn't surprised she'd climbed the ranks. As a PC, she exhibited nervous competence and efficiency. She now exuded the confidence of someone used to giving orders. Still, her demeanour also hinted at a world-weariness of a job she'd been in too long.

'Please don't be alarmed about this visit. You've nothing to worry about,' said DCI Slater. Why would there be anything to worry about? Shit, Vicky's not a suspect, is she?

'We came across something relating to Nick while investigating another case. We don't think there's necessarily any connection, but we'd like to ask you a few questions about it.'

'So you're saying you don't think Nick committed suicide?' I said.

'No, we're not saying that. But we're hoping to tie up some loose ends.' She reached into her shoulder bag and retrieved an A4-sized photograph. 'Vicky, this photograph was taken in February 2000 at a medical facility called Pickerton Hall. Can you confirm that's Nick in the picture?'

Vicky inspected the image. 'Yes, that's definitely Nick. And I know about Pickerton Hall. We considered going there for fertility treatment but couldn't afford it because Nick squandered all our money.'

'Can I take a look, please?' I asked. Vicky passed the photo.

It showed a line of people. They were celebrating something. Their clothing and hairstyles looked dated. All smiles and Champagne glasses. Then I saw it – one person, at the edge of the group, wasn't smiling. I let out an involuntary yelp, and I became dizzy. Everything else was a blur. It couldn't be.

'Are you all right, Mr Glover?' said DS Hill.

'Err, yes, I'm okay. It's just a bit of a shock seeing Nick, but I also recognise the woman in the centre, next to Nick, holding the Champagne bottle. It's Ana Steenkamp. Caroline and I met her when we were having fertility treatment.' I went to the sink to pour a glass of water.

'Okay. Vicky, can you remember if Nick ever said anything about Pickerton Hall? Nick's Foundation funded the facility – do you have any old notebooks or computer files of Nick's?' asked DCI Slater.

'We did a lot of research on Pickerton Hall, although they hadn't been going for long at the time, so didn't have much on success rates. But I know Ana Steenkamp had a formidable reputation. Nick studied them in detail. He was always really thorough about things like that. He did tell me about his work connections with them. He said they were going to be the answer to our fertility problems. How we were so lucky to have a fertility clinic, specialising in complex cases, led by a world-renowned expert, opening on our doorstep. But we never got to use it. Thanks to Nick.'

'Was there anything unusual about them that Nick mentioned?' DCI Slater asked.

'How do you mean?'

'It could be anything – inconsistencies in the financing, controversial research techniques, pushing regulatory boundaries?'

'No, nothing like that. Everything we found out was positive.'

'What are you getting at, DCI Slater?' I asked. 'Are you implying that Pickerton Hall is connected to Nick's death? Can you tell us what else you're investigating them for?'

'I'm sorry, I can't. As I said, we're just tying up loose ends. I know it was long ago, but please, can you try to think if Nick ever mentioned anything about Pickerton Hall? Also, perhaps look through some of his old things – although I appreciate this is difficult for you.'

'I can help,' I said.

'I'll try,' said Vicky. 'But honestly, I don't think I can help you any further. Anything relevant would have been on his laptop, which was stolen.'

'Okay, you have our contact details if you think of something.'

After the detectives left, I asked Vicky if I could help her look through Nick's old possessions. I was driven by a renewed motivation to seek answers.

'There really isn't much – I've thrown most of them away or given them to charity. However, a few boxes of odds and ends are in the shed. You're welcome to have a look. I need to get back to work now. Let me know if you find anything.'

I unlocked the padlock. The cobwebs indicated this was a space seldom entered. A combination of dust and mustiness made me cough. Vicky probably employed a gardener who brought their own equipment. Why hadn't she ever commissioned me for work? Four cardboard boxes were stacked at the back. They were marked and worn by time and dampness. The first one I looked at was full of Manchester City programmes. I flicked through them, including the 1981 FA Cup semi-final and final. I wondered what Nick would have made of City's newfound dominance of English football, bankrolled by money from Abu Dhabi. I think he'd have accepted the dubious moral trade-off. But there was nothing of use there – just an excuse for me to wallow in nostalgia. The next two boxes were also worthless for my purpose – mostly full of tacky holiday souvenirs, likely accumulated before their troubles. A snow globe of the Eiffel Tower and a wind-up musical Dutch windmill (which still emitted a discordant Tulips from Amsterdam). This was no good. I needed to find answers.

The final box contained assorted stationery and folders from Ebor Assurance. I rifled through notes from an assertiveness skills course. There were several orange branded pens — one of them caught my eye. It was chunkier than the others. I picked it out and pulled it open. It revealed a USB drive. I remembered it was one of the more useful gifts provided by the company to celebrate results. I wondered — could this be what I was looking for?

'I'm off now,' I shouted, passing Vicky's study. 'I've left the padlock key in the kitchen.' Hopefully, she wasn't on a video conference.

'Find anything?' she asked.

'No, you were right. There's nothing helpful there. I think if there ever was anything useful, it disappeared when his laptop was stolen.'

I entered my van. I wouldn't be joining Marcus in Acomb. Instead, a single goal consumed me — to work out what had happened at Pickerton Hall. DCI Slater's photograph changed everything. I didn't have a copy, but I didn't need one. It was etched on my brain. I could see a grinning Nick next to the arrogant Ana Steenkamp. But one image was preeminent, thundering through my mind — the melancholy figure at the end of the line. It was Renata.

Chapter 28. Jamie – 2 July 2021

Would it still work? Would there be anything useful on it anyway? I rushed into my house and fetched the laptop. Fortunately, it was old enough to have a USB-A port. I turned it on and shoved in the part of the pen that comprised the drive. Goosebumps covered my bare arms, and my heart was racing. Why does it take so long for a machine to start up? Once I opened the file explorer, it took a few more seconds for the computer to recognise the drive. Finally, the folders appeared on the screen. Bingo – there was something in it, a folder simply named 'Nick stuff'. I clicked on it, and a wave of excitement shivered through my body. There were two subfolders, one entitled 'Investment Portfolio' and the other 'Cygnus evidence'.

What should I do? I really should have given it to DCI Slater to examine. Or, at least, returned it to Vicky to make the choice herself. But I didn't trust them to do the right thing – the police let me down twenty years ago. Why would it be different this time? It might even incriminate Nick for insider dealing. And Vicky was reluctant to dig up distressing repressed memories. No, this was on me. I owed it to Nick. And I might find out what happened to Renata.

I looked in the 'Cygnus evidence' folder. Eight Microsoft Excel spreadsheets were named by month from August 2000 to March 2001. I opened February and March. Surprisingly, Nick hadn't applied any password protection. Perhaps he thought hiding the files in an Ebor Assurance pen drive was enough protection. It had sufficed for twenty years. The spreadsheets comprised tabs labelled with alpha-numeric codes, such as LB9276. Were these the code names for Nick's clients? The sheets were cash flow forecasts for different entities, but it was difficult to understand what was happening. However, judging by the size of the numbers in red font, they were making huge losses.

As well as the spreadsheets, there was a single Microsoft Word document called 'Report notes.' Was Nick drafting a report of his findings? If so, who was the intended recipient? Upon further inspection, it was more like a diary, written as a series of notes to himself – as if he had no one else to share his knowledge with.

He had constructed a table of entities financed by The Cygnus Foundation, with a summary of his findings and financial information for each. This time, he'd used an actual business name rather than an anonymous code. They all had similar characteristics, which Nick noted later. Nick forecasted all the companies to generate huge losses, not just in the short term but also over a longer time horizon. That in itself wasn't too surprising. The Cygnus Foundation were essentially a venture capitalist – focusing on biotech start-ups. The reason for their existence was to allocate capital to enterprises deemed too risky by other lenders. They accepted high risk for potentially high reward. But according to Nick's findings, there was no chance of financial reward for investors – ever. The biotech ventures weren't set up to be commercially viable. They had few sources of income. The only chance of recouping money was via a technological breakthrough, which could be licenced, or through third-party acquisition. But according to Nick's evidence, there was no prospect of this happening anytime soon.

Nick questioned whether investors were getting complete information about these companies' objectives. Instead, marketing brochures focused on the future significance of research areas such as genetically modified crops or gerontology – not how they would generate a profitable return. However, the Foundation was never short of funds to allocate to its partners.

Nick reserved his most detailed analysis for Pickerton Hall. He commented that they were an exception because of their income-generating capability – they received more than £5m a year from patient fees. However, they were still enormously loss-making. This is because their research budget dwarfed their fee income.

Nick wrote, *'I visited Pickerton Hall on 29 February 2000 to attend the launch celebration event. They were my first account, and I was interested professionally and personally. The Foundation funded Pickerton Hall to the tune of £100m, with an ongoing commitment to further funding. Even under the most optimistic scenarios, patient fees wouldn't recoup this.*

'I asked the Principal, Ana Steenkamp, for a guided tour of the facility. She had a redoubtable reputation, famed for new techniques to push the boundaries of fertility treatment developed at her clinic in Italy. But her background before that was obscure. And it was unclear why she was setting up a facility in the UK. Nevertheless, I found her dynamic and engaging – I told her about my fertility problems. She responded with complete certainty that her clinic could solve them. I believed her. From that moment, I knew I had to find the money to fund treatment at Pickerton Hall, whatever the cost.

'The tour was informative but incomplete. They had converted a stately home into a state-of-the-art clinic. The fertility treatment and administration took place in the main building. As expected, this was impressive. However, they'd also transformed outside buildings – old stables and workers' quarters – for new use. They had constructed new buildings too. I only visited one of the expansive network of outbuildings. It contained the computer servers for the clinic. Why do they need so much computing power? The other buildings were out of bounds due to needing a decontamination procedure to enter them.

'I left with the impression that Pickerton Hall was a cutting-edge reproductive technology research facility – with a side hustle in fertility treatment, which was perhaps part of the research process. What are they researching? Some of it involves animal testing – are they cloning animals? Genetic engineering? They're highly secretive, and the security wouldn't look out of place in Fort Knox.

'Something doesn't feel right about Pickerton Hall. It seems like a front for something more sinister. But some people or organisations connected with The Cygnus Foundation must know what's going on – you can't achieve that level of funding without a compelling story. Should I challenge the directors at Cygnus?'

My head was spinning. The night before he died, Nick alluded to the mind-blowing and frightening scientific developments his work exposed him to. Unforgivably I'd ignored him then. But I was starting to believe his concerns were genuine. And that Pickerton Hall was at the heart of his troubles.

Nick's later notes revealed he had challenged Cygnus. *'Arranged meeting with Claudio to express my concerns.'* I assumed Claudio was in charge of the Foundation – I vaguely remembered his name on the letter to Vicky. *'He told me working for a specialist organisation like Cygnus requires a change of mindset for new staff. Our partner enterprises are at the vanguard of scientific and technological advancement. The funding needs an ultra-long time horizon. It's only suitable for investors with vision. Fortunately, there was an abundance of such investors. He said that it wasn't my job to question where the money came from or the benefits case for investment – I was the accountant. I just needed to account for how the money was used. The meeting allayed my concerns to an extent. Claudio was very professional, but I detected a tacit threat – stick to your job and don't ask questions or suffer the consequences.'*

I was aghast at what I was reading. It was as if Nick knew he was in danger. And tragically, his notes hinted at the seeds of doom he was continuing to sow. He wrote, *'Still feel uneasy about my role at Cygnus but don't have explicit evidence of wrongdoing. I won't stay here much longer, but I can use the remaining months to reinvigorate my finances, pay for fertility treatment at Pickerton Hall and boost our savings. Perhaps then I'll go back to Ebor Assurance. I think I've found a way to make money quickly. Working at Cygnus gives me insight into future technology trends and the stock market is undervalued. I can put the remortgage proceeds to work.'*

I'd already seen what had happened to Nick's investments. It was like reading a tragic novel after watching the movie. I knew how it would unfold. I was just getting more detail. The final entry foretold his demise.

'What have I done? I've lost all our money. I can't tell Vicky. But, then, would it matter if I did? She's lost interest in fertility treatment. She's lost interest in sex. I'd think she was having an affair if I didn't know her better.

I'm trapped. I can't even leave Cygnus. Claudio called me in. He had a printout of all my investments. How did he get it? He said they needed to monitor employees' financial transactions because of the business's sensitive nature. I was under intense scrutiny because of my 'inconsistent' behaviour. Their terms of employment state that employees cannot personally invest in partner organisations or their

151

competitors. He said I'd invested in both, although I'd deliberately not chosen companies involved with Cygnus (to the best of my knowledge).

I'd committed a severe breach of employment terms. As a result, they could sack me and even report me to the police. But Claudio reassured me that it didn't have to come to that. There was an alternative. He could see I was stressed. He said I needed to enter the Foundation's reintegration programme – I was to have regular sessions with the in-house doctor (effectively a shrink), take any prescribed medication and have all my work closely supervised. After that, I'd be a genuine member of the Cygnus family.

What can I do? I'm fucked. I'm living a nightmare at work. Imprisoned at an organisation that is undoubtedly undertaking illicit activity. How much of my life are they snooping on? I'm so stupid. Why did I write this stuff on a work laptop? They're monitoring everything I do. And my marriage is failing. Who can I talk to? – Vicky's so distant, and Jamie can't even be arsed to call me. There's no way out.'

I struggled to read the last part through the tears. It was like Nick was talking to me from the grave. I should have acted on the warning signs when he visited me in distress. I should have reached out to him before then. He was right. I hardly ever called him after he left Ebor Assurance. It was as painful now as it was then. Nick's notes showed that he was on to something. The Cygnus Foundation were an uncompromising outfit, probably acting unlawfully. But I still possessed no evidence to prove it. His musings and spreadsheets weren't enough. And the Foundation didn't exist anymore – perhaps its backers were concerned that their secrets were about to be exposed. From Nick's notes, I couldn't even be sure his death wasn't suicide. He was in a dark place. There was no point in further investigating The Cygnus Foundation. It was no longer relevant. But I was clear on my next step. Another organisation, right at the heart of this sorry story, was still very much in existence. Its leader had been there since the start – Ana Steenkamp.

Would she meet me? I had been a client. Surely I could think of a reason? I remembered – we still had five unused frozen embryos, or was there a time limit for how long they could be stored? I could arrange a meeting to discuss them, although I didn't want to involve Caroline yet.

I called Pickerton Hall. 'I'd like to arrange a meeting with Ana Steenkamp, please. As soon as possible.'

'What's it about? She's very busy.'

'I want to discuss what happens to our frozen embryos. I don't think we'll have much use for them now.'

'When were they frozen?'

'May 2006.'

'Err…that's more than ten years ago. They're normally destroyed after ten years unless there are exceptional circumstances. That's the rule. We should have told you. Let me check.' We went through questions to verify my identity.

'This is odd,' she said.

'Why?'

'They weren't destroyed. Our records say they were used by your partner, Caroline Ashby, in 2016, for fertility treatment – just before the ten-year deadline. But that can't be right. You would have needed to give your consent. This is very irregular. We'll look into it immediately. Can you make a meeting with Ms Steenkamp at 2.30 p.m. tomorrow? We'll cover everything there.'

'Yes. It will only be me attending.' It was a good job they worked on Saturdays.

Chapter 29. Millie – 2 July 2021

Millie smiled as she supped her coffee. She was making a difference for the first time since starting at the police. That's why she'd joined. DCI Slater was delighted with her contribution. Millie's perseverance directly led to the interview with Ana Steenkamp. And Kyle told her they'd found a link with Nicholas Shepherd there – they were interviewing his widow as a result. So not only was her professional life improving, her love life was too. Her relationship with Kyle could really develop into something solid. Millie's only irritation now was her digital stalker – but it even seemed like he'd got the message.

Millie was waiting in a meeting room for DCI Slater and Kyle. She was used to him now; he was always late. Millie hoped they would have more work for her on the mysterious suicide cases. They entered the room. 'Hello Millie. I want to thank you for all your support on this case. You've been extremely helpful, and I'm sure we'll often need your skills in the future.' This didn't sound like good news. DCI Slater continued, 'But I've called this meeting to let you both know that we will not be investigating the circumstances of Wesley Myers's or Nicholas Shepherd's deaths any further. They are both closed cases.'

'Why? That makes no sense,' said Millie. 'We found a genuine link between the cases. That link was strengthened when you discovered a connection between Pickerton Hall and Nicholas Shepherd. Surely that gives us greater justification to continue investigating?'

'I'm sorry, Millie,' she replied. 'We've gone as far as we can. We interviewed Mr Shepherd's wife and his friend. We've obtained no further evidence to suggest his death wasn't suicide or that it had anything to do with Pickerton Hall. Now, I want to be honest about this. It's not my decision to curtail the investigation. It's come from higher up – essentially, we can't justify allocating precious police time to old cases based on scant evidence. Especially in today's cost-cutting environment.'

'But it's more than scant evidence, isn't it?' Millie said.

'It's not enough. My job is mostly about prioritising limited resources. And this just doesn't have high enough priority. The DSI also received a complaint from Pickerton Hall about us wasting their time – he explicitly instructed me to stop investigating these deaths.'

'So that's it?' Millie replied. 'What if more compelling evidence emerges that makes it a higher priority? That would justify continuing the investigation, wouldn't it?'

'Don't even think about it,' Kyle said. 'I know what you're planning. If we're ordered to stop working on something, that's what we do. You can't go rogue on this, Millie. Regrettably, you'll find that much of police work ultimately ends in frustration.'

It was Saturday. Millie was still dissatisfied after the previous day's meeting. She was beginning to realise that she couldn't yield much direct influence on cases. Millie wasn't in the police force. She was just backroom staff – a civilian. But that came with its own advantages, too, didn't it? She could behave like a civilian. So what's wrong with a few Google searches and targeted social media posts?

Millie felt claustrophobic in her flat. She wouldn't see Kyle this weekend. He was on duty last night and would watch England again in the evening with his mates. The sooner they were knocked out, the better. So Millie decided to go to the Hungate Reading Café for a coffee. It was part of her apartment complex – a brilliant amenity to have on her doorstep – a library café, where she could chill with a book or her laptop and sip a latte.

Millie sat on a stool, facing a window overlooking newly built university accommodation. She could see students were still living there, even though it should be holiday time, as they entered, hauling Sainsbury's bags-for-life, packed with groceries. The café had an urban vibe, exposed concrete pillars with angular iron and wood furniture. It wasn't too crowded. The other five window stools were empty. There was a gaggle of mums and young kids on grey sofas, facing a low table, making use of the toys available. They were noisy. That's what modern libraries should be like – a public space fizzing with life, not a mausoleum. It was the kind of racket Millie liked. She fancifully wondered if she'd be part of that club in a few years, maybe with little Kyles.

Millie opened her laptop and typed Twitter in her web browser. She wasn't a prodigious social media user, especially Twitter, but she still had an account. When Millie worked at Ebor Assurance, she used it to exchange ideas with the broader data science community, for professional reasons. That ceased when she joined the police. Millie hadn't updated her profile – it still said she worked for Ebor. That was perfect for her purposes.

Millie searched @mathsywes. The account was still there, nearly a year after his death. She found his last tweet, *'Big spike in Yorkshire COVID hospitalisations at young ages. Why?'* It included a link to his blog analysis. She clicked retweet, selected the Quote Tweet option, and wrote, *'@exonrrater did you ever find the answer?'* Millie hesitated. Was this unprofessional? No, it was separate from her job. She was just another nerd seeking to solve an interesting data puzzle. She clicked the Tweet button, sipped her latte, and let out a satisfied sigh.

An obnoxious snarling clatter from outside rudely interrupted Millie's contemplation. All the café's customers peered to see what was making the noise. This was the kind of racket Millie didn't like. It was a bright yellow, ridiculously wide sports car. Millie hated this kind of ostentation, but even she admired the sinuous lines of the muscular vehicle. She made out the bull logo. The marque of a Lamborghini, she thought. Heads remained fixated, waiting for the driver to emerge – was it a footballer? A pop-star? Perhaps a racehorse owner? They were common in York. The gull-wing doors lifted. Millie could gauge the collective disappointment as a balding, tubby, middle-aged man got out. Why are drivers of flashy cars such a disappointment? No one else in the café cared who it was anymore. They'd gone back to their scones and giant Jenga. But Millie cared. Millie cared a lot. It was her sex pest, Patrick Kemp.

What the fuck was he doing here? He went to the counter to order a drink. As the barista prepared the coffee, Patrick sauntered around the library, seemingly to browse the books. Millie dipped her head, pretending to be engrossed in reading something on the laptop. But he'd already seen her.

'Hello Millie, fancy meeting you here. What a terrific surprise.' He

156

collected his coffee and sat next to Millie without asking.

'You're infringing my personal space,' Millie said. 'What are you doing here anyway? Not many people know about this place.'

'I was driving around town and saw a sign for the reading café. Thought that seems interesting, so I came for a look. That's my Aventador outside.'

'I know. I saw you getting out, as did everyone else in the café.'

'Do you want to come for a ride in it?'

'Are you going to offer me some sweets as well?'

'You're a cold-hearted cow, Millie. I have women queuing up for me to take them out. You just think you're better than everyone else.'

'I'm not the one driving a cuntmobile. Go somewhere else, Patrick. I came here for a quiet drink by myself. I don't want you disturbing it.'

'I thought it would be good to catch up. I've not seen you since you left Ebor – that was a disaster. You were top of my office hotties list.'

Millie slammed her laptop closed. 'Okay, if you're not going, I will. I've made it clear. I don't want to speak to you, Patrick.'

'You live round here, don't you?'

Millie's calm demeanour betrayed a flash of anger.

'Why do you think that?'

'I've seen you around.'

'When?'

'Every now and then. When I'm in the city.'

Millie looked out of the window and smiled. 'Isn't that a traffic warden next to your car?'

'Fucker.' He rushed to the exit. 'See you around, Millie.'

That was a disturbing turn of events. Millie felt too sick to drink the rest of her latte. Was their meeting a coincidence, or was he physically stalking her? Since she'd left Ebor Assurance, he'd solely been a digital menace. Now he was showing up on her doorstep. How did he know where she lived? She supposed he could have found her address from Ebor Assurance HR records – but that indicated an alarming escalation in his pursuit. What should she do? She had the means to destroy his career. That dick pic was still on her phone (she had to be careful when showing her mum her photographs) and all his other harassing messages. Millie could have reported him when she was still at Ebor Assurance. She worked for

157

the police, too, and was going out with muscleman DS Kyle Hill – he'd know how to sort him out. But both those options relied on help from other people. She didn't want that. Millie's mum had brought her up to be strong and independent. She should be tough enough to deal with pathetic predators like Patrick by herself.

Chapter 30. Jamie – 3 July 2021

What had Caroline done? I was a caldron of conflicting emotions. Could I really be Sara's father? I was frightened to contemplate believing it could be true. But since the conversation with Pickerton Hall, I couldn't stop thinking about it. This was the most wonderful thing that could happen in my life.

But, if I was Sara's father, what would that imply about Caroline's behaviour? First, she must have fraudulently circumvented the requirement to obtain my consent. Then, for the last five years, she deceived me, Patrick, and, most importantly, Sara in the most abhorrent way possible. It was unforgivable. Even my sister, Erica, would be staggered at what the 'she-devil' had orchestrated.

Yet, if I was to play a proper role as Sara's father, I would have to reconcile my opposing emotions. Up to now, Caroline had kept me at arm's length as a kind of quasi-partner/paternal-figure at the periphery of both their lives. No wonder she was reluctant to tell the truth. Ironically, my disgust at Caroline's actions could drive me further away from Sara when all I wanted was to be closer. Could I ever forgive Caroline? It would be difficult, but I'd let her tell her side of the story.

The fault lines that had tortured me throughout my life converged on an epicentre at Pickerton Hall. The torment of Nick's death, Renata's disappearance, infertility, and the riddle of Sara's conception were like magma pressuring my core, ready to explode. The earthquake to trigger that eruption was coming soon.

Pickerton Hall had changed since I was last there, five years before, with Caroline. The high fences and 'Keep Out' signs generated a sinister atmosphere – like the nearby Eden Camp, an old prisoner of war camp, now a museum. Recalcitrant protestors congregated around the entrance gate. I was forced to slow down as they grudgingly unblocked my path. It would have been interesting to hear their grievances. But instead, I reflected on how unpleasant the environment was for fertility treatment compared to when I was a patient.

The receptionist escorted me to Ms Steenkamp's office waiting room and left me with a coffee. I saw it at once. The photograph drew me towards it. It was the one DCI Slater showed Vicky and me. A tear rolled down my cheek. I needed to pull myself together.

'Everything all right, Mr Glover?' Ana Steenkamp appeared from the office.

'It's strange,' I replied. 'You have a photograph on your wall with two people that were very dear to me. They both disappeared from my life long ago, and I don't think I ever recovered.'

'Life can crush you when you least expect it. I know that more than anyone. But sometimes, you get a second chance. If it comes along, you have to take it without hesitation. Show me who they are.'

'That's Nick, next to you,' I pointed. 'He was my best friend, but I abandoned him. He died twenty years ago. The police said it was suicide, but I've never believed it.'

'I remember him,' she said. 'He was the accountant for our investors. I showed him around.'

'And at the end, looking sad, that's Renata. I'm sure you know who she is. We were lovers for a brief time. Then she abandoned me.'

'Yes, Mr Glover, I know Renata. She was my prodigy. Her potential was extraordinary. I groomed her to carry on my work, but she lost her way. Lost sight of what we were trying to achieve here. She had to leave.'

'We were so optimistic when that photograph was taken. We enjoyed limitless funding and the best scientific minds. We were going to change the world.'

'Did you? Did you change the world?'

'What we've accomplished here will change the world. Few people know that yet. I think I've finally achieved what I came here to do, but I fear this chapter's ending soon.' Ms Steenkamp had lost the energy and drive she oozed at our last meeting. She appeared wistful as if finally acknowledging she was at the end of her journey.

'I don't really understand what you're saying,' I said. 'But I've come here for answers. I never knew Nick and Renata had met until I saw that photograph. I'm starting to suspect that this place has something to do with what happened to both of them. Then I discovered yesterday that my partner may have used our embryos without my consent. So I think I'm due an explanation.'

'Okay. Let's start with your fertility treatment,' she said, ushering me into her office to sit at the meeting table. She opened a folder and withdrew an A4-sized document. 'This is the consent form. That's your signature, yes?'

I inspected the form. 'Err, yes, it is.' It was unmistakably my signature – unintelligible and messy but impossible to forge. 'I don't understand. I know I didn't sign this – it's not exactly something I'd forget.'

'Have you asked Ms Ashby about it?'

'No, I wanted to ensure I had the facts before broaching it.'

'Can you remember if she ever asked you to sign any documents?'

I tried to think back. Fuck, yes, she had. There were a whole load of documents relating to the house sale in Haxby. I hardly looked at them. I couldn't wait to get away after she told me about her and Patrick. She must have slipped the consent form in. Was there no end to her deception? Tricking Patrick and me at the same time.

'I can. God, I've been duped.'

'Don't judge her too harshly, Mr Glover. Instead, look at it as a gift. You've just discovered you're the father of a most amazing child. Isn't that what you always wanted?'

'Yes, it is. And if she'd have asked for my consent, I'd have given it gladly. It's the fact she kept it from me and, more importantly, Sara. It's bittersweet for me – we were slowly becoming a proper family, but this revelation will explode everything.'

'That's for you and Ms Ashby to sort out, Mr Glover. But I've got to know Sara during her yearly visits here. She is truly remarkable. But she needs her father. So you must do whatever it takes to ensure you're there for her.'

I was becoming disorientated. Why was this abrupt firebrand proffering advice and empathy? It seemed like she meant it, but was she also skilfully distracting me from the original purpose of my meeting?

'You're right,' I said. 'I know what I need to do. Now, tell me about Renata.'

161

'I don't have much more to say. Renata was the most gifted individual that ever worked here. But we fell out. I don't usually harbour regrets, but I still have misgivings about how we parted.'

'She told me in a letter she went to Italy. Is that true?'

'Yes, I found alternative work for her at our sister facility in Italy. But she didn't stay long. She left there many years ago.'

'Do you know where she is now?'

Her head dropped, and she delayed her answer. 'No, I don't. She's not the kind of person who wants people to know where she is. Why are you asking these questions anyway? It must have happened more than twenty years ago – surely you have more important priorities than reminiscing about a youthful fling?'

I'm no interrogation expert, but her mannerisms indicated that she knew more about Renata than she was letting on.

'I suppose you're right. But that photograph brought it all back to me. And, from what you've said, I think you know that any relationship with Renata would always be more meaningful than a fling.

'All right, let's discuss Nick Shepherd. He worked for The Cygnus Foundation. The entity that funded your facility. Let me put this plainly: I think he was murdered because he discovered irregularities in how the Foundation funded its partners. The worst offender was Pickerton Hall. Am I on the right lines?'

She sounded a throaty rasp. Her demeanour changed – her muscles tensed, and her facial expression became a scowl. Her eyes fleetingly looked towards the ceiling by the door. I looked there too. Was that a camera? Was someone watching us?

'Mr Glover, be very careful about what you say. Your partner, Caroline Ashby, perpetrated the only illegal activity relating to this conversation when she forged the consent form. Whatever happened to your friend has nothing to do with Pickerton Hall.'

There was a knock on the door. A powerfully built man in a blue jacket entered the room.

'You need to go now,' Ms Steenkamp said. 'Don't come back here again.'

'Wait, I've not finished – you've not answered all my questions.'

The man grabbed my arm. 'Come this way, Sir.' He was literally

162

dragging me. I considered myself more robust than most. My build and manual occupation were an advantage. But I could offer no resistance to this guy. He took me all the way to my van and said, 'Leave the premises immediately. We have facial recognition security here. If you ever return, we'll prosecute you for unlawful entry.'

As I entered my van, I glimpsed a man in a dark suit in front of the main house. He stared at me. A recollection stirred in my mind. Had I seen him before, in the black Mercedes outside my house the night Renata disappeared? Was it Franco?

So that was it. My meeting was cut short. Steenkamp had been more forthcoming than expected, until I articulated my theory about Nick. I needed an honest conversation with Caroline to properly understand her motivations. Ana Steenkamp was right. That was the most important thing for me to focus on. But I'd found out little more about Renata. And undoubtedly, the way the meeting ended vindicated my suspicions about Nick. I was convinced Steenkamp was withholding the truth. But there was something else. She seemed scared. Shit, was I in danger? Could I suffer the same fate as Nick? My emotions were frazzled. So much so that I'd even forgotten about England's Euro 2020 quarter-final against Ukraine later that evening. It was so much simpler when football was the most important thing in my life.

Chapter 31. Jamie – 8 July 2021

I faced an agonising dilemma. Should I tell Caroline I knew she used our embryos without my consent? I would have to sometime, but as soon as I did, there was no going back. I was frightened of the outcome. It might sever my access to Sara. And, right now, I couldn't face that. So, I reverted to my default state whenever faced with a challenging decision – procrastination. I'd not seen Caroline or Sara all week, which wasn't unusual. I yearned to see Sara again now that I knew I really was her father. But I needed to control the situation – the routine formality of Caroline's Thursday night dinner seemed like the right time.

Meanwhile, Marcus focused on his succession plan for the business to deal with his departure. In reality, it was a detailed blueprint for significant expansion. He'd drafted an organisational structure with me as owner and chair, employing managers to run the business, administrators to organise it, and gardeners to do the real work. His design included seven additional employees.

We were in the front room of my house, which doubled as the HQ of Gardening Glover.

'So, will I actually have anything to do?' I asked.

'Yes – you focus on what you're good at, the design vision. And you can get your hands dirty when you fancy it.'

'How will I secure the capital to execute your expansion plan? I'm doing okay, but I'm not exactly sitting on piles of cash.'

'I've drafted a cashflow forecast. I think it's realistic. You'll have no problem securing capital based on that – you could get a business loan or try crowdfunding. But actually, I think I have a better solution – if you're prepared to cede some of the ownership. I'd like to invest.'

That caught me by surprise. I was a little apprehensive about the direction Marcus suggested taking my business. Now he wanted to own some of it too. But he sold a compelling story, and I was excited about what we could achieve. In truth, I also worried about coping after Marcus had gone. But if he was part-owner, he would be motivated to continue providing a steer.

'Wow,' I said, 'I wasn't expecting that – I'm not averse to the idea. What do you have in mind?'

'I wouldn't want to take a majority or anything – this isn't a takeover bid,' he joked. 'I was thinking something like 30%. I'll pay a fair price. I'm lucky. My family circumstances mean I have the funds to invest in something important to me like this. I've been thinking about it – I won't be able to offer much hands-on support once I'm at university or even after that. But I want to stay involved. I've enjoyed working with you over the last year and am proud of where we've taken it. However, I think this is only the start. The business has incredible potential, and I want to play a part in realising that, even if it's only to give guidance occasionally.'

'I'm touched,' I said. 'You've persuaded me. Let's do it.'

'Brilliant, we'll need all the legal stuff arranged, the memorandum and articles of association and such. But I can sort that.'

'Where will we get all these big new clients from?'

'I'm on it,' he said. 'We need to market ourselves to councils and businesses, anyone with outdoor space to transform and a sustainable vision. I've already lined us up with a potential new client. A privately owned country house called Sedgethorpe Manor, north of York. The owner wants a consultation for the redevelopment of the grounds. Are you free on Saturday?'

'I've never heard of it but sounds interesting. So yeah, I can come along – as long as it's not Sunday when the football's on.'

'Great. I'll let you know the time and the address. I'll meet you there. Right, I'm cycling home now. I'm bringing Flint to Thursday night dinner at Caroline's, to meet Sara.'

'Awesome, she'll love that,' I said. Although I was jealous because Marcus and Flint would hog her attention. 'How are you going to get him there on your bike?'

'I'll drive.'

'I didn't know you had a car. I thought you were anti internal combustion engines for environmental reasons.'

'It's my mum's, but don't worry – it's electric.'

When Sara hugged me that evening, it was special. A proper father-daughter hug. But it was as frustrating as it was wonderful. I was still her mum's friend rather than her dad. I tried to behave as I usually did with Caroline, but I'm sure she noticed my distraction. As I predicted, Flint captivated Sara as soon as he arrived with Marcus. We heard the dog barking before he reached the front door. Sara rushed to greet him and instantly started stroking him. She giggled as Flint tried to lick her.

'Careful,' I said. 'Flint might be scared of children.'

'No, he's fine. He's a big softy, really,' Marcus replied.

'Can we take him for a walk, please?' Sara begged.

'Yes. Maybe Jamie wants to go with you?' I don't know how, but Marcus seemed to sense I wanted to spend time with Sara.

'Okay,' I said. 'Let's go to Rowntree Park.'

'Take these,' Marcus said, handing a couple of poop bags to Sara.

'What are they for?'

'Picking up Flint's poo,' Marcus replied.

'Ugh,' said Sara, thrusting the bags into my hand.

As we strolled through the park and along the River Ouse towards Millennium Bridge, I was happier than ever. All my concerns and worries melted away. The strange Ana Steenkamp was right. Sara should be my focus.

We approached the bridge, and I remembered when I'd met Renata there with her sister Fleur. On that day, Renata's dog, Sandy, greeted me. He was a golden retriever too. In fact, in my memory, he looked identical to Flint. I thought I was on the verge of happiness then, but that swiftly evaporated. I mustn't let it happen this time.

When we returned to the house, Sara asked Marcus if she could keep Flint. Marcus replied enigmatically, 'You never know, maybe one day.'

I remembered his mum was ill. What would he do with Flint if she died? Marcus was sitting in the kitchen while Caroline was cooking.

'Marcus has been telling me about your expansion plans,' Caroline said.

'I think they're more Marcus's than mine. What do you think?'

'I've always wanted to marry a successful company CEO,' she replied.

Where did that come from? We'd not even discussed living together since Sara was born, let alone marriage. Was she trying to assess my reaction? It wasn't a good time. I said nothing.

Marcus clocked my taciturnity, 'I got there first. Jamie and I are entering a business marriage. And like a real wedding, the first thing I want to do is change the name.'

'Bad luck. It's not an equal marriage. I have the overriding vote, unlike when I'm with Caroline.'

Fortunately, the awkwardness dissipated once Caroline served the fish tacos. Marcus left straight after dinner to take Flint back home. I took Sara outside to say goodbye, 'I love Flint so much. Bring him to see me again,' Sara pleaded as they entered the Tesla.

After I put Sara to bed and read her a story, Caroline said, 'We really need to talk, don't we?'

'Yes, we do, but I'm not in the right frame of mind to do it now.'

Chapter 32. Millie – 10 July 2021

Millie reached for her iPhone on the bedside table to recheck Twitter. A week had passed, and there were no replies to her tweet. Not from @exonrrater or from anyone else. Did no one care about COVID anymore?

Kyle brought her a latte, 'I have to go in a minute. I'm on duty today. And remember, I'm off to the final at Wembley tomorrow, so I won't see you until Monday. Oh, and the masoor dal and chapatis were fantastic last night – but I wouldn't mind some meat next time.'

Despite her frustration, after DCI Slater told her to stand down from analysing Wesley Myers's data, she'd had a good week. Kyle had stayed at her flat three times, and they were becoming more like a regular couple. She'd heard nothing, and, more importantly, seen nothing of Patrick. Millie hadn't told Kyle about him either. She knew she ought to. Complete honesty is essential in a relationship. But stalker Patrick wasn't a complication she wanted at this stage of their liaison.

'You do the cooking if you want to eat meat,' she said. 'But I'm glad you liked it.'

He kissed her forehead. 'See you later, Millie.'

The front door of her apartment slammed. Typical. Why was Kyle so noisy? Especially this early on a Saturday. A minute later, she heard a knock on the door. And he was forgetful. What had he left behind this time? She swiftly donned a tee shirt and opened the apartment's front door.

Millie was still drowsy from sleep, so it took her a second to register that it wasn't Kyle standing outside. Startled, she took a step backwards. Patrick. What the fuck? She jerked forward to slam the door shut but was too late. He thrust his foot in the gap between the door and the frame.

'That's a hostile welcome for an old friend,' he said. He was now in her hallway.

'Get the fuck out of my apartment now, Patrick. I'll call the police or scream – my neighbours will be here in seconds.'

'No, you won't. I know you, Millie. You deal with stuff yourself. You could have reported me at Ebor Assurance – but you didn't. Now go and put something on to cover yourself up. Let's have a chat in the lounge, shall we? That cunt of a traffic warden interrupted us last week. I have something for you, as well.'

Millie froze. What should she do next? Should she call his bluff and scream? But she did what she was trained to do – determine the likelihood of the best outcome based on the available information. Millie recalled Bayes' theorem and the concept of conditional probability. She could make a better assessment based on prior knowledge of conditions related to the event. Two weeks ago, she'd have assessed the probability of Patrick sexually assaulting her as low. But the likelihood was significantly higher after he'd forced his way into her apartment. However, Millie still believed the probability was low. She could control the situation. This was her chance to get the pervert out of her life once and for all.

She quickly put on jogging bottoms and a sweatshirt and joined Patrick in the lounge. She compelled herself to appear calm and controlled rather than expose the terror seething within her.

'How did you get in the building?' she asked.

'A big coloured bloke was coming out. I thought he was burgling the place, but he held the door open for me. Is he anything to do with you? It wouldn't surprise me. I know you colonials like to stick together.'

'You've gone too far this time, Patrick. I'm not going to let you get away with it anymore.'

'Oh, come on now, Millie, we're just two friends chatting over old times. Look, I've brought this for you.' He handed her an A4 envelope. It was addressed to Millie at Ebor Assurance, marked urgent.

'What's wrong with Royal Mail?'

'Margaret in the post room likes me. I'd told her about us – so she let me know when some urgent post for you arrived. I said I'd bring it over personally. Can't trust the postal service these days.'

'There has never been an "us", Patrick, and there never will be.'

'Why not? Come out with me. Have a bit of fun. I'd treat you like a princess. You can even keep seeing your Terry Crews. I don't care.'

'Fuck off. Fuck off. Fuck off,' Millie screamed. Her composure shattered.

The buzzer for the apartment building's front door interrupted Patrick's response. Millie sprinted to the hall to grab the intercom before Patrick could respond.

'Hi Millie,' Kyle said guiltily, 'Sorry, I left my wallet. Can I come up and get it?'

Millie put the intercom down, turned to Patrick and shouted. 'Get out now. Kyle will wreck you if he finds out about you.' Patrick swiftly exited Millie's front door in silence. 'You're a coward too,' Millie said to herself.

She opened the door for Kyle. 'Who's the gammon with the yellow Lamborghini I keep passing? I've not seen him around here before.'

'No idea,' she said. 'He must be visiting one of the neighbours.'

Millie sat in her lounge. Her front door was double-locked, just in case. But she didn't think Patrick would come back. She'd heard his car going. It was time to act, wasn't it? It would be dreadful living in fear of him turning up whenever she was alone. Or would the threat of Kyle sorting him out scare him off?

Millie turned in trepidation to the envelope he'd brought her. Was this another one of his pervy games? Would she discover an A4 glossy of his shrivelled knob inside?

She opened it. It held a brochure for Pickerton Hall. What? Why would anyone send her something relating to Pickerton Hall? No one knew its relevance to her apart from Kyle and DCI Slater, and she was positive they wouldn't have sent it. Then she twigged. Could it be The Exonerator? It had to be. He or she must have thought she still worked at Ebor Assurance because of her Twitter profile. Excitement sizzled as she realised the significance of the brochure. This must be The Exonerator's way of answering her tweet and Wesley Myers's question – Pickerton Hall was the source of high COVID hospitalisations in younger people.

She opened the brochure. It was marketing literature for infertile couples. She noticed something loose inside. It was an old newspaper article. Stuck to it was a yellow post-it note, which said, *'You'll find the answer here. Be careful. Don't use Twitter.'*

It must be The Exonerator. Millie perused the article. The paper was brittle and stained by time. It was from the Eastern Daily Press, dated 22

September 1976. Millie hadn't heard of the newspaper. Presumably, it was a local rag. The article's headline was, 'Prominent Cambridge academic still missing.' Underneath was a picture of a striking woman with light hair, clearly pregnant. Next to her was a smart, handsome, younger man. They both looked contented. In love, maybe. The caption underneath read, *'Juliana and Paul Taylor at the opening of the Gemini research facility in November 1971.'*

The contents of the article brought a tear to Millie's eye. Juliana Taylor was a celebrated expert, her college's first female professor. She specialised in the field of reproductive science. There was a reference to her exploring the potential of in vitro fertilisation in animals. Juliana left the university to set up her own research facility alongside her husband, Paul. But tragedy intruded on Juliana's life in the worst possible way. Her husband and four-year-old daughter were killed in a car crash, a head-on collision with a lorry, on their way home from a holiday in Norfolk, in July 1976. Juliana was meant to present the facility's research results the day after they died. Understandably, the event was cancelled. But the article implied that the scientific community believed she had made a significant breakthrough in her field. However, Juliana hadn't been seen in public since the tragedy, and the research facility had closed. There was speculation that she had left the country in grief, possibly going back to the land of her birth – South Africa, but there was no confirmation.

The story upset Millie. Here was an inspirational woman with so much to offer. She was likely struck down by despair after a horrendous tragedy with her accomplishments lost to the world. Millie was so engrossed in the article she almost forgot why she was reading it – what was the relevance to Pickerton Hall? The only connection she could decipher was that Juliana Taylor had been a reproductive science specialist.

Millie Googled Juliana Taylor, Cambridge, and reproductive science. There weren't many hits. It was sad how notable figures before the internet age could disappear from history. But there was something, a blog on pioneering women scientists. It showcased a short essay on the life of Juliana Taylor.

Juliana Viljoen was born on 29 February 1932 in Cape Town, South Africa. Millie smiled. Juliana was born on leap year day. The poor girl only had a birthday every four years. Her parents were both academics at Cape

Town University. The author hadn't discovered much information about her early life, only that she was an academic prodigy who moved to the UK at age 20, to further her education at a prestigious Cambridge college. She became a professor in her thirties, and her scientific papers were gaining international recognition. She wrote about the potential for In Vitro Fertilisation (IVF) and how that would be a game-changer for treating infertility. More controversially, she posited that cloning, of both animals and humans, could realistically be achieved within years – and this would bring about a medical revolution.

She left the university in 1971 to set up the Gemini research facility, dedicated to furthering the understanding of reproductive science. Juliana married one of her students, Paul Taylor, and gave birth to Chloe in 1972 at forty. Millie marvelled at how Juliana continually defied the conventions of the time.

The research facility published no research in its first five years. But Juliana called a press conference on 5 July 1976 to present their findings. It was expected to be a momentous event, with national and international press invited, not just the scientific community. But the conference was cancelled after the tragic death of her husband, Paul and four-year-old daughter, Chloe. It was never rearranged.

The contents of the research due to be presented were never disclosed. Juliana disappeared from public life and closed the research facility. Her research team were known to be a close-knit group, with fierce loyalty to their leader. No one revealed precisely what the Gemini Facility had achieved. The author suggested that most of Juliana's team simply disappeared too.

After her husband and daughter died, there was no record of what happened to Juliana. However, speculation was rife. Some suggested she'd taken her own life, stricken by grief. Others claimed she'd left the UK to pursue her research in secret, perhaps in South Africa. Her work was controversial. She had already received death threats in England, so maybe she believed she'd be safer and achieve more away from the scientific spotlight. But if she had taken that route, she'd successfully hidden her achievements from the world.

Millie was fascinated but still couldn't establish a connection with Pickerton Hall. What was The Exonerator trying to tell her? What else was there? The blog had some footnotes, could there be something useful there? The first footnote detailed Juliana's parents – she was the only child of Peter Viljoen, an eminent professor of medicine, and his wife, Edith, a lecturer at the university. Edith was prominent in South African society, even before she married Peter. She came from a family of wealthy diamond mine owners. The Steenkamp family.

Chapter 33. Millie – 11 July 2021

This just made no sense. How could Ana Steenkamp be Juliana Taylor? Juliana would be eighty-nine now. Millie was freaked out at the possibility. But after studying the photograph of Ana in the brochure and the black and white picture in the article, there were undeniable similarities in their features. Their hair was obviously different – Juliana's was shoulder length and fair, while Ana's was black and cropped short. Of course, hair could be easily changed. But the shape of the eyes, cheekbones and chin appeared the same.

But Millie didn't need to rely on her untrained eye to evaluate whether the two photographs were of the same person. She had access to sophisticated facial recognition algorithms. That's why she'd gone to the police headquarters on a Saturday. She knew the photos wouldn't be a perfect match. There were two problems. One was the quality of the images, particularly the one from the newspaper; Juliana's face was small, grainy, and black and white. The algorithms could compensate, leading to lower confidence in the result. The other problem was ageing. Facial recognition software often copes poorly with an extended period between images. Millie doubted whether the programs had ever been tested by comparing a 40-year-old with a 90-year-old. But if they were the same person, the standard rules of ageing didn't apply to this comparison. If Ana Steenkamp really was Juliana Taylor, there was some weird shit going on.

Millie scanned in the images and ran the code. Her terminal displayed the result. 'What the fuck? I don't believe it,' she said to herself. The algorithm matched the photos with an 81% confidence level. Given the issues, that was astonishing.

What could it mean? She had no idea. But she was sure she had enough to grab Kyle's and DCI Slater's interest. But that wasn't all. What Millie had discovered might end up attracting the interest of the whole world.

Millie spent Saturday night at home on her laptop, trying to figure out what was happening. It was as if it was a game to The Exonerator. They had given Millie a clue to the puzzle – it was up to her to solve it. She researched reproductive science and cloning and its medical and ethical implications. This led her down other avenues like designer babies, gene editing, gerontology and organ harvesting.

She studied into the early hours. When she eventually went to bed at 3.00 a.m., a kernel of a solution formed in her mind. Had she worked out what was going on? It was far-fetched, but it kind of explained everything.

By Sunday morning, Millie was excited. She'd see Kyle again tomorrow. Hopefully, he'd be in good spirits after an England win in the final. But, more importantly, she could impress him with her discoveries about Ana Steenkamp. Millie would also tell him about Patrick.

She knew how to prepare; cook him a meal he'd enjoy. A proper meaty meal. She'd make him a Rogan Josh – an Indian lamb curry. So, Millie strolled to the Waitrose supermarket, ten minutes from her apartment, to get the lamb. She knew little about meat quality but assumed it would be okay there. She bought lamb fillets and splashed out on Champagne – hoping they'd have reason to celebrate.

But as Millie left the store, she saw something that instantly extinguished her contentment and set her heart hammering again – a yellow Lamborghini. Why can't he leave her alone? Fortunately, Patrick wasn't in the car. She looked around. She couldn't see him in the car park either. Millie decided it was safe to walk home.

Her route took her down Navigation Road, which was disturbingly quiet despite being near the city centre. It was a mixture of red brick apartment buildings and warehouses. Millie scanned for Patrick, flitting her eyes from side to side. However, she ignored the black van parked at the side of the road. Someone grabbed her from behind, and she dropped her shopping. A huge gloved hand smothered Millie's mouth to muffle her scream. The musty garlic stench of his breath pierced her nostrils, and she retched. How had she let herself end up in this situation? How had she misjudged Patrick so much? Her attacker spoke, 'Don't struggle, Millie. You'll only make it worse.' Her terror intensified exponentially. The man's voice was deep with a foreign accent. It wasn't Patrick. Her assailant spoke again, 'Who is The Exonerator?' He bundled her into the van.

Chapter 34. Jamie – 10 July 2021

I followed Marcus's directions to our mystery client. They took me near Pickerton Hall, which seeded my anxious mood. I turned towards Sedgethorpe Manor, on the outskirts of a picturesque North Yorkshire village. My sense of unease intensified as I drove through the open gated entrance. I shivered, even though the weather was balmy. The hairs on my arms prickled. I wasn't sure why, but something wasn't right.

The place looked amazing, a Georgian manor house sitting in extensive grounds. It was too large for me to survey the extent of the estate from the driveway. Still, I could see manicured lawns formed into gentle terraces, dissected by gravel pathways. There was woodland to the right and horses grazing in a paddock to the left. Why did they need my services? It was immaculate.

How does a nineteen-year-old have such well-heeled contacts? Maybe Marcus was tapping up his posh mates from his old school. He must have been well acquainted with the owners because I could see his red Tesla Model 3, plugged into a charger, in the parking area.

I parked, crunched across the gravel to the gabled porch, and banged the silver door knocker three times. A dog barked. The door opened, and the dog bounded out and jumped on me, his tail wagging frantically. It was Flint.

'Morning Jamie, you found us okay then?' said Marcus.

'This is your home, isn't it?' I said, stating the obvious.

'Well, you'd have found out where I lived soon enough. I had to put my real address on the legal documents for the business. So now seems as good a time as any to show you around.'

'But you don't need Gardening Glover here, do you?'

'We have a fantastic estate management team but want to make changes. We can do so much with the land – there are more than 100 acres of formal gardens that hardly anyone sees and woodland that no one can enjoy. But more of that later. First, my mum wants to meet you.'

Marcus showed me to the bright hallway with white floor tiles and whitewashed walls. He pointed to a door, which took me into an oak-floored reception room with enormous rectangular Georgian windows overlooking the gardens. In the corner, on an armchair, sat a woman. An oxygen mask was strapped to her face. She was thin, too thin. Her skin stretched across protruding bones like an overladen snooker pocket straining at the weight of too many balls. But her elegance and beauty outshone her indisposition. Despite the mask, I could make out a radiant smile reaching her beguiling hazel eyes. A silver chain around her neck carried a jet black swan, matching the tattoo on her wrist. It was the necklace I'd bought her twenty years before.

My eyes welled up – overjoyed and sorrowful in equal measure.

She removed the mask. 'Hello again, Jamie. Welcome to my prison.' It was Renata.

I was dumbstruck. I had too many questions. Where should I start? So I just went over and held her hand. She pulled me in for an embrace.

'Am I Marcus's father?'

'Yes, I'm so sorry I never told you, but it was best and safer for you both. I hope you can make up for it now.' This was getting difficult to comprehend. I was a boiling pot of sensations. Within a week, I'd discovered I was the father of two people, a child, and a young adult, with whom I'd already formed a strong emotional bond. But the two women I've loved most, cruelly concealed the truth of our relationships. Even so, as with Sara, I was more elated than angry.

'I'm overjoyed about Marcus,' I said. 'I already saw myself as a father figure to him, but to be honest, recently, he's been the one giving fatherly advice.'

'Let's go for a walk,' she said. 'You'll have to push me, though.' She pointed to a wheelchair.

I pushed her along the gravel path down to the woodland.

'I'm not going to get better,' she said, reading my mind. 'My respiratory condition's deteriorated, and now my major organs are packing up.'

177

'How long?'

'Weeks, probably. I'm lucky I've lasted this long.'

'Does Marcus know?'

'Of course, he knows everything.' We'd reached the woodland. Renata's own private forest. 'It's just a bit further to the lake,' she said. 'There's a bench there. My sanctuary. We can sit and talk. There's so much you need to know.'

The path opened up to a lakeside, which had been obscured by the trees. A canopied arbour on elevated ground faced the body of water to provide a complete vista of its circumference. Renata stood from her wheelchair, and we walked up to the arbour, hand in hand. She took a minute to regain her breath.

'It's idyllic here, isn't it?' I said. We could hear birds warbling and the gentle breeze ruffling the trees. Renata opened her handbag, looking for something. She retrieved a six-inch photograph. 'Look at this,' she said. 'Do you recognise anything?'

It was a family photo. An attractive family standing next to a car, possibly a Ford Cortina. Maybe they were going on holiday. The parents were of similar height. The woman was beautiful, with shoulder-length blond hair and a carefree smile. She had similar features to Renata. The man was younger, handsome, with a head of dense dark hair, nearly as long as the woman's, and a full pair of sideburns. In the middle was a girl, aged four or five, with blond hair too. Her face was obscured because she looked down at the dog she was holding, a golden retriever.

I initially thought it must be a picture of a young Renata with her parents. But a couple of details weren't right. Firstly, from the hairstyles, flares, beige tones of the clothing and the car, the picture appeared to be from the mid-seventies. I remembered the photos of my mum and dad proudly pushing me in a pram through Prospect Park. They looked similar. Renata wouldn't have been born until the late seventies. Also, she told me her father died before she was born, and where were her sisters?

'The woman looks a bit like you. And the dog looks identical to Flint. I wondered whether they could be your mum and dad, which surely couldn't be the case.'

'They are my mum and dad. Biologically, anyway. And you know the woman. You spoke to her last week, although she looks very different now.'

I tried to make sense of what she had just said. I didn't understand. 'Not Ana Steenkamp?' I said incredulously. Renata nodded.

'That's a picture of Juliana and Paul Taylor, and their daughter Chloe. It's the only photo I have of them. It was taken in July 1976, just before Paul and Chloe set off for a weekend in Norfolk. Juliana stayed at home. Tragically, this was the last time Juliana saw Paul and Chloe alive. They were both killed in a car crash, returning home.'

'That's appalling,' I said, 'So, was Juliana pregnant with you at the time?' Renata put a finger to my mouth. 'Let me tell you the story of Juliana before questions. There's a lot for you to take in.'

Her golden hair shimmered as the sun sneaked through the trees. I eagerly squeezed Renata's hand, hoping to find the answers I'd sought for so long.

'Juliana was a pioneering academic specialising in reproductive science. She left her position as the first and only female professor at her college at Cambridge University to pursue her own research at a facility she created. She was lauded for her achievements in her chosen field. But few people knew she was driven to push the boundaries of reproductive science by her own infertility.

'Juliana met her future husband, Paul, in her late thirties. He was one of her students. That was repeating history because Juliana married her professor within a year of moving to Cambridge from South Africa. But her first marriage only lasted five years. It broke down because she couldn't produce the babies her husband expected.

'But Juliana wasn't the kind to accept a doctor and a husband telling her she couldn't have children. Instead, she dedicated herself to developing new fertility treatments that could solve her own problems. However, she still sought to conceive naturally, thrusting herself into a string of relationships with what seemed like virile young students – all to no avail. Paul Taylor met the profile of her recent conquests, but he was different to the others. She saw the potential for a long-term relationship. Paul also fitted into her plans to test the fertility treatment Juliana was researching –

179

in vitro fertilisation. Theoretically, it was a relatively simple concept; fertilising eggs outside the body. She was sure she could make it work in practice.

'But secrecy was paramount. She didn't want public scrutiny of what she knew could be a controversial area. So Juliana formed a close-knit group of research assistants who collaborated to develop her IVF method. Not only that, she had the perfect patient to ensure everything remained secret – herself.

'Strangely, I don't think Paul was part of her inner research circle. He didn't know what she was planning or the critical role she expected him to play. There were several failed attempts, of course. But in 1971, Juliana fell pregnant via IVF, using her eggs and Paul's sperm.

'She was overjoyed but wary. Juliana was determined to keep the circumstances of her pregnancy secret to shield her child from the public spotlight. That's why she left the university to maintain the research under complete confidentiality.

'Chloe was born in 1972, and everything went well. She was a healthy, zestful child, adored by her parents. Juliana's research was thriving too. She helped other infertile couples achieve their dreams – but they were robustly vetted to ensure details of their treatment remained strictly confidential. Finally, Juliana sensed public opinion shifting. The world was ready to hear about her work. So, she organised a press conference to articulate her achievements and showcase some carefully chosen families who'd benefited from her IVF treatment.

'But tragedy struck the day before the conference when Paul and Chloe were killed in the car crash. Juliana swiftly cancelled the conference and swore her whole research team to secrecy.

'Everything Juliana had toiled to achieve was destroyed by the fickle hand of fate. She was understandably devastated. However, Juliana had already achieved the impossible once and believed she could do it again. But this time, she sought to rewrite the sacred laws of nature. Her ambition was to bring someone back from the dead. And not just anyone. She wanted to be reunited with her precious Chloe.'

Renata comprehended the shock and discomfort etched on my face. 'Are you okay for me to continue?' she asked.

'I need you to carry on,' I said.

'Juliana's research wasn't limited to IVF. She foresaw how her techniques could achieve so much more – including the possibility of cloning both animals and humans. All she needed to do was replace the nucleus of an egg cell with the nucleus of a donor cell. Then the DNA of the resulting baby would be almost identical to that of the donor.

'Now Juliana had fresh motivation to turn the cloning theory into reality. But she knew this wasn't a path she could travel in public. So, she closed the Cambridge facility and slipped out of public life. The world would assume she was too grief-stricken to continue her work.

'Let me tell you a bit about Juliana's background now. It's relevant to the story. Juliana was born to academics in Cape Town, South Africa, in 1932. But she also came from money. Her mother's family were one of the richest in the country, from diamond mining and other interests. The family was also instrumental in a secretive global organisation, informally known as The Bevy. The Bevy's objective was to further human achievement by evading myopic government regulations and ignoring small-minded public opinion. They were already funding the Cambridge facility. But Juliana needed something more clandestine. So, she returned to South Africa and pitched her vision to her family's contacts in The Bevy. They agreed to fund her work without hesitation because they fully understood its enormous potential for humanity.

'Juliana reverted to her mother's family name, Steenkamp. Ana Steenkamp set up a new, secretive facility in Italy, joined by her former team from Cambridge – she always commanded fierce loyalty from her acolytes. The Bevy was ingrained in her work now, ensuring they yielded good returns from their investment but also that it stayed under the radar.

'Her initial experimentation was with animal cloning. But, as with her pioneering IVF treatment, the main focus of her labour was more personal – human cloning to bring back Chloe. She had her DNA. I'm not sure how, but maybe Ana had access to her body after she died.

'Ana didn't tell me much about the early days in Emilia-Romagna, but I think that's when she finally understood the dark side of her undertaking. Her agreement with The Bevy was like a pact with the devil. But it was a bargain she was willing to accept to accomplish her aims.

'Human cloning was never going to be an efficient process. Ana acknowledged that achieving a viable pregnancy may take hundreds of attempts. And this needed access to an abundant supply of women willing to be surrogates. They were paid well and were never told of the origin of their implanted embryos. IVF was becoming an established procedure, so they mostly assumed they were acting for women unable to carry their own babies. But if any surrogates questioned their role, The Bevy ruthlessly dealt with them.

'Juliana's team experimented, tweaking the process with each attempt, like varying the time they allowed an embryo to grow outside the womb. And eventually, it succeeded. To the amazement and delight of Ana, her team, and her sponsors, they'd achieved a pregnancy from an egg containing the DNA of a deceased child, Chloe.

'On 6 June 1979, Renata Gallo was born near Bologna in Italy. Renata is a feminine Latin name meaning reborn, for it was seen by Ana as the rebirth of Chloe. Gallo was the name used for the surrogate who gave birth to Renata, although I doubt that was her real name, and I doubt she spent much time with her baby.'

'My God,' I said. 'Enough of the third person. You're telling me you're Renata, Ana Steenkamp's daughter reborn? That's crazy.' She nodded.

'Biologically. I share more than 99% of Chloe's DNA. But we're different people. Ana found that difficult to accept. She doted on me as a mother in Italy. While Chloe and I were intelligent and inquisitive toddlers, Chloe was energetic and hale. I was sickly and feeble. The respiratory problems that have plagued me throughout my life started when I was young. Differences such as health and environment have a significant impact on your personality. I was Ana's daughter, but I wasn't the Chloe Ana desperately wanted me to be.

'Ana achieved some success with animal clones, but there were problems like organ defects, premature ageing, and immune system issues. She found that the same problems occurred with human clones. I think Ana was more disappointed that I didn't emulate her cherished Chloe than she was concerned about my poor health.

'Ana wanted more. She was propelled to prove that her methods could perfectly replicate a human and, more sinisterly, improve on what had gone before. Surrogate mothers gave birth to two more clones of Chloe, my sisters, Fleur and Hazel. But they, too, suffered health imperfections. Ana still hadn't achieved her ambition – a perfect Chloe.

182

I could see Renata was struggling, getting tired. I also became increasingly disturbed by the remarkable story behind Renata's origins and the intimation that a shadowy ruthless organisation steered Ana's work. Was The Bevy responsible for Nick's death?

'I need some oxygen,' Renata said. 'Can you push me back, please? We'll talk later. If you can stay?'

Chapter 35. Jamie – 10 July 2021

I waited while Renata rested. I hoped to see Marcus, to tell him I knew I was his father, but I couldn't find him. Would the revelation alter our friendship? I hoped not. I paced around the gardens by myself. It was a truly splendid place. I reached the lake again, this time on the other side, looking towards the arbour. I chucked a stone at the water to disturb the eerie silence. Its ripples amplified towards my reflection, much like the waves set in motion at Castle Howard twenty years before.

I joined Renata again, sitting in a gazebo by the main house. 'Lucy made us some tea,' Renata said. Who was Lucy? The cook? The maid? I had trouble coming to terms with Renata's nineteenth-century aristocratic lifestyle.

Renata sipped her tea and continued her story.

'Ana believed she needed to expand her horizons to achieve her ambitions. However, the Italian operation's cloak-and-dagger approach had limitations. So, with The Bevy's blessing, Ana decided on a change of tack.

'I think this is the right time to tell you about The Bevy. It originated after the second world war as an informal group of diverse individuals from wealthy and well-connected families across the globe; scientists, economists, philosophers, and industrialists. They saw themselves as altruists. Their key objective was to protect humanity from itself. They associated swan symbolism with their motives. The white swan implied grace, beauty, light, purity, and mystery. The black swan provided balance with power and portent of profound change. That's why they're known as The Bevy.

'They viewed the world's incredible post-war economic boom with disquiet. The golden age of capitalism brought astonishing improvements in prosperity, healthcare, education, and general living standards to billions worldwide. Extraordinary technological transformations in computing, agriculture, and medicine fuelled the boom. But members of The Bevy were concerned that humanity was gorging itself on limited resources like oil, coal, metals, and timber. Unfortunately, the capitalist laissez-faire doctrine leads to a continual voracious appetite for growth and profits, which will inevitably come crashing down. When it does, it leads to war and conflict. It's always the poorest that get crushed.

'The Bevy believed that modern governments are poor custodians for the future of humanity. Like businesses, they're motivated to deliver short-term benefits. And even when they make policy decisions seemingly targeted at protecting the future, they tend to be reactionary and have the opposite effect – like banning nuclear power or pesticides.

'The Bevy believed in an alternative approach. Controlled progress and bold policy, responsibly driven by the needs of humanity in harmony with nature. But they knew this was unrealistic. Even with their level of influence in high places, they couldn't control governments. So, they sought to accelerate technological progress in areas they deemed crucial for their vision that were otherwise stifled, either through regulation or lack of a viable business case.

'They helped like-minded scientists and entrepreneurs fully develop their research through funding and by steering them past restrictive rules. But instead of secretive establishments like Ana's in Italy, they wanted to integrate more into the mainstream. This offered access to more talent and fresh ideas. The Bevy would operate on the periphery, influencing but only taking action when necessary.

'Key to The Bevy's ambitions was its funding houses, such as The Cygnus Foundation, where your friend Nick worked. These ran separately but were linked to The Bevy. They allocated funding capital to projects approved by The Bevy. Business cases weren't the primary factor in funding decisions. But the intention was for The Cygnus Foundation to be profitable over the long term, even if its investments were ultra-high risk.

'Ana's ambitions for her research aligned with The Bevy's new strategy. So Ana set up another facility in the UK. This was popular with her team and allowed access to more specialist resources. But she kept the facility in Italy open too. She initially moved here to Sedgethorpe Manor, using the outbuildings and main house. It's obviously been completely refurbished since then. The facility here mainly focused on continuing her reproductive and cloning research. But for the first time, she operated a genuine fertility clinic, helping couples or individual women have babies after they'd given up all hope. This is where The Bevy helped her adopt illegal procedures without detection. Ana continued her cloning experiments on human patients. It was relatively simple. She could pretend to offer a revolutionary technique or donor sperm to remedy a low sperm count – when she was actually creating a fertilised egg through cloning.

'As well as reproductive cloning, Ana's facility focused on therapeutic cloning. This involves creating a cloned embryo to produce stem cells with the same DNA as the donor cell. This work was more important to The Bevy because stem cells can help develop new treatments for diseases or even create organs for transplant.

'After ten successful years at Sedgethorpe Manor, Ana needed to expand. In addition, she liked the relative isolation of a research facility in a country house. So, when the nearby Pickerton Hall became available, she persuaded The Cygnus Foundation to purchase it and convert it to the desired purpose.

'The Pickerton Hall venture operated as a normal commercial fertility clinic. And most of the patients received highly expert treatment within the rules. She needed to do that to satisfy the regulators. But behind the scenes, she still pursued her reproductive and therapeutic cloning research on humans and animals. But then, of course, you've been to Pickerton Hall and met Ana Steenkamp, right?'

I was shaking in unexpurgated shock. The implications of what Renata was telling me were horrific. 'Yes, I've met Ana Steenkamp', I said. 'But there's no way she's the woman in that photograph. She must be, what, ninety now.'

'Almost, she's eighty-nine. A nice fringe benefit of running a facility researching techniques to slow ageing, and working with an organisation sponsoring other medical breakthroughs, is that you can experiment with those methods on yourself. I don't know about everything she's done to herself, but she's clearly been successful. I think she's had subtle plastic surgery to help reinvent her identity. But that doesn't explain what Ana's become – unlike any nonagenarian anyone's ever seen.'

'That's for sure,' I said. 'Why now, Renata? Why did you choose now to see me again and tell me everything?'

'Because I had to. I've always wanted to, but it was too dangerous. But now it's more dangerous if I don't tell you.'

'What are you talking about?'

'Your meeting with Ana Steenkamp last week. I understand you threatened her by saying you had evidence of financial irregularities relating to Pickerton Hall's funding.'

'Yes, I do. I found some computer files Nick worked on before he died. They represent a strong motive for The Cygnus Foundation to keep him quiet.'

'Jamie, that was so foolish. You've put yourself in grave danger. Have you told the police?'

'No, I wanted to get my facts straight first. That's why I visited Steenkamp.'

'That's good. Listen to me carefully. After you leave here, say nothing of this conversation to anyone and forget Pickerton Hall.'

'Why? The Bevy killed my best friend, didn't they? I can't just ignore that.'

'I'm not certain they killed him, but it's likely. The Bevy is opportunistic. They play the odds. If they can exploit a situation, they will. You said Nick had problems with his marriage and was suffering from anxiety. That was the perfect opportunity for them to make his death look like suicide.'

I was seething inside. This was the confirmation I sought, but to hear how they could so callously dispose of such an insignificant part of their plan was unconscionable. How could I keep quiet? 'I can't let this go,' I said. 'I promised myself that I'd find out how Nick died. Now that I finally have, I need to seek justice.'

Renata stayed silent for a minute. I was unsure if she was thinking or trying to catch her breath.

'Okay, let me tell you about my life,' she said. 'My early years in Italy were happy. Although still obsessed with her work, Ana pampered me like a firstborn child. But her time with me reduced when Fleur and Hazel came along. I think I was jealous. Soon we all spent more time with nannies and teachers than with our mother. I didn't recognise my life was abnormal. I didn't know any different. Fleur and Hazel sufficed as friends, and I loved playing the part of big sister. At that age, we never realised we were effectively prisoners in our home. Franco and his security team kept a low profile.

'We moved to England when I was ten. At the start, it was little different to Italy, just living in a country manor rather than a villa. And colder, of course. We lived here all the time, which was strange when it was a working research facility. My natural curiosity led me to constantly question what went on here, which Ana encouraged because she wanted me to follow in her footsteps. I learned about human cloning and my origin before I was a teenager – but I didn't really understand how remarkable this was.

'But as we grew older, we felt more like we were in prison. We inevitably discovered more about the outside world through papers, television, magazines, and then the internet. They were cautious about letting us go anywhere unaccompanied or the prospect of us striking up a friendship outside the house. I was always told it was too dangerous for me to be alone because of my poor health.

'The first time we were allowed out together, the three of us took the bus to Whitby. I'd just turned eighteen. Fleur and Hazel are a couple of years younger. But we all made ourselves look older. We gorged on the delights of the outside world. Drinking, smoking, gambling in the amusement arcades, and flirting with boys. All the pleasures we'd been denied throughout our lives. That's when we all decided to get a tattoo. We saw the black swan picture in the window of the tattoo parlour. It was perfect. Ana was obsessed with swans, and we thought it could be the marque of our indestructible bond.

'Ana was furious when we returned home, and she instructed Franco and his team to keep us under a tighter leash. It took me a long time to regain Ana's trust. But when the whole facility moved to Pickerton Hall, I started helping out in various areas of the clinic. Ana was impressed with what I'd learnt. I enjoyed the work, and it allowed me to meet new people, especially when I worked with patients.

'But I discovered those working at Pickerton Hall were either obedient devotees of Ana or too scared to question anything because of the implied threat from Franco and his mob. It's how Nick must have felt working at Cygnus. I became close friends with a nurse called Remi. He confessed that he was uncomfortable with the ethicality of some of the practices. Ironically, he only knew a tiny fraction of the dubious methods. One day

Remi was no longer at work. His supervisor told me he had just decided to leave. But Remi hadn't relayed this intention to me nor provided a contact address. This was out of character, and I suspected Franco's involvement.

'I looked for ways to get out of the house. However, Ana and Franco discouraged anything involving striking up a friendship outside their jurisdiction, so no courses or part-time jobs. I was limited to errands, such as taking my sisters to medical appointments. Ana and Franco were incredibly protective of me because they were aware of how much I knew about the true purpose of the clinic.

'I took up cycling and running as pursuits to allow me to leave the house without provoking Ana's concern. I wanted to get fitter, anyway, hoping it might improve my respiratory problems. I loved cycling the lanes and bridleways of North Yorkshire. It really is a beautiful place. And that's how I met you, of course.'

'Did you deliberately puncture your tyre to lure me in?' I asked, in all seriousness.

'What do you think of me? No, of course not. But I admit, as soon as you stopped to help me, I wanted you to be part of my life. It was liberating to talk freely, hear someone speak about their everyday life, and be challenged when I spouted off about the world vision I'd been indoctrinated to believe. I never wanted that morning, in the lanes around Castle Howard and the Malton café, to end. I knew I had to see you again.

'I was so excited when you agreed to come to Whitby, a place I associated with liberty from my jailors. It was a day I wanted to last forever. It was even more wonderful when it turned into a day and a night. It was the happiest I'd ever been.'

I squeezed her hand. 'I felt the same too.'

Renata continued, 'I struggled to work out a way we could keep seeing each other as a proper couple. Staying at your house gave me the taste of a life I wanted to maintain.

'Things complicated further when I found out I was pregnant. I told Ana. After the initial shock, she was excited about the prospect of me having a baby. I think, mainly from a research point of view. There's no medical reason why an individual born from a cloned embryo shouldn't

189

conceive. But, even so, I would be the first of her clones to have a baby. That was something to study. I'd be her lab rat again.

'I tried to persuade Ana to let me bring you into my life. I was having some success too. I think she did really want me to be happy. But I was worried about what that would mean for you. Exposing you to my life would cast a dark shadow you'd never banish. Then I found out about Nick when you told me where he worked. I remembered we'd met when he visited Pickerton Hall. I didn't know for sure, but I suspected the involvement of The Bevy. It wouldn't have been fair to bring you into a world responsible for your best friend's death.'

'But surely it's not fair to deprive a father of his child,' I implored. Why did this keep happening to me?

'I did consider another possibility. One that would have been riskier for us both. When I came to see you that night we went to the quiz, I intended to ask you to come away with me – anywhere, away from the UK, to Asia, South America maybe. I can speak Spanish even though I've never used it. And I had access to enough money for a comfortable lifestyle. But two things stopped me – the main one was it was too much to ask of you. When I saw you with Caroline, I realised how much she loved you. I couldn't pull you away from a good life, a normal life, with her, based on a fantasy. Then, as you saw, Franco was waiting outside your house. I was genuinely scared for your safety. I had to see him, and he told me I could never see you again. The Bevy would act if I tried to continue the relationship or let you know I was pregnant. So leaving you was the only possible option.'

'I'd have gone away with you, without hesitation, if you'd asked,' I said.

'I know. I'm so sorry you're only finding out now. I rebelled as much as I could. I refused to work for Ana or even live in the same house. Ana agreed to move to Pickerton Hall (she preferred to live where she worked anyway). I could continue living at Sedgethorpe Manor, with Fleur and Hazel, but my connections with the outside world were limited.

'I never went to Italy. I'm sorry I lied in the letter. Franco wanted you to stop looking for me, so he made me write the letter. They even posted it from Bologna to make it look genuine. Moving to Italy was one of the options Franco suggested, but I've always been in Yorkshire.

'I dedicated myself to motherhood, bringing up Marcus to be as well-balanced as possible, given his weird background. I kept him away from Ana and her work because I didn't want him re-treading my path. Fortunately, they let him lead a relatively normal childhood, with outside schooling and friends, although they never came here.

'When Marcus reached sixteen, I told him about my origin and who his father is, on the condition he stayed silent about it. I let him know the consequences if he didn't. I followed your life digitally from social media and the Gardening Glover website. It looks like things haven't always been smooth for you. When Marcus discovered who you were, he was desperate to meet you. He tracked what you were up to and eventually concocted a plan to help you with the gardening business. I disapproved as it was dangerous for both of you. But he's incredibly persuasive, and I wanted to make sure he had a family around once I'd gone, so I eventually consented to his optimistic plan. But I'm glad I did. You seem to get on well.'

'We do. I'd come to think of myself as a father figure. I hope this doesn't change things.'

'That's why you need to stop pushing Ana for answers. It's not just yourself you're putting at risk. It's Marcus too. And even Sara.'

That sent shudders down my spine. 'What do you know about Sara?' I asked.

'I knew you broke up with Caroline but got back together. Initially, I just saw some of your Instagram pictures with Caroline and Sara. So I assumed she was Caroline's child from another relationship. You'd never referred to her as a daughter. But we need to have this conversation now because Ana told me about her meeting with you last week.'

'I don't speak with Ana much now, so I knew it was serious when she came to see me about you. She told me about how you and Caroline were patients at Pickerton Hall and how Sara was born from your frozen embryos after Caroline forged the consent form. You've not had much luck with women, have you? But the reason for her visit wasn't to fill me in about what you're up to. It was to warn me. I had to stop you accusing The Cygnus Foundation of murder, or The Bevy would stop you themselves. So she gave me her blessing to speak with you, which made me happier than you could imagine. But I'm imploring you, Jamie, you need to stop, or you'll put everything you care about in peril.'

191

Renata could see from my expression that with Sara's mention, she had finally forced her message through to me. God, this whole thing was a sick mess. I'd finally found out the truth and could do nothing about it.

'Fuck, what can I do?' I cried. 'Yes, I'll stay silent. Will Franco and his friends leave us alone then?'

'Yes, Ana gave me her word.'

I heard barking. Marcus led Flint up a garden path towards us. 'Evening Dad,' he said cheerily. 'Are you staying for dinner? Lucy's cooking lamb.' His jaunty manner was discordant with the fact that Renata had just told me a bunch of ruthless assassins were out to get us.

I turned to Renata. She looked shattered. 'Yes, please stay for dinner. You can talk things through with Marcus. But I need to rest now. Why don't you stay here tonight? I'd love to see you in the morning.'

Lucy served us lamb cutlets with potatoes and vegetables. 'Why do you freeload on Caroline every Thursday when you have a personal servant to cook for you?' I asked Marcus.

'I go for the company. Not yours, obviously. Have you recovered from the shock of seeing my mum again?'

'It's going to take me a long time to get my head around everything I've learnt over the past two weeks, but I couldn't be happier to find out you're my son.'

'I thought you'd have twigged months ago. Didn't you think it strange why a teenager would be so interested in an uninspiring gardening business?'

'Maybe I did subconsciously, I don't know. How have you coped all these years with the spectre of The Bevy hanging over you if you put a foot wrong.'

'I'm lucky. Mum has done her best to insulate me from them. She's always been the go-between. I know I need to be careful, but I don't want to end up like her. She's effectively been a recluse since I was born. So I just try to keep them at the back of my mind. You'll have to do the same now.'

'It just feels wrong. We know The Bevy have destroyed lives. Literally murdered people. But we're too scared to do anything about it.'

'I feel the same. I've tried to do something when the risk was low. But even then, it often backfired. I wish they wouldn't act in such a Machiavellian way because their objectives are admirable. They foresaw the implications of insatiable capitalism – the problems the world now faces: climate catastrophe, famine and poverty, all stoking conflict. And at least they have answers. They believe the world is in such a dire state that they need to take radical action now. The long-term goals outweigh the suffering some must endure getting there.'

'It doesn't feel like that to me. I know my friend Nick didn't have to die. So, what happened to Renata's sisters? Are they dead now?'

'Fleur died of natural causes; it was nothing to do with The Bevy. Hazel stopped living with us soon after I was born. As Renata tried to distance herself from Ana and The Bevy, Hazel became closer to her mother. Ana supported her with treatment for her medical condition. I've not seen Hazel for many years, but she's still alive. It's sad for Renata, especially with little time left because they were inseparable when they were younger.'

'Yes, that must be heartbreaking for her,' I reflected. 'I met Fleur, but I never met Hazel.'

Marcus showed me to one of the guest bedrooms. I wondered how many guests ever actually stayed there. After such a substantial meal, I'd have had trouble sleeping anyway, but brooding over Renata's disclosures made it impossible. How could I live with myself, knowing the truth about Nick? How could I face Vicky and Caroline? I'd not even spoken to Caroline about Sara yet. Would I be looking over my shoulder for the rest of my life? Eventually, my turmoil must have burnt out and transformed into slumber as I awoke to the dawn chorus. That split second between sleep and consciousness in an unfamiliar place was a blessed relief, before I remembered where I was and the gravity of my situation.

I wandered down to the kitchen, 'What would you like for breakfast, Sir?' asked Lucy. In my recent experience, only police officers and security guards called me 'Sir'.

'Just toast and coffee, please,' I replied.

Marcus arrived with Flint, presumably after taking him for a morning walk. 'I'll show you my plans for the grounds sometime,' he said. 'It will showcase Gardening Glover to the whole north of England.'

193

I marvelled at his coolness, unfazed by the menace of The Bevy. Hopefully, I'd learn to live with it too. Renata didn't join us for breakfast, but she was in the garden room, where I first saw her the day before.

'I could get used to this lifestyle,' I said.

'You never know. It might be yours sooner than you think,' Renata replied.

'How do you mean?'

'I've seen the plans for the gardening business. It won't be long before you're a horticultural tycoon.'

'I can thank Marcus for that.'

We sat together in silence for a few minutes. Then I said, 'Can I come and see you here again? I want to spend as much time as possible with you.'

She touched my arm. 'I'd love that, Jamie. You can come whenever you want. Bring Sara too, if Caroline lets you.' We embraced. I hoped not for the last time.

Chapter 36. Jamie – 11 July 2021

I drove out of Sedgethorpe Manor, desperately hoping fate would allow Renata and me enough time together to get to know each other properly this time. What would my life be like if Renata had stayed with me twenty years ago? Would I be lord of the manor, imprisoned in a fantasy Elysium? Or maybe we owned a small holding in Costa Rica, with Marcus and I working the land and developing natural remedies for Renata's ailments. Or perhaps we'd sail the world, travelling from port to port to savour new experiences, Renata cured by the sea air.

The turn ahead was towards Pickerton Hall. Seeing that snapped me back to the harsh realities of my present situation. I should have put my foot down and not looked back. But I didn't. I seemed to be drawn to the place. So I took the turn. I didn't have a plan; I just wanted to find something to give me an advantage. Throughout my life, others have controlled my destiny. Caroline, Patrick and Marcus had all manipulated me, and now Renata had done it for a second time. But I wanted to be in control this time – perhaps the protestors at Pickerton Hall would have the information I needed.

I parked in a lay-by around five hundred metres from the facility's entrance. I walked along the road. The Hall's towering perimeter fence loomed to my left. It wouldn't be easy to sneak in and take a look around. So I ventured further and spotted the protesters' camp ahead. As I passed an oak tree, my heart jumped as two grotesque figures lurched out from behind the trunk to block my path. They looked like they were fleeing a Halloween party, clad in white hooded coveralls, the kind you get from DIY stores to protect clothes when painting. I suppose they were meant to represent hazmat suits. Freaky skeleton masks, one red and one yellow, covered their faces.

'Where are you going?' The one with the red mask challenged. A male voice.

'I'm walking along the road. Anything wrong with that?'

'Are you police?' Yellow mask asked. This time a female voice.

'Do I look like police? Was there a nuclear apocalypse I missed last night?'

She took off her mask. Hopefully, a signal she thought I was non-threatening. 'You need to be careful. If those Gestapo cunts catch you sniffing around, you're done for.' She pointed through the fence at two burly guards, about two hundred metres away, staring in our direction. 'Look what they did to Dojo.' She turned towards Red Mask. He removed the mask to reveal purple bruising from above his left eye (which struggled to open) down to his cheek. He looked like he'd been in the ring with Tyson Fury.

'That's nasty. Did you prosecute?' I asked.

'No point,' he said. 'They caught me trespassing.'

'What do you want?' said Yellow Mask.

'I was hoping to ask you a few questions about what goes on here.'

'Why, are you a journo?'

'No, I'm not a journalist. But I believe people at Pickerton Hall are responsible for the murder of my best friend.'

'Let's take him to Barney,' said Dojo.'

They donned their masks again and led me to the protesters' encampment. The stench of weed was overwhelming, which was probably a good thing – it concealed the stink of months of unsanitary habitation in this mini shanty town. Most protesters were similarly attired to my guardians, which was disconcerting. They took me to a portly, rough-faced man. I assumed his epithet was due to his resemblance to Barney Gumble, the beer-addled slob from The Simpsons. But the comparison ended there. He was lucid and sober. I supposed his camouflage jacket and trousers differentiated him from the others, signifying his role as commander of this strange rabble.

'I make them wear masks,' he said in a deep, throaty voice. He pointed at the security cameras on poles near the gates. 'The bastards use facial recognition technology. Every face they capture will be on a database somewhere. Cunts will do everything they can to ruin our lives. Now, tell me your story.'

I told him about Nick's death after challenging Pickerton Hall's funding model. And how the security guards threw me out and threatened me when I confronted Ana Steenkamp. I kept quiet about my conversation with Renata, of course. I told him I needed more information and evidence to nail Steenkamp and her cronies.

'I don't rate your chances, Mate,' he said. 'You'll get nowhere with the police, newspapers, the fertility regulator, animal welfare – anything official – this lot have tentacles permeating into every organisation. We've compiled compelling evidence about the activities here. Ex-employees have completed detailed testimonies, but we get blocked at every avenue. The fuzz ignore our evidence. They're more interested in prosecuting us for trespass. No one cares, so we must resort to blogging and social media. But even that gets taken down, or we're labelled conspiracy theorists. I'm telling you, this place is run by people with influence in high places. Even their security thugs act with impunity. That's why I post lookouts like Dojo and Ivory, to protect our little community from sabotage by their Stasi henchmen.'

I was weary of people telling me to give up. 'Why are you still here then if it's a lost cause? Why don't you quit protesting?' I said.

'It's what I do, isn't it? And I have nothing to lose. But I didn't say it was a lost cause. Things change. It will all come crashing down eventually. Maybe we'll have to take direct action ourselves.' He looked around. 'We'll be here when the time's right to act, but you look too soft to stay the course.'

'You know nothing about me. I'm trying to right a wrong that's haunted me for twenty years, so don't lecture me about staying the course. I won't be intimidated. I want to help you bring it down,' I said. 'Please, tell me what goes on here.'

'Okay, they're trying to genetically engineer the future,' he said. 'They're performing cloning and gene editing experiments to create animal super-breeds. They believe for humanity to have a future, it needs to be sustained by a new kind of food chain, including livestock that won't drain resources or contribute to carbon emissions. So, for example, they're trying to create cattle that generate less methane, eat less, and produce more milk. Sounds great, doesn't it? Well, it's not. They're not elevating us to a new utopia. Instead, they're plummeting us into a terrifying existence where life is simply a currency to be manipulated by the powerful. Pain and suffering are necessary by-products.

'As well as being illegal, their experiments inflict untold misery on their lab animals. Female cows, sheep, dogs, mice, and horses are harvested for their eggs and cast aside. Embryos are genetically edited to deliver offspring with the required characteristics, but it's not an exact science. The process is acutely inefficient, meaning countless infant animals are born deformed, with compromised immune systems or major organ problems. These consign them to a life of suffering. It's like something out of *The Island of Doctor Moreau*.

'And then there's the human experiments. Animal research is so intense because they want to apply the learnings to humans – I don't even know the main objective, but the implications are horrific. Are they trying to create a master race?'

Barney's explanation made me feel sick. Yes, he was a conspiracy theorist. His story was probably exaggerated. But if only half of it was true, the consequences were shocking.

'If that's all true, how do they get away with it? Surely their regulators would have picked up on these practices from routine inspections.'

'They're untouchable. First of all, the fertility clinic functions as a front. They operate as a conventional clinic to make it look like that's the main activity. Then, because of the influence of whoever is backing them, no one looks any harder at what's happening – even though we've clearly set out the evidence.'

'Look,' I said, 'I think I can help you bring them down. I know information about who might be backing them. Let me work out my next steps.'

'You know where we are, and we're not moving. But be careful. I know what happens to people who get too close, and I think you do too.'

I walked back to my van, content that I had made some progress. Barney's story was consistent with Renata's but articulated more detail about Pickerton Hall's nefarious practices. What should I do? I was now more determined than ever to take action. But I had promised Renata to stay silent, and there were Sara and Marcus to consider. So I would need to tread carefully.

I passed the tree where Dojo and Ivory had intercepted me. It didn't look like they'd returned to their posts. My van was visible in the lay-by ahead, but as I moved closer, my heart sunk. The front tyre was flat. Typical, I thought. A punctured tyre on a North Yorkshire lane was how this first started. I reached the car and inspected the wheel. A six-inch nail protruded from the side wall of the rubber. It was clearly an act of sabotage.

'Having trouble, Sir?' said a deep voice behind me. I flinched in shock and jerked my head around. It was the brawny security guard who had dragged me out of my meeting with Ana Steenkamp. Another blue-jacketed man of similar build joined him. Were they cloning the staff too? 'I told you to stay away,' he said.

'I'm on a public road. What I do here is nothing to do with you.'

The guard laughed. 'Just taking a Sunday stroll, are we?'

Despite all the warnings from Renata and Barney, I wasn't scared. Surely, they wouldn't do anything to me outside the perimeter fence? These weren't The Bevy's assassin crew. But, not for the first time, I misjudged the situation.

They grabbed me, and given the big guy had previously managed to drag me to my van alone, they had little trouble moving me, despite my struggling.

'What are you doing? Fuck off. Get off me now,' I shouted as loud as I could. Hoping Barney and his disciples would hear and come to my rescue. But they were too far away. The guards swiftly transported me through a concealed gate near the lay-by. My heart was pounding due to anger and fear. I was on their turf now, and, no doubt, Franco was controlling their actions behind the scenes. What were their intentions?

I stopped struggling, realising I wasn't going to get away. A small part of me wanted this to happen, I think, to bring everything to a head, but the rest of me was terrified. 'Where are you taking me?' I screamed. They were silent. But I could see where we were going, towards an isolated brick barn. Once inside, I could smell animals, but there were none there now, although straw was still on the floor. They pushed me to the side and handcuffed me to a ring chained to the wall.

'You can't leave me here,' I shouted as they left the building.

'Here, you can use this if you need a piss or a shit,' the bigger guy said as he threw me a bucket. I don't want you messing the place up like an animal.

Chapter 37. Millie – 11 July 2021

They had been travelling for about twenty minutes. Where was he taking her? Millie battled to compose herself. But being gagged and handcuffed in the back of a van was about as bleak as it could get. A small blessing was that she now knew her kidnapping was something to do with Pickerton Hall. At least it wasn't some random psycho. Or Patrick. Actually, out of the three possibilities, abduction by Patrick was probably the least bad outcome. Terrifyingly, though, she knew what her captor was capable of.

What should she do? How should she act? He hadn't harmed her yet. That was a good sign. He wanted information; to know who The Exonerator is. She didn't know. What would he do when he found out she couldn't help him? Would he eliminate her like Wesley Myers and Nicholas Shepherd? He'd have to make it look like an accident. No one would believe Millie could take her own life. She tried to focus on something else, something happy, somewhere safe. Like when the doctor told her mum she was cancer-free or dinner with Kyle. But it was no good. All she could think about was the hopelessness of her situation – her captor had gone too far. As Millie lay shaking, curled up in the foetal position, she realised he'd never allow her to escape alive.

The van slowed. Probably moving at less than ten miles an hour. The ride was bumpy. Were they reaching their destination? It stopped, and after thirty seconds, the doors opened. She squinted her eyes, reacting to the sunlight. Her captor was a tall man in a black suit, his dark hair slicked back like a Mafia gangster. He was comfortable letting her see his face, which was not a good sign.

The man tore off Millie's gag. 'Go on, scream,' he said. 'No one will hear you.'

'I work at York Police,' Millie shouted. 'You're fucked now.'

He looked at her quizzically. 'You're not *pula*,' he said. 'No one's coming for you.' He waved a mobile phone at her face. Millie's phone. He dragged Millie into a brick building and handcuffed her to an iron manacle on the wall. She heard movement inside the building.

'What is this place, your dungeon?' cried a man's voice from the gloom. Then, as Millie's eyes became more accustomed to the dark again, she saw a man handcuffed to the opposite wall. Her captor started to walk out of the building.

'What do you want?' Millie shouted.

'*A presto*. See you soon,' he replied.

'Help. Help,' Millie screamed. She yanked the cuff that shackled her to the wall. Pain surged through her wrist, but she ignored it. Trying to find a means of escape was her only focus.

'I've tried,' said the man chained to the opposite wall. 'I thought I could wrench the manacle from the wall. These are old bricks. But it's in too tightly. I doubt we're the first people they've imprisoned here.'

'Where the fuck are we?'

'We're in an outbuilding, a barn maybe, at Pickerton Hall. Somewhere that advertises itself as a fertility clinic. But it's a front for illegal animal and human reproduction research.'

Millie's head dropped. It was all becoming clearer. 'I know about Pickerton Hall, and I think I have a good idea about what goes on here,' Millie said.

'Who are you? What do you do?' asked the man.

Millie remembered the self-development courses she'd attended while working at Ebor Assurance. How often had she answered those questions, inhibited by a slight sense of awkwardness? What she'd give to be in one of those sterile meeting rooms now. 'Sorry, I forgot to put on my name badge. I'm Millie Kumar, and I'm a data scientist.'

The man laughed, obviously in tune with Millie's gallows humour. 'You're not Shiv's daughter, are you?'

Millie hesitated before answering. This was getting weirder. 'Yes, I am,' she whispered. 'Who are you?'

'My name's Jamie Glover. We met once before, although I doubt you'd remember it. You must have been about five then. Shiv brought you to see me at Ebor Assurance, so I could tell you about pensions.'

'I do remember,' Millie said, laughing and crying simultaneously. 'You showed me how to play Minesweeper on Windows. That was the only thing I learnt that day. And the only thing I remember. Ironically, I've been playing a real-life game of minesweeper this week. It's like that situation where you have two covered squares. You know a single mine is under one of them, but you don't have enough information to know which one. So you have to make a guess. Unfortunately, I think I just guessed wrong and hit the mine.'

'It's not game over yet. We're both still alive. We just need to be smart when they come back, make sure they know we're more useful to them alive than dead.'

'Why are you here, Jamie? What could they want from a Pensions Manager?'

Jamie laughed again. 'I'm not a Pensions Manager anymore. I'm a gardener. But I don't think they care much about their victims' occupations. It started for me when they killed my friend Nick. And he was an accountant.'

'Is that Nicholas Shepherd?'

'Yes, that's right.'

'That's kind of why I'm here too,' Millie said. 'I work as a data scientist for York Police. They asked me to look at some data analysis carried out by a maths teacher called Wesley Myers, who died in 2020, in a similar fashion to Nick.'

Millie told Jamie about discovering Pickerton Hall linked Nick's and Wes's deaths.

'Wes's data analysis identified a spike in COVID cases at young ages,' Millie said. 'He connected it to a super spreader event here, a celebration of the twentieth anniversary of the fertility clinic. But there was more to it than that. Why were the hospitalisation rates for young people so high? I have a theory that might sound outlandish, but everything revolves around the facility's Principal, Ana Steenkamp.'

'Nothing you can tell me about Ana Steenkamp will surprise me,' Jamie said.

'What if I told you she's eighty-nine years old?'

'I'd say you're spot on. Steenkamp's research and connections give her access to technology and treatments that slow down some of the effects of ageing.'

Millie was shocked. Firstly, at confirmation it was true and secondly that someone else knew about it, but she continued. 'I believe Pickerton Hall is experimenting with human cloning and gene editing, sometimes on unsuspecting fertility patients. Animal clones often suffer health problems not present in their donors – like major organ defects, premature ageing, and immune system issues. I think Ana Steenkamp cloned humans but found they suffered the same health problems as animals. But she was driven to perfect her technique, so she experimented with different procedures, such as gene editing, to improve the outcome.

'Here's where I might be overthinking things, but I believe Ana Steenkamp is uncompromising. She'll stop at nothing to achieve her aims. When COVID-19 came along, Steenkamp looked at it as an opportunity rather than the health catastrophe most people viewed it as. Nature had given her the perfect situation to evaluate the robustness of her work. Could her superhumans stand up to COVID? I think she deliberately manufactured events that would cause COVID to spread among her patients' children. For example, the anniversary celebration here. But I also found out that Steenkamp has another facility in Italy. There was an event there in February 2020, which also resulted in a spike in hospitalisations at young ages. Wesley Myers was close to exposing this on social media. That's why they silenced him.'

'Everything you say is consistent with what I know,' Jamie replied. 'I was a fertility patient here with my partner. Unlike other fertility clinics, one of their selling points is that they monitor the babies' health after they're born. They even arrange yearly medical assessments for children until they're twelve. That always struck me as strange, but it makes sense now. They're studying the effectiveness of their experiments.'

'I don't know for sure. I'm making a lot of assumptions. Tell me your story, Jamie. It might help me understand better.'

'Okay, but you might find it even more remarkable than yours.'

Jamie told Millie how Pickerton Hall had played an almost supernatural role in his life. He never believed Nick took his own life, but the police, including Rosemary Slater, ignored him. He eventually connected Nick to Pickerton Hall when DCI Slater showed him a photo from the facility's opening. It showed Nick with Ana Steenkamp and included Jamie's ex-girlfriend, who'd disappeared twenty years ago. He saw that same ex-girlfriend yesterday for the first time since then. The ex-girlfriend told Jamie she was created as a clone of Ana Steenkamp's first daughter, who died in a car crash in 1976.

'That's remarkable,' said Millie. 'But from what I've already found out, I believe it. I know about Juliana Taylor and Chloe. I'm sure the events of July 1976 caused Steenkamp's zealous obsession to recreate a perfect daughter.'

'How did you find out about Juliana and Chloe? I didn't even know about them until yesterday?'

'Strangely, I think that's why I'm here now. Wes Myers used to collaborate with a follower on his Twitter COVID analysis, who called themselves The Exonerator. The Exonerator only interacted with Wes and stopped posting after Wes died. I thought I was clever when I forwarded Wes's last tweet to The Exonerator. It asked if they had formed any conclusions about Wes's Yorkshire COVID spike analysis. Frustratingly there were no replies to my tweet. But a week later, I received a Pickerton Hall brochure and an old newspaper cutting about Juliana Taylor. It was like a clue to a macabre game that I assume was from The Exonerator. I found the rest out myself.

'I think my interaction with The Exonerator alerted Pickerton Hall. They were interested in whoever it was because they could potentially spill the beans about Ana Steenkamp and her work. But, catastrophically, my post also aroused their interest in me. They saw my profession and thought I was a danger too. They want to know who The Exonerator is, and I don't know. How are we going to get out of this, Jamie?' Millie sobbed.

'It's not as bleak as it seems. Pickerton Hall is just a piece in a much bigger jigsaw. It's run by an organisation with colossal resources and ruthless practices. They call themselves The Bevy. The man who kidnapped you is named Franco. I believe he does the bidding more for The Bevy than Ana Steenkamp. And I don't think everything is rosy between Steenkamp and The Bevy. I met Ana Steenkamp last week to challenge her about Nick's evidence of financial irregularities at the facility. She was being monitored by a security camera and looked scared when a guard entered to evict me.

'I also met with the leader of a bunch of protesters outside. They've a good idea about what's happening here, so it will not stay covered forever.

They can see cracks in the Pickerton Hall operation and are ready to take direct action – although I don't know what and when that will be.

'When they come back for us, our best hope is that it's both Ana Steenkamp and Franco. We need to play them off against each other to take their focus off us.'

'Okay, but I'm so scared about Franco returning. It's ironic. Last week I was petrified when a stalker from when I worked at Ebor Assurance forced his way into my apartment – I thought that was the pinnacle of fear. But this has reached a new level.'

'I know it's something you won't want to think about – but who was it? I might know him,' Jamie said.

'It's funny. I've not told anyone about it. Not even my boyfriend, and he'd kick the shit out of him. I thought I could deal with it by myself. But I should have reported him. I'm sure he's done it to others. But sitting here now, keeping it to myself seems ridiculous.'

'Who is it?'

'Patrick Kemp.'

'Fucking hell Millie, Patrick Kemp joined Ebor at the same time as me. He's always been a sex predator but gets away with it because the business turns a blind eye. He went out with my partner, but when they split up, he acted like a complete nutter and threatened me with a shotgun. I'm aware he's currently under disciplinary investigation for offering a promotion to someone if she'd sleep with him. Millie, when this is over, promise me you'll let me help you sort this.'

Millie had stopped shaking, and she was breathing more easily. The conversation provided a trace of cathartic relief at a time of jeopardy. 'Yes, I promise,' she said. 'When do you think they will come back for us?'

'Soon, I hope. I'm getting thirsty.'

'How long have you been here?'

'Not long, maybe a couple of hours before you arrived.'

'You don't think they're listening to us, do you? Franco ripped my gag off when I came in here. Do you think they deliberately put us together to talk, to find out what we know?'

Millie yelped as bulbs on the ceiling flooded the barn with unaccustomed light. She shivered with revulsion as Franco entered. Behind him was a woman Millie recognised as Ana Steenkamp. Ana started speaking. 'It's a small world, isn't it? Who'd have thought you two would know each other? But your conversation has been enlightening. You have been doing your homework on us, haven't you? So, I think you both know what happens next.'

Chapter 38. Jamie – 11 July 2021

There had to be a way out of this. But Ana and Franco heard everything we'd said from the hidden microphones. There was nothing left for us to tell. We were much safer to them dead than alive. Could I leverage my relationship with Marcus and Renata? Surely Ana Steenkamp must have empathy for her daughter and grandson? But everything I knew about her indicated she was a psychopath.

'Just let us go, Ana,' I pleaded. 'I promised Renata I'd keep quiet about everything – and I meant it. I'm sure Millie will do the same. What else are you going to do – try and make it look like we've joined in some kind of cult suicide pact?'

'You are a simple person, aren't you? I still can't believe you are Marcus's father. You think you're smart and worked everything out. But you really haven't a clue about how important what we do is and how insignificant your little problems are.' Her South African accent had become stronger. She'd shed the wistful demeanour she displayed at our previous meeting – Ana Steenkamp had reverted to demented zealot mode.

'All I know is you're a crazy witch who's willing to fuck with people's lives and fuck with nature for something unattainable. You can't get Chloe back. Face it, she died.'

Ana sniggered. 'What will the world be like in fifty or a hundred years? Does it matter to you? You'll be dead, and those you love will be old or deceased.'

'But you'll still be around, Ana, won't you?' I taunted. 'Even more shrivelled and crazy, if that's possible.' She ignored me.

'Individuals don't matter. People die, and they soon become irrelevant. But humanity continues. Unhappily, the world is changing too quickly. If people don't adapt, life will become unsustainable. We're seeing the effect of climate change and resource depletion now. Crop failure, famine, mass migration – it will only get worse. Many areas of the planet will become uninhabitable. So how does the world react? Countries squabble between themselves to gain some insignificant strategic advantage while, simultaneously, the structure that has underpinned their existence collapses.

'The only hope for humanity is a paradigm shift. The concept of "survival of the fittest" is broken in an economic and biological sense. Nature, including humans, can't adapt quickly enough to what's coming. That's where we come in. We're the invisible hand, steering the world to make the necessary changes. But we're not the calamitous invisible hand economist Adam Smith envisaged. He believed unregulated competition would somehow lead to widespread benefits for all. No, we act behind the scenes because the public and governments are made up of small-minded idiots like you, who can't comprehend the inescapable necessity of what we do. But our work is planned and deliberate – including providing a helping hand to evolution to keep pace with the environmental disasters spawned by humans.

'Do you have any idea what that means, Jamie? You probably have heard of genetically modified crops, selective breeding, or genome editing to improve livestock. These changes could enhance humanity's prognosis – yet, public opinion still rails against marginal actions to help itself. Can you imagine the outcry if there were widespread human genome editing? But it's essential to survive what's coming – humanity needs to be more robust, productive for longer, more fertile, and consume less. That's what we've achieved here. That's my gift to the world.'

'No way, I don't want to turn into a freak like you,' I said.

'You know, it's sad,' Millie said. 'You could have been such a positive force for humanity if you hadn't been corrupted. How many more people could you have inspired to help solve all these problems through collaboration? But you decided to go underground and become a mad scientist. As a result, you cut yourself off from technological advances that could have helped you. For example, the rise of data and artificial intelligence. You didn't need to carry out scores of Frankenstein-like experiments on unsuspecting patients. Most of it could have been modelled.'

Good, Millie was playing along now too. The tactic of stoking Ana Steenkamp's vanity, to play for time, was the only strategy I could think of. But to what end? Who was coming to our rescue?

As if reading my mind, Ana Steenkamp addressed Franco and, in a cold toneless voice, said, 'Enough, we need to deal with them now. No one knows they're here. It should be simple. You've done it enough times before.'

Millie shuddered. All I could think about were Sara and Marcus, my children who'd never get to know me as a father. Franco withdrew a pistol from under his jacket and raised his right arm to point it at me. He hesitated. Everything seemed in slow motion. God, why was it taking so long? It was as if they derived sadistic pleasure from the psychological torture of delaying the death bullet.

But then Franco seemed disturbed by something. He reached into his jacket again, retrieved his phone and looked at it. Was he reading a message? *Il Cigno Nero*,' he said, 'Coming here.'

A momentary flicker in Ana's facial expression betrayed anxiety. It was the same as when she looked at the security camera at our last meeting. Someone was watching her, someone she feared. Who was *Il Cigno Nero*', The Black Swan?

I perceived an opportunity to act due to the confusion. Franco was still near enough for me to reach him. I sprung from the floor and stretched my left arm to grab his gun. I'd caught him unawares, and my fingers gained traction on the barrel. But Franco had the reflexes of a professional fighter. He was too quick. He swung his left arm around and smashed his elbow into the side of my head. Pain exploded like a hand grenade detonating in my skull. I fell to the ground, and Franco stamped on my head. Dirt from the floor crunched between my teeth. Had I fucked up our last chance?

'You're getting sloppy, Franco. Clear this mess up NOW,' yelled Ana.

He glared into her eyes and asserted his reply, 'Wait.'

The next fifteen minutes passed in silence. I was dazed by Franco's blow, but the dynamic had changed. Ana was no longer in charge. Instead, Franco was awaiting the orders of The Black Swan. Was this a reprieve or a stay of execution? I looked at Millie. I tried to smile in a way that indicated hope. But, more likely, my pathetic state projected panic. She didn't react.

New movement registered in my peripheral vision. Someone else entered the barn, and I simply stared in astonishment. Had I shifted to some alternate reality? The striking face, the radiant flaxen hair, and the graceful poise were all features boldly etched in my mind for twenty years. Renata's features. But this wasn't the frail, sickly version of Renata I was reacquainted with the day before. This was the stunning, vivacious, effervescent Renata in her early forties I'd imagined. What was this miraculous transformation?

She motioned toward me. 'So, this is the legendary Jamie Glover? You look out of sorts. I apologise for the boorish behaviour of your hosts.' She reached to hold my handcuffed hand. Her warm touch was comforting. The black swan tattoo peaked out from under her sleeve. But the eyes betrayed her. These weren't the compassionate, enigmatic eyes of my lover. They were the frenzied eyes of a fanatic. 'You have a lot to answer for, Jamie. It was never the same after you entered her life.'

I immediately realised who it was: Hazel, the third sister I'd never met. Twenty years before, Renata gave me the impression that Hazel was the weakest of the sisters. Not anymore. Today she was the antithesis of infirm.

She let go of my hand. 'No matter, that was a long time ago. The question for now is, what will we do with you two?' She reached into her shoulder bag and handed me a water bottle, then walked over to Millie and did the same. I took a couple of gulps, and immediately the pain dissipated.

'You know more than anyone that this has to be cleaned up rapidly,' Ana said icily. 'What are you waiting for?'

'You're right. But I fear we've reached the stage where the situation needs a purge rather than a spring clean,' declared Hazel.

'What are you talking about?' Ana replied.

'I think you know, don't you, Ana?' Hazel said. 'This place has had its time. We've indulged you for too long. You were truly pioneering in your day, but that day was so far in the past no one remembers it anymore.' She looked at Millie, 'The data boffin's right. Science has moved on, and you've done your bit for fertility, but iPS cell technology is replacing therapeutic

211

cloning. You're an anachronism that used to produce results, but you've become too risky. We can't carry on covering up for you.'

'The Bevy would be nothing without me, and I created you. You'd have expired long before Fleur if it wasn't for my work,' Ana replied in anguish.

'That's always been your weakness, Ana, God delusions. You succeeded in cheating nature once. Then, you thought you could continue repeating it. But you're not God. You can't outwit death.'

The antagonism disappeared from Ana's countenance. Her soft smile and distant stare suggested a restful resignation to her fate. Ana turned to look Hazel in the eyes, 'Yes, I can,' she declared defiantly.

'Don't worry. Your legacy will be protected.' Hazel nodded in Franco's direction. He lifted his pistol again. But Franco didn't aim at Millie or me. Instead, he pointed it at Ana and shot her in the head, this time without hesitation.

With the gunshot still echoing in my ears, Franco turned to me and grinned – exposing his crooked, blemished teeth. I stared into the face of the devil. *'È ora di morire,'* Franco said. 'It's time to die.' BANG.

Was this it? Was I dead? No. I was still in the barn. Ana and Franco both lay on the ground, dead. Hazel had shot Franco.

I looked towards Millie. How would she cope with witnessing such a horrific spectacle? But she was lying motionless on the ground too. Her left arm was suspended aloft by the handcuff.

'What have you done?' I screamed at Hazel.

'Go on, drink up too. It will be better for you,' she replied. Next to Millie's body was the bottle Hazel had given her, now empty. Had she been drugged or poisoned?

I looked at my bottle. I'd drunk about a third of it. I was feeling dizzy.

I emptied the water on the floor, but nausea overwhelmed me. There were noises outside. A commotion and people shouting. The stench of smoke lingered in the air – was this Hazel's purge? Were they torching the place? I think the panic was the only thing keeping me conscious. I looked for Hazel to plead for our release, but I couldn't see her. Had she fled?

Smoke entered the barn, and I started choking. I tried to scream, but all I managed was a whimper. No one would hear me. I transformed into a semi-conscious state; the noise, sounds, and smells registered but didn't mean anything. Had I become like Ana, resigned to my fate at the moment before death? I sensed movement in the building now, and the noises, there was something transcending the shouts. Was it a dog's bark?

Someone was holding me. I looked up to face her. It wasn't Hazel, I was sure. Those eyes, that smile, the feeling that everything would be all right. It couldn't be, but it was. It was Renata. I motioned to embrace her. Miraculously, my right hand was free. Was I dreaming? We hugged. Renata was with me now. With me forever. She whispered in my ear. 'It's time for me to go now, my love. Please forgive me. Look after Marcus. He's not as clever as he thinks he is. *Ti amo tanto*'. All was darkness.

Chapter 39. Jamie – 12 July 2021

A coughing fit signalled my return to some form of consciousness, likely triggered by the acrid stench of burning. I tentatively opened my eyes. Flames and smoke surrounded me. Panicked voices pleaded for help while others cheered. I closed them again. Had I been banished to the underworld as penance for a life of inaction? Punished for neglecting the plight of my best friend. Something licked my face. Either I was still alive, or it was a weird start to my afterlife. 'Leave him alone, Flint.' It was Marcus's voice. He was trying to stop Flint from slobbering all over my face.

'Renata, Renata,' I babbled. 'She's here.'

'Wait up. The paramedics will be here soon,' Marcus said. 'You're suffering from smoke inhalation, Jamie. Maybe you're hallucinating. My mum is too unwell to leave the house.' I choked again. I could see more now. In the distance, the main hall was ablaze. The outbuildings were smouldering too. The barn that had been my prison for most of the day was reduced to rubble. No one could have survived in there. 'Where's Millie?' I screamed. Marcus pointed. There she was, lying on the ground. The paramedics reached her first, administering oxygen, she appeared conscious. Someone placed a mask on my face and said, 'Can you hear me, Jamie?' I nodded.

The next few hours passed in a haze. The paramedics took me to a hospital in York. The doctors undertook numerous tests and kept me overnight for observation. The following day my head pounded, and I was emotionally drained. Still, I wanted to leave the hospital as soon as possible. The doctor said I'd suffered no concussion, burns or lasting effects from the smoke inhalation. She said the blood tests revealed I had been drugged, but there was no long-term impact. She explained I was lucky. Someone pulled me out of the building (I presumed it was Marcus, but what was he doing there?). I asked about Millie, and she said she was fine too, as good as she could be, considering her ordeal. That was an enormous relief. I was worried my reckless goading of Ana may have inadvertently put Millie in more danger. The doctor said I could go but shouldn't be alone for the next twenty-four hours. Then she told me the police were there to question me.

DCI Slater and DS Hill entered the room. 'How's Millie?' I asked. I presumed they'd seen her first.

'Like you, it seems, a little worse for wear but lucky to be alive. So, tell me, Mr Glover, how did you end up in the grounds of Pickerton Hall, when everything was burning around you?' asked DCI Slater.

'What, are you accusing me of starting it? Do I need a lawyer? You must have spoken to Millie. Didn't she tell you what happened?'

'Don't worry, we're not accusing you of anything, although you have a strong motive to damage Pickerton Hall. But you are a key witness to serious crimes. Murder, potentially, and arson. We found the remains of three dead bodies in the building near where the paramedics treated you. Luckily, the facility had only a minimal workforce as it was Sunday. They were all evacuated before the fire destroyed the main house and other outbuildings. So please, can you give me your account of how you ended up where the paramedics found you?'

I was relieved there had been no other fatalities. But why did DCI Slater say they found three bodies? Franco and Ana were executed, but I was convinced Hazel had disappeared before I lost consciousness. What about Renata? Surely she was a hallucination?

I wanted to be as truthful as possible with the detectives. But I had to be careful to prevent any scrutiny on Marcus or Renata. The doctor said the police didn't know how I'd escaped the burning building. She'd made no reference to Marcus. So what had Millie told the detectives of our conversation? In retrospect, I'd gone too far in my exchange with Millie in the barn. I shouldn't have told her about Renata or The Bevy, but at the time, I thought the gravity of our situation meant there would be few consequences. Now my loose tongue could lead the police and, even worse, the media to Marcus and Renata, turning them into a public freak show. That was, of course, if Renata was still alive.

215

I decided to keep quiet about Marcus and Renata. I told the detectives about finding Nick's USB drive and how examining its contents led me to a confrontational appointment with Ana Steenkamp. Understandably, DCI Slater was furious about me withholding evidence. I told her it was my decision, to deflect any blame from Vicky. After I met with Steenkamp, I explained that I was still short of answers and evidence. Of course, I left out the bit about finding out I was biologically Sara's father.

I gave them an abridged version of the events at Pickerton Hall. But I didn't mention the executions of Ana and Franco. I was pretty sure Millie was unconscious then, so she didn't witness them. I said I didn't know how the fire started or how we ended up outside the building.

DCI Slater and DS Hill took all this in without expression. I think they suspected I was holding information back, especially as I'd already withheld the evidence on Nick's hard drive. But, possibly out of sympathy for my ordeal, they didn't push it any further. Instead, they told me I would need to come to the station to make a statement once they had progressed with the investigation. And I would need to hand over the USB drive, of course.

I was relieved to see them go and looked forward to returning home. My clothes were in a bag beside my bed, but my phone was missing. I couldn't remember, but I assumed Franco or one of his security guards had taken it. I was surprised Marcus hadn't come to see me, but perhaps he wanted to distance himself from the events at Pickerton Hall. I'd speak to him about it later. Despite the doctor's instructions to be with someone for the next twenty-four hours, I decided to check myself out. My van was still at Pickerton Hall, but my house was only a short walk from the hospital.

The stench of my clothes made me gag, caused by the acrid odour and the traumatic memories it triggered. I couldn't wear those. There was a knock at the door. Someone coming to my rescue. But it wasn't Marcus, it was Caroline. Tears rolled down her face. She approached and hugged me for a full two minutes.

'I'm so relieved you're okay,' Caroline sobbed. 'I don't know what I'd do without you, Jamie. I don't know what Sara would do. Promise me you'll never be so reckless again.'

'Have you spoken to Marcus?' I replied.

'Yes, he told me you were caught up in the fire at Pickerton Hall and had been taken to hospital. It's all over the news. They're saying the protesters caused it. They found bodies. It could have been you, Jamie. What on earth were you doing?'

'Didn't Marcus tell you?'

'Not really. Marcus was a bit strange. He didn't say much. He just said he was walking Flint and saw the smoke from Pickerton Hall. So he went into the grounds to see if anyone needed help. He said he discovered you lying semi-conscious on the ground. You were so lucky he found you and attracted the attention of the paramedics. But he said he needed to sort some things out, so he asked me to come and see you.

'I've brought you these. Marcus said you'd need them. I hope they fit. I haven't bought you clothes for a long time.'

Caroline handed me beige chinos and a blue polo shirt from Marks and Spencer. She was still trying to dress me like a mid-market Patrick. But I guess they were appropriate for a middle-aged man. I was relieved Marcus had been circumspect in his communication with Caroline.

'The doctor said I could go now,' I said. 'Can you take me home? We need to have that talk.'

'Yes, of course, Sara's at the nursery. We can have as long as we need.'

Caroline drove me home. I realised I'd need to find my keys as we approached my front door. I groped into the plastic clothes bag the hospital had given me. I usually kept them in the side pocket of my cargo pants. And fortunately, I could feel the angular rigidity of my keys under the fabric. But I felt something else irregularly shaped and hard in the pocket. What could it be? I retrieved the keys, which were entangled with a thin silver chain. And at the end of the chain was a small piece of black Whitby jet carved into the shape of a swan. It was Renata's necklace.

Chapter 40. Jamie – 12 July 2021

Caroline was speaking to me. Asking if I was okay, probably, but I wasn't listening. All I could think about was how Renata's necklace had ended up in my pocket. It's possible she could have put it there as we embraced before I left Sedgethorpe Manor. But surely I'd have noticed it? Could my apparition of Renata at Pickerton Hall have been real? Marcus had some explaining to do.

I untangled the keys from the necklace and unlocked the front door. Caroline led me to the front room and left me on the sofa while she brewed a tea. When she returned, she asked, 'Are you okay to talk, or do you need to rest?'

'I've been in bed for eighteen hours. I don't think I could tolerate much more rest.'

'Can you tell me what happened, Jamie? What were you doing?'

'Only if you're completely truthful with me, because it involves you and Sara. No more secrets.' She nodded.

'Okay. It started when DCI Slater showed me the photograph at Vicky's. It was from the opening of Pickerton Hall in February 2000. Nick was next to Ana Steenkamp in the picture – but the image had an extra significance for me the others didn't know about.'

'What?'

'Renata. She was in the lineup of people celebrating. She worked there.' Caroline squeezed my hand. 'I was foolish, but the link to Renata increased my conviction to find answers and not tell the police.

'DCI Slater asked Vicky if she knew of any connection between Nick and Pickerton Hall. The police were also investigating a recent death, in similar circumstances to Nick, which had a link to the fertility clinic.'

'Fuck, Jamie, are you saying Nick was murdered?'

'I'm sure of it. But there was no evidence, so I ended up at Pickerton Hall. I didn't trust the police after they ignored me back in 2001. I found an old Ebor Assurance USB drive in Vicky's shed. Nick used it to save his spreadsheets and diarise his concerns about The Cygnus Foundation. He challenged the financial integrity of the Foundation and the Pickerton Hall facility. The Foundation and its backers had the motive to silence him. I didn't tell Vicky or the police about the files. Unwisely, I wanted to interrogate Ana Steenkamp myself. I tried to arrange an appointment on the pretence of a discussion about what to do with our frozen embryos.' I looked Caroline in the eyes. 'But you know what they told me?'

Caroline looked broken, disconsolate in a way I hadn't seen her since Nick's death. 'The embryos had already been used,' she whispered.

'How could you do it, Caroline? You messed with so many people's lives, me, Sara…even Patrick.' We were both in tears. 'I can't continue until you've explained everything to me.'

'I was desperate. You know how much I wanted kids. It destroyed our relationship. We couldn't focus on anything else. That's why I went with Patrick, to break away from the torment of being unable to conceive. I didn't love him. But it was fun. I admit I enjoyed the lifestyle, and, most importantly, I didn't have the pressure of trying to get pregnant.

'I didn't think Patrick wanted children, but I was wrong. He did. One of the reasons for his marriage breakdown with Elaina was his inability to have children, even though they weren't together long. He knew from his sperm test that he'd be unlikely to ever fertilise an egg.'

'Fucking hell, rutting rooster Patrick's a Jaffa. I'm stunned he let that slip to anyone.'

'Well, at least it put the relationship on an equal footing. There were no expectations about children. But I knew that wasn't enough for me, and we wouldn't last. He was bound to be unfaithful eventually. So when Pickerton Hall sent the reminder that our frozen embryos were reaching their ten-year limit, I saw it as a sign, an opportunity. My last chance.'

'Why didn't you tell me, Caroline? I'd have gladly consented for you to use them?'

'I couldn't risk it. I know how much you hated Patrick. Would you really let me use our embryos after I'd been with him?'

'So you forged the consent form?'

'Yes, I'm sorry, Jamie, I put it in a bunch of other forms to do with the house. I knew you would be distracted and wouldn't be bothered to read them. But it didn't feel real. It was a last-ditch attempt to have the baby I wanted. I didn't believe it would work.'

'And you had the temerity to stay with Patrick while doing it. What was his reaction?'

'I didn't tell him, of course. As I said, I didn't really believe it would work. I was meticulous to ensure he didn't know what I was doing. All the correspondence from Pickerton Hall went to the nursery. I could cover my appointments by making excuses about nursery business.

'I followed up on the letter by meeting with Ana Steenkamp to seek her advice about the likelihood of me conceiving this time. She said they'd improved their techniques and reckoned I had a greater than fifty per cent chance of pregnancy.'

'What techniques?' I said with alarm.

'I don't know. I didn't ask for details. I didn't care as long as it worked. The procedure was the same as before. Implanting two embryos. Amazingly, I conceived. I was so happy, but I also knew my problems were only starting.'

'What did you tell Patrick?'

'I told him I was pregnant. I thoughtlessly pretended it was his — a miracle conception. I played on his vanity because, sometimes, even compromised semen can fertilise an egg. He was overjoyed. His wishful thinking got the better of him. He believed what he wanted to think — I was bearing his son.

'But I realised I was weaving a convoluted web that would eventually unravel. I had to find a way out. That's why I asked to see you at Café Concerto. I fantasised about us getting back together again — with the child, our child, we were always meant to have. But I knew it was unrealistic. Surely you'd have moved on and built a long-term relationship with someone else. But when you told me you were returning to York, I was so excited. Perhaps we did have a future together.'

'Why didn't you tell me about using the embryos when we met at the café?'

'I wanted to make sure if you ever took me back, it was because you genuinely wanted it. I didn't want to trap you — especially after all I'd done already.'

'It's funny. My sister Erica nailed you. She said you've been manipulating me all my life.'

Caroline was now in floods of tears. 'I'm so sorry, Jamie.'

'You know what, Caroline, I'd have taken you back, despite everything. I hoped for that when I met you in Café Concerto.' I paused. 'We should be meeting there now, shouldn't we? That's where we normally have these heart-to-hearts.'

Caroline chuckled through the tears. 'We can't meet there anymore. It's closed down. Another casualty of COVID.'

'So what happened with Patrick? What did you say to get him so riled?'

'I told him he wasn't the father, of course. It was indescribably cruel but the quickest way out of the relationship. I think he knew all along, but he couldn't believe he wasn't the one in the partnership being unfaithful. He just didn't know I'd cheated on him with ten-year-old embryos.'

'That is a shitty way to treat someone, but I suppose if anyone deserves it, it's Patrick. I guess that explains his behaviour at the time. But I can't understand why you've continuously kept it a secret from me. You've prevented Sara from getting too close to me the whole time. It's unfair on both of us. There's nothing I want more than to be Sara's dad, regardless of whether I'm her biological father or not.'

'I know, I was scared. I could never find the right time to tell you. The longer it went on, the more difficult it became. I didn't know how you'd react. And things have been working okay. I thought you liked having space to yourself.'

'Don't you think you should have allowed me to decide that? So, where are we going from here?'

'Complete honesty Jamie, you still haven't told me how you ended up unconscious in the grounds of Pickerton Hall.'

'Fair enough. Incredibly, what I'm about to tell you is more shocking than your sordid revelations, but at least I've only just found out. I've not concealed secrets from those entitled to know. Also, there's danger in what I'm about to tell you. People have died to keep what I now know quiet. Are you okay with that?'

She nodded. 'I don't have much choice, do I? No secrets.'

I told her about the meeting with Ana Steenkamp and being thrown out by a security guard.

221

'Why did you go back?' Caroline asked.

'I had to – after discovering that Marcus is my son with Renata. They both feared retribution from the organisation that controls Pickerton Hall.'

'Oh my God, I thought Marcus's relationship with you was strange. Now I know why. But why are they in danger?'

'Because Renata is a clone of Ana Steenkamp's daughter, who died in 1976. Ana Steenkamp is eighty-nine. She's benefited from her own pioneering treatments to slow the effects of ageing. Renata and Marcus needed to be controlled to keep them quiet. You see, Caroline, you're not the only one with secrets.'

I told Caroline about Marcus's invitation to Sedgethorpe Manor under false pretences, how I was reunited with the ailing Renata and discovered Marcus was my son. I tried to explain Renata's life, how she was conceived, and the roles of Ana Steenkamp and The Bevy – but I empathised with how difficult it all was to comprehend.

I described my abduction by the security guards after meeting the protestors at Pickerton Hall and my ordeal in the dungeon barn with Millie, then Ana, Franco, and Hazel.

'And I regained consciousness outside, with everything burning around me. Marcus and Flint were by my side. I've no idea how Millie or I escaped the fire. We'd both been drugged. But I'm sure Marcus had something to do with it – although he denied it.'

Caroline's blank expression showed she was still trying to grasp the implications of what I'd just told her. But it didn't take her long.

'What about Sara?' she mumbled. 'Pickerton Hall carries out yearly medical assessments on her. Does that mean she's the product of one of Steenkamp's little experiments?'

'One thing we don't need to worry about is Sara. We know she's a wonderful, healthy, inquisitive, effervescent child. Nothing we've learned about Pickerton Hall changes that. I'm proud to be her dad.'

'But are we safe? You paint the picture of an organisation that can murder people without consequences. Are you, we, in their sights now? Doesn't what you know put us in danger?'

'Honestly, Caroline, I don't know. I think if they wanted me dead, I'd be dead already. But, somehow, I survived. They must have allowed that. I'm unsure how much of what I know will be revealed by the police investigation into the fire and the deaths. We need to speak to Marcus. I'm sure he knows more than he'll admit.'

'This is scary. I don't know what to think.'

'I want to make a go of it,' I said. 'I'm sure this will bring us closer together, no more secrets. I love Sara, I love you.' We kissed.

A white van pulled up outside my house. My van. Marcus emerged from the driver's door. Caroline let him in.

'How are you holding up, Jamie? I thought you'd want your van back. I've changed the tyre.' I'd forgotten he had spare keys to the van.

'I'm not too bad,' I replied, 'Caroline's been looking after me. But I don't think I'd be here if it wasn't for you. Thanks, Son.'

'I didn't do anything. I just found you there. You were stupid to return to Pickerton Hall after everything my mum told you. Did you tell Caroline?'

'Yes, Caroline knows everything I know, but I'm sure that's not a complete picture – I don't know what happens next.'

'Yes, we've a lot to discuss, it's important, and we haven't much time.' Marcus's demeanour had changed. The insouciant confidence had shifted into a voice of self-assured authority.

'Listen, I didn't just come here to return your van. There are things I need to tell you. But, firstly, I have some sad news. Renata, my mum, passed away, in her sleep, on Sunday night.'

It took a few seconds for the news to sink in. Although it's strange, my reaction wasn't shock or surprise – but a calm acceptance of the confirmation of a sad event I subconsciously knew had already happened. Was my dreamlike memory of Renata in the burning barn some kind of psychic foresight of her death, or was she really there with me? If she was, Marcus obviously had his reasons to deny it.

'I'm sorry, Marcus,' I said. 'We were going to spend her last days together. It's heartbreaking we can't do that now.'

'Don't be sad, Jamie…Dad, she wouldn't want that. She was extremely ill. Seeing you again before she died was her last wish. She died contented.'

'What are you going to do now, Marcus?' I asked. 'What happens to Sedgethorpe Manor?'

'That's something else I need to tell you. Sedgethorpe Manor is yours now.'

'What?' I exclaimed.

'My mum left the estate to you. Well, us, actually. She bequeathed Sedgethorpe Manor to Gardening Glover. We're joint owners. We can do with it what we want. I'd like to execute my rewilding plans, but it's up to you – you're the boss.'

'That's crazy. How can we afford to maintain an estate that size?'

'Mum thought of that too. She also bequeathed an allowance for the maintenance of the estate. You can choose what you want to do. You can live there if you want. Have you ever fancied being lord of the manor?'

'Sorry, I can't get my head around this now. We'll talk about it later.'

'It sounds like an amazing place to bring up Sara,' Caroline interjected. I was having my mind made up for me again.

'The most important thing for us to understand now is, are we safe? I've just been abducted, chained up, drugged, elbowed, stamped on and nearly incinerated by an organisation that thinks I know too much. I know they've murdered other people, too, like Nick. What happens now? Will they come for me again?'

'I don't know exactly what happened,' Marcus responded. 'But this is my interpretation. Those in charge at Pickerton Hall have been acting semi-independently of The Bevy. They've run their own security operations, led by Ana Steenkamp, but delivered by Franco and his crew. Franco and Ana are old-school. They're accustomed to the uncompromising approach they used to operate with The Cygnus Foundation. If the opportunity arises, they silence or eliminate anything that's a threat to their objectives. But The Bevy has changed over the years. They're ruthless when they need to be. But they're more risk averse. I think Ana, Franco and the whole Pickerton Hall setup became a liability. Its time had passed.'

'Yes, that's essentially what *Il Cigno Nero* told Ana, who I assume was Renata's sister Hazel.'

'You saw Hazel?' He looked surprised.

'She's a senior leader in The Bevy now. They tasked her with cleaning up Ana's mess. The Bevy knew the truth of the operation would come out soon, so the time had come to end it.

'It's likely the fire was started deliberately by The Bevy, not the protestors. Although the presence of the protestors will provide a convenient cover-up excuse. We'll probably find that all evidence of the facility's operations has been destroyed, including all computer records.'

'That conforms with Nick's diaries,' I said. 'He visited the computer server room, which was onsite.'

'That's part of how they closely guard their secrets,' Marcus continued. 'It also means they can quickly destroy all evidence if necessary. I suspect it means there's no longer any evidence of the patients treated by the clinic or of Ana's experiments.'

I looked at Caroline. She was still in shock, but I was relieved if that meant all records connecting Sara with the clinic had been destroyed.

'But surely what took place at the clinic, the cloning, Steenkamp's quest for immortality, will be exposed after the fire and the deaths.'

'I doubt it. The Bevy is extremely effective at tying up loose ends. That's the other thing we need to talk about, Jamie. What exactly do you remember from Sunday, and what did you tell the police?'

'This is getting sinister now, Marcus,' I replied. 'How close are you to The Bevy's operations?'

'My life's been inextricably linked to The Bevy because of who my mother and grandmother were. I disapprove of the methods Ana and Franco perpetrated and tried my best to stop them, but they were loose canons. I do, however, believe in The Bevy's objective to strategically harness technological progress for the benefit of the planet. Hazel, known as The Black Swan, stood for the more enlightened side of The Bevy, seeking to integrate with mainstream scientific research rather than operate illicitly.'

'That's not true,' I responded. 'I witnessed Hazel's ruthlessness. She ordered Ana's execution, her own mother, for fuck's sake. Then Hazel eliminated Franco. She's a crazed psychopath.'

'You're only here today because Hazel spared your life. It would have been safer for them for you and Millie to go the way of Ana and Franco. But she knew you were both largely innocent, and your connection to my mum, her duplicate, swung it in your favour.'

'That's not what I remember. First, Hazel drugged Millie and me. Then, after Ana and Franco died, she left us to burn alive in the dungeon.'

'Why didn't she shoot you and Millie too, then? She saved you, and I suspect she sacrificed her own life.'

'What are you talking about?' I said.

'There were three bodies found in the barn. Two of them are Ana and Franco. I expect the third one will be identified as Hazel.'

'But I saw Renata when the barn was burning. It could have been her body.'

'You were drugged and concussed, Jamie. Your memories aren't reliable. My mum was gravely ill at home.' I wasn't sure I liked this new version of Marcus, so I didn't mention Renata's necklace. 'Did you tell the police all of this?'

'I told the police everything I remembered about the interactions in the barn before the executions. I said I was unconscious, so I didn't see anyone killed. I didn't say I knew who Hazel or Franco were. I didn't mention Renata, you, or The Bevy.'

'Good. It will have to stay that way. The past crimes will be blamed on Ana and Franco, who are dead. All the evidence about the activities at the facility is likely destroyed. The protesters will be blamed for the fire. I think a line will be drawn. I'm sure we are all safe, but it's important to keep everything else we know between ourselves.'

'It's not as simple as that, is it? The police will investigate, and I told Millie about Renata and The Bevy. She works for the police.'

'I think you'll find the police will be happy everything has been resolved satisfactorily. The Bevy wields a certain influence in the establishment. Like you, Millie was drugged, so her recollections are unreliable. However, it might be worth a chat with her to straighten things out.'

Marcus went home on his bike, which he'd brought in the van. Caroline left to collect Sara. They were coming over later to stay the night, which excited me – how would Sara react to finding out I was her father? Would she call me Daddy? I opened my laptop to read the news about Pickerton Hall. I saw the sports headlines. England lost the final on penalties. I'd forgotten about the match. It was reassuring to get a dose of normality after my crazy few days.

Chapter 41. Millie – 22 July 2021

Millie's boss at the police headquarters insisted she took a couple of weeks off to recover from the ordeal. Millie followed his instruction, partly because she felt guilty for spending so much time on the Pickerton Hall case. It wasn't, strictly speaking, her core work. However, Millie thought she would have recovered more quickly had she returned to the office. She declined the offer of counselling.

Millie wasn't sure what to do with herself. Kyle had been great, spending as much time with her as possible, but his job meant it was limited. At least he had kept her up to date with the investigation – although it sounded like that was pretty much complete. Her mum, Shiv, had been supportive, too, staying with Millie when Kyle was away.

It was Thursday, Kyle and Shiv were at work, and Millie was relieved to have time alone. However, she was annoyed at herself for accepting the dinner invitation. It was a surprise call from Vicky Shepherd, the director of her old department at Ebor Assurance. At first, Millie thought she might be trying to poach her back to the financial services company. That wouldn't have been an unwelcome proposition if it wasn't for a certain individual who still worked there. But, instead, Vicky invited Millie to dinner – not to her house or a restaurant, but to the home of Jamie Glover's partner. Millie was caught off guard. She accepted the invitation without thinking. It may still be a recruitment pitch, but with Jamie in attendance, it was more likely related to the events at Pickerton Hall. Perhaps Vicky wanted to discover what Millie knew about Nick. She shuddered at the thought of reliving those memories.

Millie ambled alongside the River Ouse, in her own world, oblivious to the dog walkers, cyclists and joggers. She turned through Rowntree Park and found the house at the address Vicky provided. She knocked on the door. There was no going back now. Jamie answered and greeted her with a hug.

Jamie's partner, Caroline, was in the hallway with Vicky. They also embraced Millie. She found it simultaneously awkward and comforting. Caroline showed Millie through to her spectacular kitchen and introduced her to their daughter, Sara, and dog, Flint. Sara followed the lead of her parents and hugged Millie too. Sara's energy, natural happiness and playful interaction with Flint lifted Millie's spirits.

After uncomfortable small talk with no mention of Pickerton Hall, over wine and crudites with Mexican dips, Jamie and Sara left to take Flint for a walk. Millie noticed Vicky's and Caroline's expressions instantly transform from vacuous grins to stern frowns, signalling a shift in the conversation to more serious matters.

'I hope you don't mind,' Vicky said. 'We want to talk to you about Patrick Kemp. He's been harassing you, hasn't he?'

Millie was cognisant of the significance of her answer. An affirmative response meant she was all in. Millie tilted her head to relay, what she hoped, was the merest hint of a nod. She wasn't ready to commit herself yet.

'Let us tell you about our experiences with Patrick Kemp,' Vicky said. Vicky told Millie about how Patrick had seduced her at a vulnerable time when she was having marriage problems. They had a brief fling, but it ended soon after Vicky's husband, Nick, tragically died.

Then Caroline described a strikingly similar experience to Vicky's. Problems with her partner, Jamie, due to infertility. Seduction by Patrick at a vulnerable time. An explosive end to the relationship, which involved Patrick threatening Caroline and Jamie with a shotgun.

These stories irritated Millie. They presented a picture of an unscrupulous and unstable individual. Still, their experiences did not bear any resemblance to Millie's torment. Caroline and Vicky both acceded to his solicitation. They knew what they were doing. Millie had told Patrick 'No' at every stage, and still he persisted. Millie was unsympathetic to the grievances of two spurned middle-aged women. She actually felt sorry for Jamie, stuck with conceited Caroline. Vicky perceived Millie's annoyance and swiftly tried a change of tack.

'We just wanted to get everything in the open to let you know about our personal experiences with Patrick, so you can make your own judgment about our impartiality and whether you help us ensure he gets punished for his actions.' Vicky leaned towards Millie and looked into her eyes. 'Patrick's behaviour has undoubtedly crossed the line over the last two years. I think he's always been inappropriate, at least by today's standards. I know of four women at Ebor Assurance, all considerably younger than him, who he has harassed and threatened to elicit sexual favours – taking advantage of his position of seniority. I'm sure there are more women, but they are too frightened to come forward.'

'Why do you need to talk to me then?' Millie asked. 'If you already have the testimonies of four women?'

'We don't have enough evidence to be certain we can sack him. As you'd expect, he's supported by expensive lawyers.' Vicky described the experiences of women, some younger than Millie, who had been denied promotions, threatened with spurious disciplinary action, or been told their career was 'fucked'. All because they hadn't given Patrick what he wanted. Millie had more sympathy for these individuals. Millie thought she had been lucky. She'd bagged an exciting job elsewhere. But the others may not be in that position. They'd be stuck with the impossible choice of working for a perverted boss or having no job. Would Millie have left Ebor Assurance if it wasn't for Patrick? And getting a new job hadn't ended Millie's turmoil. If anything, it made it worse. Yes, now was the right time to unburden herself. Maybe she should go to the police, but she didn't really want her new colleagues to know about this episode of her life. If Patrick was sacked in ignominy, losing his power and beloved job, she knew it would hurt him.

'I can provide evidence from when I worked at Ebor Assurance,' Millie said. 'But if I do, I need you to promise me two things. Firstly, anything I tell you and the evidence I give you must remain confidential. Secondly, Patrick must be properly sacked, with Ebor Assurance providing a press release stating the true reason for his termination. I don't want him getting some cosy settlement where the reason for his departure is ambiguous. His reputation must be tarnished enough for him to never work in a senior position again. In fact, if I give you the evidence, and he isn't publicly trashed, I'll expose Ebor Assurance for knowingly protecting a sex pest and continuing to tolerate his harassment.'

'I know Ebor Assurance's behaviour over his tenure at the company has been deplorable. It has been culpable in creating an environment for him to thrive. The company acknowledges that now. They won't try and cover anything up. I can't make any promises about the nature of Patrick's dismissal. But I will do everything I can to ensure that the true nature of his departure is made public.'

'Okay,' said Millie. 'Here goes.' She took her phone from her back pocket and swiped the screen for a few seconds. Then, she handed the iPhone to Vicky, 'Recognise this, ladies?'

Vicky's cheeks turned salmon. Caroline emitted a short gasp. The caption read, *'You've had the hors d'oeurve. Time for the entrée?'* It was under the photo of a semi-erect penis.

'That was one of his early, less threatening efforts,' Millie said. She showed them the hundreds of WhatsApp messages, which became increasingly sinister over time. Millie told them how it started, with a drunken snog at the Christmas party, and after that, how he wouldn't take 'fuck off' for an answer. She then described his recent behaviour, stalking her at the café and forcing entry into her apartment.

Both the women listening looked genuinely shocked. Vicky appeared angry. 'I'm so sorry you had to suffer all this, Millie, and you felt you had to keep it to yourself. Rest assured, I will make sure he is suitably punished. But isn't this a police matter? Stalking and forced entry are more like criminal offences.'

'They happened after I left Ebor Assurance,' Millie replied. There should be enough material in my photo library and message history to expose him for what he is. But I don't want to go to the police.'

'He really had it bad for you, didn't he?' Caroline said. 'He was in a position of power over all the other women and was more cautious, careful not to leave evidence of his behaviour. With you, it was different, you weren't in his direct reporting line, and he was reckless with texts and photos.'

Millie glared at Caroline, not deigning her with an answer. She still wasn't sure whether Caroline fully understood the vileness of Patrick's actions. Was she jealous of his all-consuming obsession with Millie?

Chapter 42. Millie – 22 July 2021

Millie was relieved when the dog walkers returned. Sara's joyful devotion to Flint was an antidote to the gloomy dialogue. Also in tow was a young man Jamie introduced as his son, Marcus. She thought back to her conversation with Jamie at Pickerton Hall, and his admission of a relationship with a woman he thought was Ana Steenkamp's cloned daughter. Could Marcus be Ana Steenkamp's grandson? It was abundantly clear he was Jamie's child. There was a striking resemblance, Marcus had inherited his dad's good looks, but he was smoother and more confident than Jamie.

Caroline sat everyone down for a burrito supper. Fortunately, Vicky had obviously remembered Millie was a vegetarian and alerted Caroline. And, to be fair, Caroline's veggie burritos were delicious. The conversation mainly centred around Millie's career. Vicky did hint that there were potential opportunities for Millie to return to Ebor Assurance if she was interested. Marcus appeared enthralled in Millie's description of what being a data scientist entailed, especially in its potential uses for her work for the police force.

After dinner, Jamie suggested they move into the lounge. But Caroline and Vicky stayed in the kitchen with Sara. Had they choreographed the evening? It was as if the four adults had planned every scene to get what they wanted from her. And, sure enough, once they sat on the sofas, Jamie asked, 'Can I talk to you about Pickerton Hall? There are still things I don't understand.'

'Yes, okay,' said Millie. 'Although you probably remember more than I do.'

'I remember you were already there when I was forced into the barn; how we talked for a long time, and Ana Steenkamp joining us, as well as the brute that abducted me. After that, it gets fuzzy.' Millie shivered. 'I think the man pretended to shoot us, and another woman entered the barn.

She gave me water, which I later found out was drugged. After that, I don't remember anything until I regained consciousness outside when the paramedics treated me. I don't know how I escaped the barn.'

'It's similar to what I remember,' said Jamie. 'I became unconscious too. I was hoping you could shed some light on how we escaped the barn.'

'The police told me what they believe happened,' said Millie. 'The protestors were becoming increasingly aggressive, and the police expected they might take direct action. However, the police didn't anticipate they'd go as far as torching the place, but that's what they think happened. We were lucky because the ensuing confusion surrounding the fire created the conditions for our escape. They believe some protesters probably pulled us clear of the barn. But they kept a low profile, not wanting to draw attention to themselves, as they were also complicit in arson.

'The police found the charred remains of three bodies in the barn. They positively identified them using DNA evidence. They were Ana Steenkamp, Franco Barella and Hazel Gallo. Barella had known connections with organised crime in Italy in the 1990s but had slipped under the radar since then. The discovery of the other body, Hazel Gallo, alerted the attention of security agencies throughout Europe. Apparently, she was something of a legend in the counter-intelligence community. She was suspected of numerous nefarious activities, including being a spy, a femme fatale, a terrorist, and even an assassin. All working for various organisations. She's known as the Black Swan, due to a tattoo on her wrist and the fact that her appearance is a portent of doom. The security services thought of her as a ghost. They would have loved to have captured her alive.'

'What do the police think she was doing at Pickerton Hall, and how did she die?' Jamie asked.

'They think those running Pickerton Hall employed Barella and Gallo to ensure their illicit activities stayed secret. Barella was Steenkamp's normal head of security. But the police believe that Gallo was brought in for the special task of quashing the protestors. They had become too big a threat to the facility. Their charismatic leader, known as Barney, was the driving force behind the rabble. If Gallo could make him disappear, surely the rest of the protest movement would dissipate?

'However, it seems like the Black Swan was too late, and Barney struck first. The police think the three of them remained in the barn to destroy evidence of our kidnapping. But they were overcome by the speed of combustion. Another possibility is that Barney executed them as retribution for the facility's animal cruelty. Barney does have previous convictions for violent behaviour. But there isn't enough evidence to charge Barney with murder. He has, however, been charged with arson and manslaughter. He denies it, of course.'

'What are the police going to do about Vicky's husband, Nick's, death? And what about the other similar death you were investigating?' asked Jamie.

'They're sure Franco Barella was responsible for both murders. They were not suicides. He was working under the orders of Ana Steenkamp. But both are dead now, and the Cygnus Foundation no longer exists. The Pickerton Hall facility is completely destroyed, including any evidence of what happened there. So the police investigation is effectively over. The security services will likely investigate the involvement of Hazel Gallo, and the fertility regulators and relevant government organisations will examine what went on and interview the staff who worked there. But as far as the police are concerned, it's case closed.'

'What did you tell the police about our discussion in the barn?' Jamie asked.

'I told them everything I told you of what I'd discovered about Ana Steenkamp. She was really Juliana Taylor, conducting experiments to clone humans and prolong life. In case you're worried, I didn't say anything about your relationship with Ana Steenkamp's cloned daughter. I wasn't entirely sure of my recollections, and I thought you were probably bewildered then too.

'It's strange. I've been warned from speaking about the case publicly. However, certain covert government departments seem to be analysing the implications of Steenkamp's scientific breakthroughs. It's probably a good thing. I don't think the public is ready to embrace human cloning or immortality yet.'

'Yes, I think it makes sense that none of us mentions what we know about what went on at Pickerton Hall. We know people have died for possession of that knowledge.'

'I agree. Although it's a shame, it would be a good ice-breaker story,' Millie joked. 'At least DCI Slater is satisfied that she has finally been vindicated over her doubts about the two cases.'

'That's a bit rich,' said Jamie. 'She ignored my protestations about the suspicious nature of Nick's death for over twenty years. But I don't suppose I'll get an apology.'

'Sorry, I don't know much about that,' Millie replied. But I am glad we've set the record straight over Wes Myers's murder. He was tragically slaughtered, simply for trying to keep the public informed about COVID.'

'I knew him,' interrupted Marcus. Jamie looked shocked. 'Mr Myers was an inspirational maths teacher. I used to go to the maths club he organised. He helped us appreciate what could be achieved through mathematics. It's because of him I'm going to study maths and computing at university. His COVID analysis was brilliant. I was devastated when he died.'

Vicky popped her head around the door. 'I need to go now. Thanks for coming. It was good to see you again, Millie. Let me know if you're ever interested in returning to Ebor Assurance.'

'Wait a second. I'll walk down the road with you if that's okay,' Millie said. 'I need to tell you some things about Nick's death.'

'Yes, of course,' Vicky replied. 'But I think I already know how and why he died. It wasn't suicide. DCI Slater asked to see me next week, which I assume is to confirm the revised cause of death.'

As they approached the front door, Marcus got up to see them out. 'Before you go, I wonder if you could both do me a big favour. I'd like to do something to properly recognise and remember Mr Myers's life and dedication to educating young people about the beauty of mathematics. I have some ideas but would be grateful for your help.'

Chapter 43. Jamie – 25 July 2021

I'd found my answers – I knew why Nick died and Renata abandoned me. But, somehow, it felt unsatisfactory. There were still loose ends. No one had been brought to justice for their crimes. Franco's and Ana's deaths at Pickerton Hall were all too convenient.

I hadn't yet solved the riddle of Renata's necklace. Marcus still insisted she died at home. My theory, however, was that Hazel alerted Marcus and Renata to the events unfolding at Pickerton Hall. Renata, knowing she was dying, sacrificed her life. Renata realised the police would mistakenly assume it was Hazel because they had Hazel's identical DNA on file. Perhaps Renata struck a bargain with Hazel; she would take her place as the dead body in the barn so the security services would believe the Black Swan had died. In exchange, Hazel and The Bevy would leave my family alone. I wasn't sure what had happened. Still, I clung to the romantic notion that Renata sacrificed her life to protect Marcus and me. And that she was with me at the end.

We didn't arrange a funeral for Renata. She wasn't religious, and besides Marcus and me and the staff at Sedgethorpe Manor, she didn't know anyone. So instead, Marcus suggested we scatter her ashes at the lakeside in the grounds of the Manor.

Marcus and I ventured down to the waterside early on Sunday morning. We were joined by Lucy, who had been Renata's cook, cleaner and personal nurse. Mist loomed from the lake, creating an eerie scene. It was reminiscent of the hazy vista that day I met Renata at Castle Howard. The three of us stood by the arbour where Renata had told me about her life less than two weeks before. Marcus carried an urn, which contained what he said were her ashes. He tipped it up and dispersed its contents in the lake. There was no eulogy or farewell speech. Instead, we stayed at the shore in silence, reflecting on her extraordinary life and what she meant to us.

Distant movement disturbed the lake's murky blanket. Someone else was on the opposite side. I could just about make out her features through the fog. I shivered, was it the morning chill or because the figure on the far side of the water looked like Renata? I turned to Marcus and Lucy, but they stayed static and expressionless. Surely they could see her too? I stared again at the ghostly apparition. She lifted her right hand to her temple in a half salute, half wave, then turned and disappeared into the woods.

If I had faith in the supernatural, I might have believed I'd just seen Renata's soul passing into the afterlife. But, despite the incredible events in my life, I still needed to explain everything rationally. So I interpreted the phantom vision as Hazel coming to pay her last respects, keeping her distance out of necessity. I optimistically translated her gesture as a signal everything was good now. The Bevy wouldn't pursue us anymore.

Rustling in the reeds stirred me from my trance. I looked down to glimpse a white swan emerging from the vegetation, carrying four fluffy grey cygnets on her back. I imagined it symbolised Juliana and her four daughters. But a fifth downy bundle appeared behind them, swimming by herself. It was as if she was showing off her ability to make her own way without her mother's help.

Part 8: August 2021 – July 2022

Chapter 44. Jamie – 17 August 2021

When we told Sara I was her father, she was happy but unfazed. She took it in her stride and said, 'I've always known you're my dad. I thought "Jamie" was your special word for Daddy.' In fact, we had slipped into proper family life more quickly than I'd expected. I stayed at Caroline's house most nights and took Sara to the nursery when Caroline wasn't working there.

However, I wished the transition into a family relationship with Marcus had been as smooth. If anything, the paternity revelation had created a wedge between us. Previously we enjoyed an effortless matey banter, and I thrived on his enthusiasm and confidence. But now I was almost resentful of him. Perhaps I was envious of the time he spent with Renata. He also still had secrets. One such surprise was when he said he knew the maths teacher murdered by Franco. It made me wonder how much else he knew about the events surrounding Pickerton Hall.

At least the admission about Mr Myers seemed to pique Millie's interest. I was concerned that the dinner at Caroline's had become too overwhelming for Millie and that she was on the verge of walking out. In retrospect, it was too planned, and we tried to cover too much. But it was vital that we found out how much she had told the police and implicitly warn her about The Bevy. The dinner had achieved those objectives, and Patrick was about to get a deserved comeuppance by the sounds of it.

Marcus was desperately seeking means to commemorate the life of Mr Myers, as if he felt some responsibility for The Bevy's actions. I suspected Marcus's invitation to the pub had something to do with Mr Myers. He'd invited Millie and Vicky too. He'd chosen the Old White Swan as the venue. I couldn't remember telling him it was the last place I went out with Renata. He probably didn't know and chose it for its convenient central York location.

Vicky and Millie were already at a table when I arrived. I hadn't been there since the pub-quiz night with Renata. It hadn't changed much since then. It hadn't changed much in three hundred years. Did it bring back painful memories for Vicky? It didn't look like it. She and Millie were happily chatting. Seeing Millie cheerful and relaxed after our recent ordeal at Pickerton Hall and the awkward dinner at Caroline's was fantastic.

They both enthusiastically greeted me. 'Millie's thinking of coming back to work at Ebor Assurance,' said Vicky.

'I'm surprised to hear your unsubtle recruitment pitch has worked on someone,' I replied. 'Are you sure, Millie? I couldn't wait to get out of that place. Surely your work's far more interesting with the police?'

'If I remember correctly, it wasn't your choice to leave,' taunted Vicky.

'I haven't definitely decided to return. But Vicky has offered me a top job. The police work hasn't given me the opportunities I expected, and it's become complicated since I started going out with a detective.'

'The good news is Millie, or anyone else for that matter, won't have to live in fear of sex pest Patrick anymore,' said Vicky. 'I shouldn't say this yet, but he's been sacked, and the company will issue a press release tomorrow stating why. So he'll never work in the financial services industry again.'

'Yes, I suppose that is good news,' I replied. 'It should have happened years ago. But, honestly, it's not something I feel like celebrating, either. It's just a horrible business.'

I went to get a drink, and as I returned to the table, Marcus entered the pub alongside a skinny lad wearing a grey hoodie. He had dyed blond hair, cut short at the back and sides but longer and curly on the top. He sported two gold chains around his neck and chunky rings on each hand.

Marcus said, 'Hello everyone. This is Nathan. I met him at Mr Myers's maths club.' He introduced us all to Nathan, highlighting our connections with Ebor Assurance. Millie hugged and greeted him like a long-lost buddy. The poor kid looked overawed.

'Nathan's a brilliant mathematician,' Marcus continued. 'But he suffered with the teacher-assessed grades last year. Nathan wants to attend a good university, so he decided to buckle down and retake his A-levels this year. Unfortunately, COVID and woolly education policy meant he didn't get a chance to take proper exams this year either. But even so, he achieved three A-Star grades.

'Well done, Nathan, congratulations,' we all declared warmly, in what I thought was a slightly patronising manner.

'What are you going to do now?' Vicky asked.'

'Maths at Warwick Uni,' Nathan replied in a broad Yorkshire accent. Good on him, I thought. I just hoped he didn't end up like Warwick alumni, Patrick.

'Have you considered what you want to do after university?' Vicky said, articulating her well-worn recruitment pitch.

As if following a script drafted by Marcus, Nathan said, 'I'm thinking about a career in data science.'

Millie talked about the things she'd done at Ebor Assurance, and the broader opportunities having the right skills can bring, such as her work for the police force. I had to admit, she made it sound interesting.

Slightly to my surprise, Vicky provisionally offered Nathan an Ebor Assurance scholarship, if he passed the assessment criteria, as they still had places left. Nathan was clearly gifted enough, but he didn't fit the clean-cut, dull persona of the typical financial services graduate trainee. I was impressed Vicky was prepared to accept candidates from more diverse backgrounds. But I suspect Nathan would have never considered an insurance career if it wasn't for Marcus.

I was pleased with Marcus too. He'd engineered something I think Mr Myers was genuinely trying to achieve with his maths club – broadening the outlook of its members to increase their opportunities in life.

Nathan was the first to leave the pub. It was difficult to gauge his expression, but I think he was chuffed he had a great career and paid-for course fees in the pipeline. Once he'd gone, Millie turned to Marcus and said, 'You know Nathan was connected to Wesley Myers's death? Nathan abandoned Wesley after his brother, Troy, pushed him off his bike. As a result, Wesley had an epileptic fit and was badly cut and bruised. He could have died even before Franco Barella got to him.'

'Yes, I know,' said Marcus. 'But I don't blame Nathan. He was the one that called an ambulance. And Troy's a pernicious influence. Fortunately for Nathan, his brother's in prison now.

'It doesn't always work out as planned, but I aim to see the best in people and help them when possible. I try to believe they're free from blame.'

'You mean you try to exonerate?' Millie said.

Marcus grinned and nodded.

Chapter 45. Jamie – 12 October 2021

Things were looking up after our tumultuous summer. Caroline, Sara, and I swiftly adapted to our new life together at Sedgethorpe Manor. Caroline had taken little persuasion to leave her Bishy Road house to make the switch to lady of the manor. I remembered when I rescued her from Patrick's country house near Easingwold. Well, Sedgethorpe Manor was on another level. No wonder Caroline loved it. We'd had no sinister missives from The Bevy and no follow-up from the police after the Pickerton Hall fire. We hoped we could consign that episode to the back of our minds.

Renata's staff, including Lucy, continued to expertly manage Sedgethorpe Manor's house and grounds, leaving Caroline and me time to concentrate on our businesses. We both made use of the outbuildings to create offices. Taking Marcus's advice, I changed the name of our company – it was now Glover's Eco Landscaping. I worked on Marcus's plans to transform the estate, which included removing some formal gardens, planting different oak species, and introducing more ponds and wildflower meadows. I had planned to remove the paddock, but Sara loved the horses, so that would stay. Ultimately, we wanted to open the grounds to the public, because we believed such a magnificent landscape should be accessible to all. In addition, it would serve as an excellent advertisement for my company's services.

My relationship with Marcus wasn't what it was before I knew he was my son. However, he still felt like part of the family, being especially close to Sara. I think she missed him more than I did now that he'd departed for university. We didn't expect to see him again until Christmas, despite only living down the road in Leeds. I realised I'd have to get used to Marcus having secrets. I supposed this wasn't any different to the normal state of affairs between a young adult and their father. It's just that most teenagers aren't in collusion with a bunch of assassins. I'd also heard, through

Marcus, that Nathan had taken his place at Warwick, funded by the Ebor Assurance scholarship.

Sara relished her new life, and no wonder – she'd moved from a house with a tiny backyard to one with limitless outdoor adventure on her doorstep. Sara started at the local village school in September and settled well, making many new friends.

One of my biggest worries was explaining my life's gargantuan transformation to my mum, Susan, and sister, Erica. But, as it turned out, my mum took it in her stride, unlike Erica, who now thought Caroline was even more of a she-devil.

Out of the blue, being told that you happen to have two grandchildren, aged four and nineteen, may have fazed some mothers. But Susan was overjoyed, which I should have expected as she'd already overcome many more traumatic shocks. I took Sara and Caroline to visit my family in Reading in September. Now Mum was enjoying her first visit to Sedgethorpe Manor, with her husband, Mike. When I first greeted her on the driveway, she remarked on how different it was to our two-bedroom council house in Reading. We encouraged Susan to perform typical grandmotherly duties to make up for lost time – such as looking after Sara while Caroline and I went out for a meal or picking her up from school. Mum and Mike were due to pick Sara up from school on Tuesday, allowing Caroline and me to work through the afternoon.

I first realised something was wrong when Mum called my mobile phone. 'Is Sara with you, Darling?' she asked tentatively. I'd been in the office all afternoon, so my initial reaction was she'd forgotten to pick her up.

'No,' I grunted. 'We agreed you would pick Sara up so Caroline and I could work. Where are you now?'

'I'm at her school, of course. But she's not here. Her teacher said her uncle's already collected her.'

'What the fuck?' I screamed. 'I'm coming over now.'

Caroline emerged from the adjacent office to find out what the commotion was about. I told her. We both raced to the Tesla in a blind panic. As we accelerated up the driveway, a call from an unidentified number appeared on the car's screen, connected to my phone via

Bluetooth. I pressed to answer so Caroline and I could hear the conversation through the car's speakers. 'Hello,' I said.

'Hello Jamie,' came the happy response. It was Sara. Caroline and I looked at each other in relief.

'Where are you?' I said, trying to stay calm, hoping she was at a friend's house. 'Didn't you remember Grandma Sue was meant to pick you up today?'

'Uncle Patrick came to get me instead. So I'm at his house.' she chirped. I froze momentarily, trying to process what she'd just uttered.

Patrick's voice droned in the background. 'Please go and watch television in the lounge, Sara. I want to talk to Jamie.'

'What the fuck are you doing, Patrick? I swear I'll kill you if you harm her,' Caroline screamed into the car's microphone.

'You're there too, bitch, even better,' he responded. 'You've both conspired to destroy my life. I saw Jamie meeting those conniving slags in the pub. I'd still have my job and career if it weren't for you. So now I will devastate your lives by taking what you love most.'

We were speeding to Patrick's house. Hopefully, he hadn't moved since Caroline lived there. She entered the address into the Tesla's navigation and said it would take sixteen minutes. I felt more terrified and helpless now than I ever did at Pickerton Hall. During that ordeal, I was resigned to my fate and only responsible for myself. Now I had to figure out the best strategy to preserve the life of my beloved daughter, who was in the hands of an unhinged maniac. Caroline, usually so calm in a crisis, was wailing uncontrollably. I endeavoured to stay measured in my response to Patrick.

'Don't do anything stupid, Patrick,' I urged. 'If you think things are bad for you now, just imagine how grim they would get if you harmed a four-year-old girl.'

'It doesn't matter anymore, Jamie. I won't be around to suffer the consequences. But you and Caroline will have to live the rest of your lives in pain and suffering, for which you will always hold me responsible. Just think, you spent your adult lives struggling to have a baby, Caroline even tried to rope me in on her sordid games, but nothing worked. But then, miraculously, the bitch spawned satan's child and shacked up with her spineless lover boy. What sweet revenge it will be when I terminate that life.'

Thirteen minutes.

'Look at her, Patrick. I understand your hate for us but don't take it out on Sara. She's blameless. If you really have to take a life, take mine.'

'You do have a point, Jamie. She doesn't seem much like you or Caroline. She has far more personality and intelligence. But I don't really care. One thing I've learned about myself over the years is that I lack empathy. My shrink told me that. Others might call me psychopathic. Which is a good thing, obviously. It's meant I've obtained things that others are too timid to pursue, like nearly every woman I've desired. Compare that to wimps like you who settle for the first woman who comes along, and are so mediocre at their job that they hang around until their employer has to pay them off to get rid of them. Another advantage of my psychopathic tendencies is that it doesn't matter if I hurt people. Even children. I've never been afraid to torture individuals emotionally, but I've not yet had the need to exact physical harm. But now seems a good time to start.'

Eight minutes. The car's computer hadn't allowed for speeds so far over the limit.

'Don't do it. She's your child,' Caroline screamed.

'Ah, you're trying to make that play once more. It worked the first time, more fool me, but you won't catch me out again. She can't be mine. I'm incapable of having children. The doctors told me that in no uncertain terms. I know she's Jamie's. No one would react that desperately unless it were their own child.' I heard a door opening and the sound of television.

Six minutes.

In the background, Patrick said, 'Come back in the kitchen, Sara. Time to say goodbye to Mu...' Something must have distracted him.

A cacophonous bang echoed around the car from the speakers, after which – silence.

'Sara, my love, speak to me. Tell me you're okay,' implored Caroline to the microphone.

'Patrick, are you there? What's happened?' I shouted. But it was no use. We were disconnected. Caroline tried phoning again, but there was no dialling tone. Patrick had obviously changed his number, but she did have the presence of mind to call the police.

Two minutes.

We were on the road to Patrick's house. Fortunately, traffic was quiet, but a motorbike, haring around a corner in the middle of the road, caused the car's automatic braking to engage. We screeched through the open gate and up his driveway. As we came to a halt, a most beautiful sight greeted us. The front door opened, and Sara rushed to Caroline. Caroline hugged Sara so tightly that I feared she would crush her. I tried to join in.

'What happened, Sweetie?' Caroline asked.

'I ended his life,' Sara replied in her usual cheerful manner.

'You shot him?' I said, not believing I was asking my four-year-old daughter that question.

'Not me, silly,' Sara replied. 'It was the lady.'

'What lady? You said *you* ended his life.'

'The lady said she was me from the future. She looked like me. She said she'd come to protect me from harm.'

I ventured into the house to determine whether everything was safe. The gruesome image in the kitchen informed me that Patrick was no longer a threat. His supine body lay on the floor, but little of his head remained. Most of it appeared splattered around the walls and appliances. Next to him was a shotgun.

I couldn't linger there any longer without throwing up, so I quickly inspected the rest of the house. There was no sign of anyone else. As I returned to Caroline and Sara, three police cars dashed up the driveway.

Chapter 46. Jamie – 15 July 2022

One of the established rituals of parenthood is the family holiday. It was a pleasure denied me in Sara's early years by Caroline's reticence. I fondly remember my summer trips to Cornwall as a child with Dad, Mum, and Erica. I wanted to replicate that experience with Sara. We'd booked an Airbnb near St Ives, Cornwall, although I nearly baulked at the English school holiday prices – something I'd need to get used to. As a rehearsal for our summer vacation, Marcus had organised a weekend trip to Norfolk, where he'd decided to spend his university summer break. He'd been vague about precisely what he was doing or why he'd chosen to go to Norfolk. He mentioned something about helping out in a retirement home. All very laudable, but it wasn't how I'd expected Marcus to fulfil his spare time, especially when I knew of his passion for commerce. However, it would be great to catch up with him, as we hadn't seen much of him since he started university. He seemed to have lost interest in the eco garden design business, even though he owned thirty per cent of it.

We really needed the time away together as a family. It had been a challenging year, trying to come to terms with what happened when Patrick kidnapped Sara on top of the episode at Pickerton Hall. So naturally, we were super protective of Sara after her ordeal. But surprisingly, it didn't appear to affect her. Caroline regularly took Sara to a child psychiatrist, one of her contacts from the nursery. We both believed it would be impossible to emerge from such a harrowing incident psychologically unscathed, particularly at such a tender age. Sara still claimed a woman entered the house and killed Patrick to prevent him from harming her. The woman told Sara she was her future self whose job was to protect her. The psychiatrist reckoned this story was Sara's coping mechanism. Sara had made it up to repress her memories of the incident.

However, I wasn't convinced Sara's tale was imaginary, given I'd experienced ghostly apparitions I believed were real. But the police had thoroughly investigated the incident, and there was no evidence that anyone else was involved. Moreover, they retrieved Patrick's security camera footage, which proved Patrick and Sara were the only people in the house until I arrived with Caroline.

We managed to piece together the likely course of events that day, from a combination of the Police, Vicky and Sara. Patrick had taken a job as a caretaker at Sara's school, which his conduct at Ebor Assurance hadn't prevented because he didn't have a criminal record. Here, he befriended Sara and convinced Sara and the teachers that he was her uncle, perhaps because he knew so much about Caroline. He collected Sara from school without opposition from either Sara or the school staff. Patrick told Sara he was looking after her for the evening because Mummy and Daddy were going out. We drummed the perils of stranger danger into Sara, but her gregarious nature was difficult to curb. Sara said she never felt in danger at Patrick's, and he didn't threaten her. However, in Sara's version of events, her future self told Sara to lock herself in the bathroom while she dealt with Patrick. I prayed that Sara didn't witness the scene in the kitchen. It scarred me, so I couldn't comprehend the effect it would have on her.

The police were convinced Patrick had taken his own life. His were the only fingerprints on the shotgun. Also, as part of the deal Ebor Assurance granted for Patrick's termination, they agreed they wouldn't take their evidence to the police if Patrick saw a psychiatrist. His psychiatrist revealed Patrick had admitted to suicidal thoughts. Needless to say, Caroline and I were incandescent at the parts played by the school and Ebor Assurance in her ordeal. Both could have prevented it if they'd acted differently. Caroline and I were gradually coming to terms with what had happened. Sara was her usual joyous self.

Marcus booked us a static caravan for the weekend, which was significantly cheaper per night than our St Ives apartment. Still, the weather forecast predicted record-high temperatures, so it was perhaps a poor accommodation choice. We set off on Friday after picking Sara up from school. I expected the journey to Norfolk to be less wearisome than the later trek to Cornwall in school summer holiday traffic. But I hadn't counted on the A17, a single-carriageway road that weaves its way through the Lincolnshire fens. Mile after mile of ponderous progress behind crawling agricultural vehicles across a flat, featureless landscape. The backdrop was almost apocalyptic. Scorched yellow grass lined the road's embankment. We spotted a vast dust cloud ahead, which wouldn't have looked out of place in the Sahara. But as we approached, we could see it was simply a tractor disturbing the arid farmland baked by the unceasing summer sun. Was this a vision of the world to come? Despite their ruthless methods, I pondered whether there was some merit in The Bevy's goals.

We stopped to charge the car at King's Lynn, which jolted me from my reflection. Then it was a short drive to our destination, the Victorian seaside resort of Hunstanton. I wasn't sure what to expect, but the place made me uneasy. Maybe I was affected by the tiresome eerie journey through the fens. Perhaps it was because so much about the place was a contradiction. It was an east coast resort where the sun set over the sea. There was a pier entertainment centre, but no pier. I saw signs for the 'Wash Monster'. It wasn't a mysterious creature to rival Loch Ness's but an amphibious vehicle for seal tours.

We checked into our static caravan on a large caravan park near the sea, then took Flint for a walk along the promenade. The expansive sandy beach looked enticing, somewhere Sara would enjoy playing.

The resort itself was faded, it had clearly seen better days, but it failed to dampen Sara's excitement. It was like she'd been there before, dragging us along the promenade. 'Can we go to the fair, please, Jamie?' I looked at Caroline. Sara had worked out I was more likely to accede to her requests than her mum. Caroline nodded.

The fairground was a small-scale assortment of classic rides and amusements, which had unlikely changed much since the 1950s, but it was perfect for a five-year-old. It was wonderful to bond with her away from Yorkshire, with its still too recent traumatic memories. Sara giggled all the way through the ghost train and beamed as she descended the Helter Skelter. I was delighted Caroline had let Sara's hair grow longer. It suited her. Caroline was now wearing her hair to shoulder length too, and had dyed it blonde as if trying to demonstrate to Sara how alike they were.

We passed a stall selling henna tattoos as we exited the fairground. 'Can I get a tattoo, please?' Sara begged. This time Caroline refused. Sara studied the stall's display and said, 'That's okay, Mummy. They don't have the one I want anyway.'

We met Marcus for fish and chips in the town. He was in good spirits, staying with a university friend in nearby Burnham Market and spending his time on various volunteer activities, including helping at a retirement home in Hunstanton. I told him how well the business was doing. 'All thanks to my business plan,' he crowed.

'More like Renata's inheritance,' I countered. But he didn't pick up on that. Our conversation stayed respectful. He never mentioned The Bevy anymore. After dinner, Marcus returned to the caravan, as he was staying with us for the weekend. Sara was overjoyed to see him and excitedly donned the orange sun dress he'd bought her as a present. Marcus spent most of the evening with Sara and Flint. Then he joined Caroline and me for drinks on the veranda while Sara played with her colouring books in the caravan.

'There's someone I'd like you all to meet tomorrow,' Marcus declared enigmatically. 'And I know he'll be thrilled to meet Sara.'

Sara overheard the mention of her name and joined us on the veranda.

'Who are we meeting tomorrow?' Sara asked.

'It's a surprise,' said Marcus.

'What's that mess on your wrist?' Caroline bellowed at Sara. She grabbed Sara's hand to inspect a mark on her skin. Sara had drawn a shape on her right wrist using a black marker pen.

'They didn't have the right tattoo at the fair, so I drew my own,' Sara explained. 'I want to see what I'll look like in the future.'

When viewed from my seat, it was just a messy black splodge on her arm, so I moved closer. It slowly dawned on me that the shape wasn't some random scribble. I shivered, despite the heat, and the hairs on my neck prickled. Sara had drawn a black swan on her wrist.

Chapter 47. Albert – 16 July 2022

Why did he choose to live out his life in Hunstanton? Albert repeatedly asked himself that question. It was where he'd been happiest, playing with his granddaughter, Chloe, on the beach and watching her savour the thrill of the fairground rides. But it was also a place of unspeakable sadness, where he'd last seen Chloe and his son, Paul, before their fatal journey back to Cambridgeshire. Nevertheless, the resort seemed to draw him in.

Nothing was the same after Chloe and Paul died. It couldn't be. Albert and his wife, Peggy, just went through the motions. Peggy passed in 1986. Her death certificate said cancer, but Albert knew she had died of a broken heart. Albert often tried contacting his daughter-in-law, Juliana, to find solace in her connection to Chloe and Paul. But Juliana simply vanished.

After Peggy died, Albert regularly visited his static caravan in Hunstanton. He lost his job after the factory closed, so he had nothing tying him to Newark anymore. He was a member of a golf club in Hunstanton, which provided a social life of sorts. When Albert turned 75 at the turn of the millennium, he decided to move to a retirement home in Hunstanton, into a self-contained two-bedroom apartment, with a warden on call. He didn't think he needed sheltered accommodation yet, but it was an investment for the future. And the retirement home organised activities like quizzes and bingo, as well as trips to local attractions. It was an excellent opportunity to meet new people.

But more than twenty years later, Albert was still at the same retirement home. He'd outlived everyone he cared for. His golf partners had all died, and most of the fellow residents he'd befriended had gone too, as had many wardens. Was this penance for the way he treated Paul? He was so proud of Paul's achievements, but he'd never properly told him. That's not what men did in those days. So, here he was, a lonely 97 year-old-man, stuck in a never-ending purgatory of coffee mornings and trips to the pantomime in Norwich. He didn't even find the COVID lockdowns much of a burden, as he was already living his own self-imposed lockdown.

But this all changed last month when a strange young man called Marcus started helping at the retirement home – collecting shopping and running errands. He took a special interest in Albert, taking him out for fish and chips and to the pub. They had long chats. Marcus wanted to know about Albert's family, especially Paul and Chloe. At first, Albert was reluctant. He'd kept those painful memories repressed for so long. But Marcus had an engaging way about him, and Albert found it cathartic to talk about old times. He showed Marcus his old photo albums, snaps of Paul, Chloe and Juliana with Rocky on the beach, at the fairground or enjoying a meal outside the caravan. Incredibly, Marcus was entranced, taking an age to study each image – especially those pictures with Chloe in.

However, Marcus said something that raised Albert's suspicions. Marcus told Albert he was his great-grandson. Albert knew this couldn't be true after the fatal crash had erased his bloodline. Was Marcus a scammer, preying on ancient pensioners to claim their inheritance? If he was, Marcus had selected a perfect target, Albert had no heirs, and his time was surely soon.

Although Albert knew it was impossible, something about Marcus reminded him of Paul. Not just his looks, but his manner too, and he was smart – just like his Paul. Whoever Marcus was, Albert was overjoyed he'd introduced some happiness and companionship at the end of his old life.

Now Marcus wanted to introduce Albert to his family. His dad, little sister, and step mum. Marcus led Albert along the promenade. Albert could still walk unaided, but he used his walking frame today in case he was overcome by heat exhaustion in the searing sun. The sweltering temperatures reminded him of the weekend he last saw Paul and Chloe. Back then, forecasters said temperatures could exceed one hundred degrees. They never did. But they were expected to comfortably surpass that benchmark over the next week.

Marcus hollered to a family on the beach. A golden retriever, barking excitedly, bounded across the sand. Albert leaned on the walking frame as his legs turned to jelly. It could almost be Chloe's dog, Rocky. A girl called, 'Come back, Flint.'

Albert spotted her. Wearing a bright orange sundress, she scampered after the dog. He gaped at the girl in amazement. It couldn't be. It wasn't possible. His decrepit mind must be playing tricks. Tears gushed from his eyes. He never cried. He didn't believe in ghosts.

She came closer. 'This is my great grandpa, Albert,' Marcus said to the child.

The little blonde girl hugged Albert. This was no phantom.

'Hello, Grampy,' she said as he stared, spellbound, into her hazel eyes.

Acknowledgements

Thank you for reading Dark Swans. I hope you enjoyed it.

Special thanks to my wife, Jenni, for her support and patience while I hid away for hours, offering the dubious excuse – 'I'm writing a book.' Jenni painstakingly read and reread Dark Swans countless times, spotting numerous errors and inconsistencies. Thanks to Christine, Wendy and Tony, who were among the first to read the manuscript, and Jeremy, who read Dark Swans while climbing Aconagua in Argentina. I'm incredibly grateful for Tony's constructive comments, suggestions, ideas, and insight from the publishing world. Also, many thanks to my sisters, Clare and Emma, for their feedback. Clare's positive comments on an early draft helped maintain my confidence in the book, and Emma's teacherly critique of the last draft was what I needed before publication.

Dark Swans is my first book (hopefully not the last). I've thoroughly enjoyed the process, but it's been a steep learning curve. Thanks to Nicky L, whose developmental editing report significantly improved the structure and pace of the story.

When I tell people I've written a book, their initial reaction is usually enthusiasm and respect. Thank you so much to everyone that provided encouragement along my journey.

If you enjoyed Dark Swans, please take a few moments to write a review of it. Thank you!

About the author

Stephen Jackson writes suspenseful, exhilarating stories with authentic characters and jaw-dropping plot twists. After a career as an actuary in financial services, he took redundancy in 2022. This freed him to focus on his passion for writing thrillers influenced by the human consequences of paradigm shifts in technology and big data.

Stephen's writing considers how unexpected changes incite fear, greed, guilt, betrayal and conflict. But it's not all about a dystopian future – hope and love are key ingredients too. Sometimes a quantum leap can elicit a miracle so incredible it could almost be supernatural. His debut novel, Dark Swans, explores these themes. It's set mainly in Gothic North Yorkshire and York, where he lives with his wife, son and cat.

To learn more about Stephen Jackson and find out about new books, check out his website, stephenjackson.info

Follow Stephen Jackson at
Twitter – @goalprojection
Facebook – facebook.com/stephenjacksonwriter
Instagram – instagram.com/stephenjacksonwriter

Printed in Great Britain
by Amazon

20562727R00150